# THE KINGMAKER CASE

## THE STATE VS. CALEB ESCUETA

H. VALENCIA

Order this book online at www.trafford.com
or email orders@trafford.com

Most Trafford titles are also available at major online book retailers.

Printed in the United States of America.

ISBN: 978-1-4907-3136-0 (sc)
ISBN: 978-1-4907-3138-4 (hc)
ISBN: 978-1-4907-3137-7 (e)

Library of Congress Control Number: 2014905516

*Trafford rev. 03/21/2014*

www.trafford.com

**North America & international**
toll-free: 1 888 232 4444 (USA & Canada)
fax: 812 355 4082

# CHAPTER ONE

Coach has a zero tolerance policy towards tardiness. The team bus leaves promptly at noon and we've been instructed to arrive ten minutes prior to its departure. Piece of advice, if you're going to be ten minutes late to anything team-related then you might as well not show up at all. The last time a player had the audacity to show up to practice late the entire team was sent home. Coach called the whole thing off. At any rate, I get to the bus five minutes earlier than the mandated ten minutes prior; that is to say that the time is 11:45. The first thing I see is Coach having a discussion with the bus operator. Immediately, I take note that Coach's hands are placed on his hips. He has a unique way of putting his hands on his hips. When most people assume that posture, their thumbs are placed on the back of their bodies. When Coach does it his thumbs are placed on the front of his body. It looks as though Coach is trying to keep himself from floating away. As an athlete you learn to read body language. Whenever Coach places his hands on his hips it means something isn't meeting his high-minded expectations.

The players all file onto the bus; at least, most of us do. A few minutes after twelve o'clock a player named Javaman decides to grace us with his presence. Javaman's real name is Vinton but only his mother calls him that. Even Coach has become accustomed to calling his player Javaman. Javaman went to college to become a grave-robber or something like that. If you go to his residence you'll see a bunch of old things that were supposedly dug up from all corners of the world. He calls them artifacts but I call them old things. I never had a brother but I imagine he and I fight like brothers; truth be told, Javaman fights like a sister—a little sister. He gets all snarly when I tell him that his old things should be put in a museum with the rest of the world's old things. He'll tell me that I have no class and I'll tell him that class isn't some old thing you keep locked up in your house. He'll tell me that I have no culture and I'll tell him culture isn't something you have to dig up. Then he'll tell me that he is appalled by my content for a world older than our own. If I hadn't left his house at that point he would no doubt kick me out. Sundays with Javaman, that is.

Javaman may be quiet on the outside but the guy has got a beast in him; a sexy beast ha—ha-ha. He may not talk so much but the locker room never stops gossiping. There are so many stories in that locker room. The word is that the season before I joined the team Javaman tweaked his big toe. The Forces of Reaction [team management] told him that he couldn't participate in a certain Charity Basketball Game. Keep in mind Javaman plays in this Charity Basketball Game every year. Javaman took offense to being told what to do with his personal time. In his mind, The Forces of Reaction were treating him like property. The Forces of Reaction must've forgotten that as basketball players we all have the proverbial Love the Game Clause in our contracts. The Love the Game Clause states that we can play this game anytime and anyplace we see fit because we-love-this-game.

Not only did Javaman play in the Charity Basketball Game but he made a concerted effort to score 36 points. To get even with The Forces of Nature, Javaman put off his toe surgery until the continuation of the regular season. In an interview he stated, "I got a flat tire on company time so I should get it repaired on company time." After surgery, Javaman went to a place where he had never gone before—the injured list. Being a player myself, I have a natural compulsion to take the side of other players (as opposed to taking the side of management). After all is said and done it's the players who have to play the game. While I don't totally agree with the manner in which Javaman handled the situation I support the decisions he made. It's too easy to stand at a safe distance and say Javaman should've done this or Javaman could've done that or Javaman took it too far. It's not so easy to find the right move(s) when you're in the middle of the action. Right or wrong: when the pressure was on Javaman he did what he thought was right. To me, that speaks volumes.

So, Coach is barking at Javaman because he's late to the bus and this-and-that. Coach tells him that it's disrespectful to the team and it's not fair to all the other players who were able to arrive on time. Javaman tells Coach that he is on time and proceeds to tell Coach that he should get his watch fixed. Coach shakes his head in disapproval and gestures for Javaman to get on the bus. I know Coach isn't really upset. Javaman broke a team rule and Coach doesn't have any choice but to go through the motions of reprimanding him. With his players watching Coach has to try to save face. As the tardy man, with a quiet disposition, takes his seat one of the players tell him he should've used that feistiness in the game we just lost. "Settle down ladies," Coach looks worried but, then again, that man always looks worried. "We all know it's going to be one of those long drives home. I strongly suggest you get some sleep." He's got his hands on his hips, again. "I'll see you all at the first stop."

When I arrived in this town, and met the team, I said to myself this won't do. In college we had our fun and, so long as we were winning, the coaching staff pretty much stayed out of it. I think it's important to have camaraderie with the guys you play with. It's not mandatory but it helps. So, when I joined this team I took the initiative. I started what we now refer to as Team Meetings. I'm not even supposed to be telling you this because the first rule of Team Meetings is to not talk about them. A Team Meeting is code for guys' night out. These semi-secret events are for players only: The Forces of Reaction are not allowed. Most importantly, if a player were to tell The Forces of Reaction about the specifics of our Team Meetings we'd find a creative way to emasculate the traitor. It's comic. Sometimes we'd be right in front of Coach asking one other: "Are you going to make it to the Team Meeting, tonight?"

We'd get together and, in that old-fashioned way, paint the town red. Any restaurant we went to they'd let us eat for free. Granted the only thing we'd ever order is salad-freaking-salad. I remember at our first Team Meeting we all went bungee jumping. Now, bungee jumping is something The Forces of Reaction would never allow us to do. Keep in mind these are the same micro-managers who didn't want Javaman to play in a Charity Basketball Game. However, the beauty of Team Meetings is that the people who would oppose our extra-curricular activities weren't there to object. In order to ensure that no player was going to turn around and rat us all out every player had to make that leap (a leap of faith, as it were). Through our Team Meetings I got to see another side of the town and another side of the guys I was playing with. On another occasion we treated ourselves to a massage parlor/karaoke bar. We paid escort royalty to walk up and down our backs and stuff.

On our way to another Team Meeting we saw a couple of kids playing one-on-one basketball at a local park. We pulled over—I remember we were using taxis that day because the taxi driver looked nothing like his photo—and spent the better part of the day there. We shoot around with those kids, let them score on us, picked them up so they could dunk . . . it was impromptu. I found it odd when the kids gleefully kissed our hands. It's a form of respect you'd never see from kids where I come from. In spirit, Coach was always with us. If he were there he'd say, "Different fields, different grasshoppers; different seas, different fish." In town, people of all ages greeted us with smiles and words of support. We were there team. Apart from a league championship what more could we players ask for? At any rate, I bet we shocked the hell out of those kids. I bet those kids shocked the hell out of their friends and parents, too, when they showed them all of our pictures and autographs.

We've been having our fun this season, both on and off the court, but today's loss was a something we'd all just as soon forget. Coach always reminds us that true love comes from being fully present in every moment and not just when things are going our way; that if we can accept the good then we can deal with the bad.

During the day the town is like any other major town: traffic, pollution, prostitution, and homelessness. It's got enough to keep your head on a swivel. Did you know, in this town, people are actually allowed to smoke cigarettes in hospitals? How could you know? Anyway, where I come from you, can't even smoke cigarettes in bars (not that I'm a smoker). As I look out the window of the bus I see an old lady, on a three-wheeled motorcycle. The ancient lady is carrying cages filled with chickens. A little farther down the road, I see a donkey cart over-taken by a brand new sports car. One time I saw some punk kid running down the street. He was chasing down some elderly man. Now, I thought for sure the punk kid was going to assault the elderly man. It turned out that the punk kid stopped the elderly man to tell him he had dropped his wallet. This town will surprise you.

On the bus ride home (despite Coach's advice to sleep) my teammates are busy little beavers. The players usher me into a little huddle. One of the players—Arief—is sharing a boggle that he's been keeping close to his chest. By the time I get into the huddle Arief can no longer contain himself. He hits the entire team across the bow saying, "You guys said we were a family. We're supposed to be a family, right? We're supposed to be like brothers. Not like brothers . . . but actually brothers, right? This whole thing is going down for me and mine and not one of you called me."

"I did call you." A player tells Arief.

"I called you twice." Another player tells him. "You never answered the phone."

As the new guy who initiated Team Meetings I feel the need to step in. "Look, Arief, we reached out to you but you never reciprocated. I'm not blaming you for that—I understand—but you're way off base on this one." Arief is the loudest person on the court but, as is the culture, he rarely says much off the court. He's the kind of player who rarely complains about things. I think if Coach were to ask us to play an entire game in our pajamas Arief would play the game in his pajamas. The rest of us would undoubtedly seek advice from the Player's Union. It's as though basketball is an assembly line job, to Arief. He shows up, punches the clock, and goes to work. We all have jobs to do on the assembly line. Arief's job is to come off of screens, spot up, and knock down open jump shots. As the team's point guard it's my job to get the ball to him, in rhythm, and in his shooting pocket. No waiving towels. No high-fives. No one gets accolades for doing what they're supposed to be doing. When the game is over Arief punches out, and goes home . . . or wherever he goes when he's not with us.

It's a shock to hear that Arief is offended that we didn't probe into his personal affairs. Here I didn't think he cared what we knew or didn't know or thought about his private life. You see, Arief is one of the team's veteran players. Is he a bit cynical about the game? Possibly. Is he jaded, as well? Most likely. As the oldest player on our team's roster, Arief has seen the ugly part of this game we care deeply about. To veteran players like Arief, basketball isn't so much about friendship as much as it's about winning. When considering the big picture it's difficult to argue with that kind of logic. If there's a choice between young and old, the game will choose young. Ultimately, the game uses you up and—when you have no further value—dumps you (in a nice way). In that sense professional basketball is like any business. If you don't understand or are unwilling to accept that then you're setting yourself up for disappointment. I may have only been doing this for two years but

I already understand that it's difficult to find genuine loyalty in professional sports.

Arief points his finger, kind of, in my direction. I can tell he's about to go off on me. "You never called me, Caleb." As he says this he wags his finger, "You of all people."

"You kept me out." I plead. "I don't know how it was for the others but you kept me out. You never told me anything. I still don't even really know what happened. All the information I got about your situation was second or third hand. You never told me a thing."

Leave it to my best-est friend Javaman to back me up. He probably feels compelled. If it were not for Javaman I would have never hitched my wagon to this hectic town. Javaman and I met at a point guard camp that my college coach staff was holding. During scrimmages at that camp Javaman and I were matched up. These were only pick-up games but we went at one another. On the court, I wasn't going to give him anything easy and he wasn't going to give me anything easy either. After practice, we would get to talking about past games and that. Thus began our bro-mance. At some point Javaman told me that his team was a player or two away from winning a league championship. At that point I was going into my senior year in college. I told him that I might be interested and Javaman arranged a meeting between me and The Forces of Reaction. I was so impressed that the team owners were willing to fly out to camp just to meet me. Granted The Forces of Reaction, in all likelihood, had some other business to attend to as well. Nonetheless, I like to believe that they came all the way out there to scout little-old me. The Forces of Reaction were very supportive of me and my future. They went on to tell me pretty much everything I wanted to hear which brings us to back to the present.

Like I said; I'm Javaman's best-est friend. He brought me out here so he feels a little responsible for me (and vice/versa). When I found bed bugs at my place, it was Javaman who called me up.

He offered to put me up until we got the bed bug situation squared away. Javaman tells Arief, "You know the rules. Caleb invites everyone—except the coaching staff—to our Team Meetings. I know for a fact that he invited you, too. We've been going out all season long but you're always a no-show. That's not our fault. When Muhammad got married you attended the wedding but left before the reception. Everyone stayed for the reception—except you. We all love you but what could we do? You froze us out."

After having set Arief straight we saw it fit to address the "Bo issue". Bo is the big man on the team. At least, that's how he likes to think of himself. He loves to push us around. I'll give you an example. Muhammad made the cover of a local sports magazine. We took the cover of that magazine and hung it up in the locker room. Bo took the photo and signed his name right on Muhammad's face. What a horse's ass, right? Bo is the same way on the court. He tries to be some kind of enforcer and, for reasons unknown to me, Coach lets him get away with it. It's, sort of, alright when Bo intimidates the opposing teams but even that is questionable. It's not the brand we want to put out. This isn't to get Bo mad at me if he reads this monologue but he was the player solely responsible for the loss of our last game. Whenever we find ourselves in striking distance, that is whenever the game is close, Bo feels the need to abandon our set offense and he tries to take over the game. It's hero ball. This totally goes against our team's concept because no one or two players are supposed to be above the system. It's how we'd like to define ourselves a team. It's supposed to be our identity. Our team's system is supposed to be bigger than any individual player.

Now, I'm talking about basketball. I'm not talking about constitutional law or comparative religions. When you basketball the right way it's not a difficult game. "Find the open man." They tell little kids that in grammar school. "Help one another out." Most of us learn these things before we learn to tie our shoes. It's inconceivable to me that a professional, like Bo, can go through his entire career without these basic concepts ever getting through his thick skull. With some players, you can tell the right thing to do and they'll make the adjustments. Horse's asses, like Bo, need to hit rock bottom. Horse's asses, like Bo, have to completely break down in order to break through.

He loves to remind us that he's the player with the most experience; that he's the vet [veteran] on this squad. Well, let's take a minute or two to explore that claim: Bo lost at the high school level. Bo lost at the collegiate level. Thus far, Bo's lost all eight years of his professional tenure. So, in a sense, he's absolutely right. Bo is a "vet" and, now, he's gracing us with all those years of losing experience. I'll probably never understand why The Forces of Reaction put up with his shenanigans ha-ha-ha. My guess is that Bo knows where some of the proverbial bodies are buried.

We tell Bo how we feel about his tanking the game—again. He took 29 shots and made only 9 of them. Upon hearing our grievances the "vet" did what he always does: he denies everything and makes counter accusations. Escueta needs to get him the ball, more. Coach needs to call more plays for him. The player Arief was guarding was taking advantage of him. You see, nothing is ever Bo's fault. It's upsetting. I'm upset that we didn't make any progress on the Bo—front but I'd be even more upset if we stopped trying. It's as though the man is oblivious to his shortcomings. You would think that a player who wants to be the man would *own it* (his shortcomings). That's what I want to tell him, "*Own it* you horse's ass. If you want to be the man then you have to man up." You know what? I don't even want to talk about it anymore.

Whether we win or lose the distance, from the arena to home, is equal. It's not as though we take a long route if we lose and a short route if we win. It's all the same. Nonetheless, after a loss, bus rides home always seem to be so much longer.

\*

I've been here two years and I don't own a car. I ask Coach to give me a ride home. It may not seem like it but he and I are very close. As critical as I am of him—if he were writing this book—it'd be far worse. The way I see it the point guard is an extension of the coach's will. Coach is the General and I'm his Lieutenant. It's my job to keep this unit running smoothly. For the moment there is dissention in the ranks. When it's not basketball Coach has a calming demeanor. He's got so much more *life* experience than me but he has a way of making you feel comfortable in your ignorance.

Coach has got his grandson on the phone.

"Is what I hear true? Your tooth finally fell out?" He asks his grandson. "That's fantastic."

(Pause.)

"No. I can't say we did win. We lost but, nonetheless, we put up a valiant effort."

(Pause.)

"No. That would be a tie score. There are no ties in basketball: someone has to win."

(Pause.)

"I don't know why. It's just the way things are in basketball. That's how the game has been played since it was invented. It's a competition. There has to be a winner and there has to be a loser. Am I on speakerphone? Take me off speakerphone, baby-boy."

(Pause.)

"Really? Tell papa again who your favorite player, is?"

(Pause.)

"Kingmaker? So, now, Kingmaker is your favorite basketball player? The other day you told me Bo was your favorite player?"

(Pause.)

"So you think Kingmaker is the fastest, huh? Tell me, now, how old do you think Kingmaker is?"

(Pause.)

"Five, huh? You think Kingmaker is five, like you ha-ha-ha? Well, that's very forthright of you."

(Pause.)

"Yes, 'forthright' can be a good thing." Coach turns to me and says, "My grandson thinks you should consider retiring all those unnecessary left-handed passes."

"Tell him 'I don't care'." I joke. "Tell him, Coach. You tell him that Kingmaker said, 'I don't care ha-ha-ha'." Coach shrugs me off.

"I don't think there'll be time for all that, baby-boy. You'll probably be asleep by the time I get there." Coach tells his grandson. (Pause.)

"Really. You want to hear a story, huh? I can do that. Okay, I can tell you a story. Get under the covers, now, okay?"

> Now, there once was a shepherd girl who was bored as she sat on the hillside watching the village sheep. To amuse herself she took a great breath and sang out, 'Wolf. Wolf. The Wolf is chasing the sheep.' The villagers came running up the hill to help the girl

*drive the wolf away. But when they arrived at the top of the hill, they found no wolf. The girl laughed at the sight of their angry faces.*

*'Don't cry wolf, shepherd girl,' said the villagers, 'when there's no wolf.' They went grumbling back down the hill.*

*Later, the girl sang out again, 'Wolf. Wolf. The wolf is chasing the sheep.' To her naughty delight, she watched the villagers run up the hill to help her drive the wolf away.*

*When the villagers saw no wolf they sternly said, 'Save your frightened song for when there is really something wrong. Don't cry 'wolf' when there is no wolf.'*

*But the little girl just grinned and watched them go grumbling down the hill once more. Later, she saw a real wolf prowling about his flock. Alarmed, she leaped to her feet and sang out as loudly as she could, 'Wolf. Wolf.' But, this time, the villagers thought she was trying to fool them again, and so they didn't come. At sunset, everyone wondered why the shepherd girl hadn't returned to the village with their sheep.*

*They went up the hill to find the girl. They found her weeping.*

*

One minute I'm listening to Coach mangle a classic bedtime story. The next thing I know I'm being interrogated by a couple of police detectives. When I arrived home there were unmarked police units in the driveway. The detectives aren't here to arrest me but they strongly urge me to accompany them to the precinct. Apparently, not going with these detectives would be perverting the course of justice. I hop into the backseat of one of the unmarked cars. The detectives seem like nice enough fellows. There's an old detective and a young detective. The duo seems thick as thieves. "It (referring to my last basketball game) wasn't what I expected" the younger detective says.

"I know," I admit. "It wasn't pretty. During warm-ups they (the opposing team) were dunking in the lay-up line. They got the crowd into it early." Despite our lackluster performance we were still within five points at the beginning of the fourth quarter before the bad guys pulled away for good. "I'm disappointed we didn't win," I say shrugging off our performance. "I'm thinking if we make a couple of threes (three point baskets) in the second half and we walk away with a win."

"And that's the way you've got to look at it." The young detective adds.

"We didn't lose." I jest. "We just ran out of time."

"Right, you see, it's all in the phrasing" the young detective quips to the old detective. "We need to laugh otherwise we'd cry."

"You'll (my team) find your way." The older detective chimes in. "You've got all the pieces, you guys just need a little tweaking—and maybe a new coach." I don't respond. The older detective goes on to give me a little pep talk. "Think about Hadrian's Wall." I think about the wall that the Roman Empire built in England. "That was a turning point in Roman thinking.

They changed from being an expansion-minded culture to being a defensive-minded culture. In a way Hadrian's Wall is a symbol. It stands as a huge white flag of surrender. You guys have to keep expanding and exploring new horizons and pushing yourselves. You keep going. You keep going or it'll be like The Dark Ages." I'll think more on that tomorrow. The older detective glances at me in the rear view mirror. "You're looking a little pale, there, Mr. Escueta."

Perhaps I'm reading the situation incorrectly when I take the detective's previous statement as a term of endearment. "It's the ice water in my veins, detective." I respond.

The older detective tells me not to worry about going down to the police station. He says "I know it's difficult to be answering all these personal questions about you and your wife but you understand why we have to ask them, don't you?" Actually, I don't understand why they have to ask them. "It's got less to do with the truth and more to do with the proof of that truth."

"So, tell me, how do you prove a negative?" I ask but neither of the two responds. I rephrase the question, "How do I prove that something didn't occur; that is, how do I prove I didn't do something?"

"That's big of you to ask, Mr. Escueta. The burden of proof is with the accuser. We (the detectives) are but a cog in the machine of justice. We're here to collect the evidence, the District Attorney evaluates that evidence, the lawyers argue that evidence, and the jury determines the truth of that evidence." It takes me the rest of the ride, and more, to digest all those tidbits.

It worries me when the detectives write things down before I say anything. At one point I get so frustrated from answering the same sets of questions that I say, "Spell that, tough guy." Four score and seven-thousand-and-one-questions later, the detectives present me with a 5 page form. Though it's single-spaced I read the document over. The form states that by signing I'm consenting to have a medical exam performed. The detectives tell me that after the exam they'll take me home. Against my better judgment I sign the consent form.

The medical examiner—a woman with hands I can only describe as masculine—asks me if I have any history of this disease or that illness. She's got a copy of *Twelve Angry Men* sticking out of her purse. The doctor wants to know everything there is to know about my medications: what the names of them are, what the dosages are, how often I take them, who are the prescribing doctors, what shape and color they are . . . . I feel as though I've been answering questions all afternoon long. I'm hungry, I'm frustrated, I really need to use the restroom, and I'm still a little upset about not having enough time to win the basketball game. The medical examiner asks me if I've ever been physically abused or if I have ever abused anybody. I'm so tired that I tell her everything. She shows me some of my clothes and asks me if this is what I was wearing on December 12th.

After the questions, the examination starts to get real personal. The examiner takes fingernail scrapings, hair standards, oral swabs . . . I'll spare you the details and just say the doctor takes a sample of everything she could possibly take a sample of. Keep in mind I'm just about naked at this point. She goes over every inch of my body with a fluorescent lamp. Then the examiner tells me that she's going to have to do a penile exam. I have never even heard of a penile exam. I'm not even sure that a penile exam is a legitimate test. All I know is that I want to go home. I tend to talk a lot when I get nervous, "So you like reading the classics" I ask her?

"Are you familiar with it?" The medical examiner is referring to the Reginald Rose play about a jury of twelve men. In the play these guys have just finished listening to 6 long days of trial proceedings. A 19-year old man is on trial for the murder of his father. The defendant has a criminal record and a lot of circumstantial evidence piled against him. The defendant, if found guilty, would receive a mandatory death penalty. It's up to a jury of twelve men to decide the fate of this young man.

"Try not to sound too surprised, Doc." I tell her. "I watched the play. You know, I've got a degree and a library card and everything . . . ?"

"I'm sorry, Mr. Escueta. I didn't mean to imply . . ."

"It's fine, huh." I cut her off. She still has a look of amazement. I guess I'm not as dumb as the doctor thought. She seems disappointed. "You guys have been asking me questions all afternoon but nobody asked me about my education. Anyway, I had to write an essay about *Twelve Angry Men*. I like when the man says 'I beg pardon . . . '"

"Well remembered." She encourages. "And the other juror yells, 'What are you so polite about?'" She stops what she's doing to recall the lines. "'For the same reason you are not.'"

"'It's the way I was brought up.'" She and I say in chorus. "I love that line." I tell her. "It's a good play, Doc."

She nods and says, "'Tis."

"I imagine it must be strange to be examining a live one, huh, Doc?" She doesn't respond. "So, you're a forensic pathologist? Did I get that right? I hope I did."

"Yes, you did."

"Do you testify in court, at all?"

"Yes, of course I do." She reveals. "I wouldn't say I testify a lot, though." "So, you're all about the science, huh?"

"I am, today."

"I guess it gets boring in the lab." I say thinking out loud. "That's probably why you read the classics? It's a good way to pass the time." She doesn't respond. "Ever serve on a jury, Doc?"

"Yes, I have" she recalls. "It must've been, oh my, it must've been before you were even

"I never served on a jury before." I inform. "Tell me, was serving on a jury anything like Reginald Rose's play?"

"How did I know you were going to ask that?" The doctor finishes her examination.

"You can get dressed, now. We're about finished, here." Using the medical examiner's toiletries, I do a little washing up. I ask her a few questions about the evidence she's just collected but she neatly avoids answering. The detectives come back and the good doctor lady leaves without saying goodbye.

On further reflection, I've come to understand that it was probably in my best interest to have a lawyer present through this entire facade. I find that erring on the side of caution tends to lessen the fall. With the poking and prodding concluded the detectives keep their end of the bargain. As I get dressed, the younger detective offers to give me a ride home. I've had enough of their hospitality for one day "No. Thank you, though, really." I tell him "If it's all the same to you, I'll take a taxi." The detective calls a cab and lets me go.

# CHAPTER TWO

I'm willing to bet that there's never a good time to be accused of spousal rape; having said that, my number one priority is to consult a criminal defense attorney. After coming home from the police station, last night, I called three people whom I unequivocally trust and respect. Each of whom provided me a list of defense attorneys who they believed to be the best defense attorneys in town. One name in particular stood out. It was the name of a lawyer who showed up on each of the three lists. This person had been a full-time professional rape prosecutor who had prosecuted more than 50 rape cases. Now, one might rightly question why a man, accused of sexual assault, would want to be represented by a woman who spent the better part of her life putting rapists in jail. Well, the thing is that with all her legal experience, with actual rapists and actual rape survivors, I figure this woman could easily spot a fake. It's only a theory. Armed with this knowledge I then placed a call to *The Law Office of Gisele Taurasi*. It's such a powerful name. Whenever I refer to *The Law Office of Gisele Taurasi* I do so in a "five gold rings" manner. The only problem is that *The Law Office of Gisele Taurasi* has yet to call me back.

When you're the point guard of a basketball team they teach you to always be aware of the time and the score. Right now, the detectives are investigating and the District Attorney's office is putting together a case against me. The clock is winding down. I have no alternative but to take an assertive/proactive approach against the crazy allegations. Right after the team's morning shoot around I hail a taxi. I ask the taxi driver to get me over to *The*

*Law Office of Gisele Taurasi* as quickly as reasonably possible. I'm surprised that the taxi driver recognizes me. It, no doubt, has got something to do with me wearing the team's warm-up uniform. The taxi driver tells me that he and his wife have been following the recent and unfortunate events of my life. He increases the volume on the radio and we listen intently.

LOCAL RADIO STATION:

CALLER:

>   Law enforcement officials seem to have sought attention for themselves in investigating this professional athlete . . . . is it really necessary to say that Caleb Escueta is of good character and has no previous criminal convictions.

DISC JOCKEY:

>   I'm sorry but this isn't quite the case. Caleb Escueta has displayed the sort of aggression on the court that wouldn't be tolerated off the court. Indeed, for a player in only his second professional season he has already had his share of altercations.

CALLER:

>   In all fairness, the game of basketball is so different from the game of life. Had Caleb Escueta been a schoolteacher or an automotive technician—a talent of less physical nature—I'm sure we might not be having this debate.

DISC JOCKEY:

>   Whether he likes it or not, accepts it or not, he's a public figure. To many youngsters he's a role model. This is clearly evidenced by the media attention the investigation has

already attracted. Some of these professional athletes have managers and publicists. They make it a point to keep people like this in the public eye. I say that comes with a huge responsibility. When young people see the Kingmaker extending his aggressive behaviors beyond the court it sends altogether the wrong message.

CALLER:

These professional athletes are human beings just like you and I. Whose life, when under the microscope, is perfectly-perfect? Athletes like Caleb Escueta are brought right out of college and they're suddenly thrust into the public eye. Surely, you can understand that they are at far too young an age to cope with that sort of attention. Mistakes will be made. We can't prop Caleb Escueta up as role models then make an example out of him when he doesn't live up to our high expectations. I believe what our professional athletes require effective support and encouragement, not criticism. We're all in need of examples of selflessness, not critics.

DISC JOCKEY:

What he's dealing with is merely the consequences of his aggressive behavior when the stakes are so high. This man was not set up to fail; that he did on his own. Let us not forget that Caleb Escueta is being investigated for sexual assault. When young people see that he can't get away with that sort of behavior then they will realize that neither can they.

*

The taxi driver is doing a fine job negotiating his way through traffic. "Have faith in the system, Kingmaker." He offers. "The system might surprise you." I thank him for his intelligent and forthright assessment. Then I ask him to change the radio station. I've heard enough. As he fiddles through the radio stations I'm reminded that the last trial case Mrs. Taurasi lead involved a drunk driver and a dead father. Her client was a police officer. I remember that case because everyone seemed to want that police officer's head on a platter. Mrs. Taurasi found a way to win the case. To many observers, including me, the win was nothing short of a miracle. Fate would have it that the victory would take its toll on Mrs. Taurasi. It's my understanding that, following the narrow victory, she has gone into what was described to me to be lawyer's block. In the six months that followed her big victory, and up until today, Mrs. Taurasi has rejected every case that has come before her. I bet the poor woman's been banging her head against the wall with guilt.

It's a heroic effort but traffic eventually gets the better of my taxi driver. I look out the window and see that we're a mere 2 blocks from *The Law Office of Gisele Taurasi*. After having weighed the risks and benefits, of continuing the journey on foot, I hand the taxi driver a wad of cash. "Thank you." I say. "It's such a nice day. I think I can walk the rest of the way."

The taxi driver holds the cash up with two fingers and says, "Dare to think better thoughts, Mr. Escueta."

I'm on foot patrol. About a half-block up the road an adorable-little creature creeps out of the bushes. After a few clumsy steps the animal crosses directly into my path. I stop and get a good look at the thing. The furry thing is a little-white dog with black patches. The helpless animal—which has no dog tags and looks worse for wear—gets a good look at me. Stuck somewhere between hope and despair the creature lets out a bellow. I can't speak for the animal but, for me, it is love at first sight. Suffice it to say, I can't be distracted by a little thing like puppy love. I have a clear objective and that objective doesn't involve squishy things. I walk around the little dog and press forward to *The Law Office of Gisele Taurasi*.

Just when I I'm feeling like a man on a mission my conscience gets the better of me. I turn around to get one last look at the lovely-little animal. Alas, my little love has already scurried, back into the bushes, from whence it came.

In good time, I reach my destination. An elderly gentleman has me stewing in the reception area of *The Law Office of Gisele Taurasi*. I feel like a schoolboy who's waiting to be reprimanded by the principal. With the clock is ticking, my impatience takes a hold of me. Despite the elderly gentleman's best efforts, I guerilla my way into Mrs. Taurasi's office. I put my hands on my hips—Coach style—and declare "Now I know why Shakespeare said first kill the lawyers."

"Mr. Escueta . . . ." Mrs. Taurasi says getting the ground beneath her feet. "I thought I recognized you from the television. My husband is a follower of your league." I'm not impressed. "We've been trying to get in touch with you."

"Really?" I ask rhetorically. "Really." I say it, again, but more as a statement of fact. "*The Law Office of Gisele Taurasi* has been trying to get in touch with me?"

She states the obvious. "I see you're upset." Mrs. Taurasi is, I don't know, in her mid-sixties . . . ? Though she's obviously of African descent; she's rather light-skinned. When she speaks she does so with an unrushed drawl.

"You know, people complain that there are too many lawyers. Now that I'm in need, I can't even find the one I want."

"Well, there are never too many *good* lawyers." Don't look now but the attorney-and-counsel-at-law is making an argument. "I doubt you came all the way over here to vent? Would you like a glass of water, Mr. Escueta?"

"You guys haven't responded to my case." I say as if vomiting the words. *"You've* been trying to get in touch with *me?* You guys never even called me back. What kind of lawyering is that?"

"I'm so sorry, Mr. Escueta. I'm truly sorry." She pleads. "The decision isn't personal."

"The decision isn't personal?" When I get upset I tend to parrot. "I'm in a coffin here and my wife is nailing it shut. For me, it doesn't get more personal than this."

"I'm actually relieved you came here." She tells me. "I am. I know you're feeling some kind of way about our not taking your case and I'd like to clear the air if I could."

"That's a nice way of putting it, huh. You're going to let these people lynch me? You're really going to let me burn? It sounds like these guys want to lock me up until the apocalypse. You didn't let that cop burn and he killed that guy. Next to him I'm choirboy."

"We're currently inundated with cases. My husband is overwhelmed. If you were in my position . . ."

"That guy, in the waiting room, is your husband? I thought he was a client." I'm shocked. "I'd never be in your position because I would never turn my back on an innocent man."

"'Never' is such a strong word." She argues. "It's not so clear cut." I give her the opportunity to get it all out. "Let's say I review 100 cases. We might only take 2 or 3 of them. We actually hire people to help us screen cases and filter cases." She explains. "I have to pick and choose cases that have the most merit. Now, if you like, I can refer you to a few defense attorneys who specialize in sexual assault cases."

At the moment she says all that my selective hearing kicks in. "Cases with the most merit, huh. Now, what's that supposed to mean?" Call me naïve but don't think it should matter if a case is popular or unpopular. It shouldn't matter if a case is big or small. The only thing that ought to matter, when selecting a case, is whether or not the client is innocent. "You're killing me."

"In order for anyone to get paid a case has to be, first, won. A single trial can carry on for as long as six weeks. We get complex cases, such as yours, all the time and we have to choose the most promising among them. You have to take into account that our cost to pursue a case is substantial. We provide quality representation. We reach into our own pockets to properly represent a client in court. There is no revenue in frivolous cases." She backpedals. "Not that your case is frivolous. I'm not implying that your case is frivolous."

"Stop." I don't want to hear this. "Stop talking."

She clears her throat. "I'm so sorry, Mr. Escueta. I know you said you don't want me to say that I'm sorry but I am. I'm truly sorry."

"Just stop." I repeat. The apologetic attorney gestures for me to take a seat. She hands me a glass of water. I take three huge gulps then say the first thing that comes into my head. "You know, I saw a little dog, just outside. The damn thing looked so . . . sad." I tell her this as I adjust myself in the seat. "How can anyone argue that suffering is some type of divine . . . some type of punishment? Divine? I'm sure people would like to believe that the good—in this world—outweighs the evil. Seeing that little dog I wonder if believing that is an insult to those who are suffering. What justification can there be for that? I mean, what amount of good has to come from suffering in order for the suffering to be justified? How would we begin to even measure that sort of thing?"

"Excuse me. Counselor?" Her husband beckons. "Can I borrow you for a moment? It won't take but a minute." The two lovebirds make their way into the reception area. I take a look around Mrs. Taurasi's office. She has a newspaper clipping on her desk. I can't resist the urge to read it.

LOCAL NEWS REPORT:

A police sergeant arrested for allegedly causing a deadly drunken-driving crash, last May, was ordered yesterday to stand trial on all charges. Terrance Singh showed no expression at his preliminary hearing, during which testimony was given that he was driving at more than 100 miles per hour when he slammed into a van being driven by Marcus Harrington. "Singh was traveling at almost three times the speed limit" Assistant District Attorney James Guthrie said.

The collision which occurred shortly before midnight left Singh with a broken wrist, while Harrington was ejected from his van and mortally injured. Harrington, a father of 4, died 3 days later of blunt-force injuries. Just before the crash, Singh and a friend had been drinking at *The Silver Tattoo*. "The rate of speed at which Singh was traveling was obtained from an onboard crash-data-recording device, similar to an airplane's black box" an officer of the Accident Investigation Division testified. He said that 5 seconds before the crash, Singh was going 73 miles per hour and he reached 101 miles per hour at impact.

Judge Karen M. Sampson held Singh for trial on 2 counts: homicide by vehicle while DUI; and involuntary manslaughter. Defense attorney Gisele Taurasi sought to get the lead charge of homicide by vehicle while DUI dismissed, arguing that the accident resulted because Harrington ran a blinking red light. Judge Sampson dismissed the charge of homicide by vehicle while DUI. Singh, a cop for 21 years, was fired immediately following the crash. He is now serving 8 years for involuntary manslaughter. He is expected to serve only 2 of those years.

\*

The conversation between Mrs. Taurasi and her husband gets a little hot under the collar. Somehow seeing them argue pleases me. Then, without warning, their discussion ends and the two of them break away. Her husband enters the office armed with some paperwork. He explains to me that, before discussing my case with *The Law Office of Gisele Taurasi*, I should first to fill out something called a retainer. This document, as her husband explains to me, ensures attorney—client privilege. Mr. Taurasi emphasis the point that a retainer does not mean *The Law Office of Gisele Taurasi* is going to take my case. The retainer only means that our conversations, about the case, are secured or privileged while they have time to make that final decision.

My selective hearing clings to the part where he said *The Law Office of Gisele Taurasi* have not, yet, decided to take my case. As with last night's delightful medical examination I, again, sign my life away. Mrs. Taurasi and her husband insist that I keep a copy of the retainer. When Mr. Taurasi leaves the room Mrs. Taurasi asks me if I know what I'm being charged with. I tell her that my wife Sojey is claiming that I raped her. "My wife Sojey is claiming I raped her."

"Well, at this point, it's only an allegation." She says. "Don't forget that. It's important. Allegations are not evidence and *unsubstantiated* allegations are irrelevant. Have you attempted to contact your wife, since the investigation began?" She asks.

"No, I didn't. Should I?"

"Absolutely not." Mrs. Taurasi advises. "In doing so you'd be opening the door to witness intimidation."

"That's good to know." I encourage. "See? Now, we're getting somewhere."

Mrs. Taurasi breaks the situation down, for me. "Spousal rape takes place when one engages in an act of sexual intercourse with the other without consent. The good news is that, in our jurisdiction, the penalties for spousal rape are *less* than those for rape of someone other than a spouse. The bad news is that rape laws protect spouses from unwanted sexual intercourse in the same way that they protect everyone else."

"Well, my wife told the detectives that the sex took place *without* her consent."

"So, there was intercourse?" She asks. I don't respond because it's embarrassing. She reminds me that I have attorney-client privilege but I'm not altogether convinced. She tells me that I have no idea the great pains she goes through to ensure that privilege. "If I'm going to represent you then you're going to have to answer all of my questions to the best of your ability. I'm going to need to know everything about you. Remember, you chose me." She tells me that this isn't basketball; that there are no make-up calls in criminal court; that we have to get this right the first time. I have to admit Mrs. Taurasi makes a convincing argument.

"The answer to your question is yes." I respond. "Yes, there was intercourse."

"Did you accomplish this through the use of force? Do your best to keep in mind that this is not an accusation—it's a need to know."

"No. I didn't force her." "Did you use violence?" "It wasn't like that."

"Mr. Escueta, did you make any type of threat?" "Of course I didn't threaten her, no."

27

"Did you know her to be on any drug, alcohol, medication, or any other intoxicating substance?"

"My wife isn't like that."

"We'll have to confirm that with her toxicology test. Was she unconscious of what was going on . . . how can I say this . . . was she awake at the time?" "I wouldn't do that." I respond. "Sojey was awake."

"I have to ask, Mr. Escueta. Was your wife aware that the act was going on?"

"She certainly was." I tell her. "If they convict me what kind of sentence would I be looking at?"

"We'll get into greater depth later but, for the purposes of this discussion, spousal rape is a felony." I can feel the air come out of the room. "Penalties may include fines, formal probation, up to ten years in the gulag—even more if it is determined that you inflicted a great bodily injury—and a lifetime requirement of registration as a sex offender."

On paper, Gisele Taurasi is a very impressive attorney. She completed her undergraduate work at the nation's premier school of journalism. After several years of covering trial and appellate courts, she graduated cum laude from her Law School. After her stint as a prosecutor she began assisting clients with an extensive array of offenses ranging from traffic violations to homicide, murder, and serious sex and drug related cases. I understand she's also a top appellate litigator and has been involved in many successfully acquired appeals. "Are you good at what you do?" I ask her point blank.

"Let me explain this to in terms you might appreciate." She says. "If you want to play the game, you had better know the rules. If you want your opponent to play by those rules, you'll not only have to recognize the infraction, but you'll have to complain to the referee and tell him exactly which rule was violated by the opposition." Wow. "I'll be frank. I don't think this is going to just go away. We can also expect that everybody involved in this case is going to act differently because it's going to have media exposure. With the press second-guessing everyone's every move we can *also* expect the prosecutor to (1) not entertain any deals and (2) push for the maximum penalties. The last thing the District Attorney's office wants is to be accused of being too lenient on a high-profile defendant such as you. The state doesn't want the public to think they're soft on crime."

I tell Mrs. Taurasi that I'm not interested in making any kind of side-deal; that I don't want to plea-bargain; that I don't want to settle this out of court. Quite the contrary, I want my day *in* court. I want to go on the stand and set the record straight. After all, I did nothing wrong. I then ask that Sojey not be dragged through the mud. "You know what I mean?" I ask her. "I've seen what happens to women who cry rape. It's an ugly thing and no one deserves that. It would only be *two* wrongs. I don't want you making her out to be something she's not. I mean, she's still the mother of my children."

I realize that taking such a stance can have injurious effects on my case but, then again, this is *my* case. Mrs. Taurasi doesn't respond to me either way. She simply jots notes down on yellow Post-Its. "If you do take my case I want it clear that we're not putting my wife on trial. That's all I ask, really. I want you guys to find another way to win this case." Once again, Mrs. Taurasi doesn't respond. In fact, neither of us says a word for what seems like 24 seconds.

Mr. Taurasi sticks his big head in the office. He informs us that he has The Forces of Reaction (namely the head of my basketball team's legal affairs) are holding on line one. The gentleman from my team informs us that this is a public relations nightmare but they're going to stand behind me. In fact, for the duration of the ordeal,

The Forces of Reaction are going to continue to pay my salary. In addition, he tells us that The Forces of Reaction are going to reimburse me for legal fees should I be acquitted. I wonder. If I didn't average 11.5 assists per game would we even be having this conversation?

Don't answer that.

The gentleman proceeds to inform us that the team is prepared to do whatever they can, within reason, to help during this troubling period. "All we ask for in return is that you keep us in the loop." Mrs. Taurasi tells him that she'll be in constant and close contact. Obviously she wants to ask his 1000 questions, about me, but she wants to do this when I'm not in the room. Fair enough. She then tells the gentleman that she needs to hang up; that she has to prepare me to go county jail and surrender myself.

How one would prepare himself to go to jail, I don't know. The conversation begins simply enough. I ask Mrs. Taurasi if I'll be handcuffed and she says "Most likely. At the precinct, a police officer will interview you and ask for pedigree." I ask her what pedigree means and she informs, "Information, including your name, address, date of birth . . . so take two forms of identification with you. You'll be fingerprinted and photographed. You'll be searched and they'll take away whatever you have in your possession. They'll give you a voucher for your property. Keep the voucher. It'll make it easier for you to retrieve your property once you're released."

I hear the word *released*. "And how long is that?"

"Processing can take up to 9 hours. During that time, you'll be held in a cell. There may or may not be pay telephones, in the cell, for your use. Know that anything you say in the presence of a police officer might be used against you. They can even use statements that they overhear you make during a telephone call or while you are talking to other inmates. Mr. Escueta, if you hear nothing else hear this: Be extremely careful what you say while you're at county jail. Don't be naïve. The guy in the cell with you is not your friend. Don't talk about your case with anyone; especially, if I'm not there to protect you. Get it?"

"I got it."

"Good. If you think you have information, that'll help your case, you tell me and only me. Do you have any questions, so far?"

"So, I'm going to jail without a trial?" "That's the way it works."

"I thought people were innocent until proven guilty?"

"Take it up with the Legislature, Mr. Escueta." She tells me. "It's in the interests of public safety."

"Okay. So, say I turn myself in and the court rules in my favor. I don't see an easy way, for the state, to restore to me the time I spent in jail."

"How about . . . let's just try to think productively."

"And won't it make it difficult for me to build a case, for myself, if I'm locked up in county jail?"

"I know this is a difficult time, Mr. Escueta, but it doesn't have to define you."

"This is the lowest point in my life." I tell her. "And it doesn't help that I have to share it with the local media. You know, I bet my wife wouldn't tell this lie if her name were *also* published by the newspapers."

"I understand the double standard, in the media, Mr. Escueta." "Do you?" I ask

"I know it all too well, and I believe the stigma inherent in identifying a husband as an alleged rapist is worse than that inherent in identifying a wife as an alleged victim." She states.

"Yes . . . I mean . . . what?" She gives me time to process. "How is it that the accused doesn't have the same protection, from the media, as the accuser?" I ask. "I'm innocent yet this chicken—liver disc jockey is attacking me as if I were a registered sex offender. Maybe, if I were a minor, the media wouldn't attack me like this. It's so confusing. Who tells them this is right?"

She hands me a pocket-sized version of *The Constitution*. "I don't mean to sound cruel but I hope you didn't retain my services simply because I'm a woman?"

"Hmm . . . now which one of us is being be naïve?"

# CHAPTER THREE

I couldn't sleep at all last night. The Taurasi's gave me an annotated version of *The Constitution* but I couldn't get past page ten. Then, I made the rookie mistake of watching television. With my private life being made a public reckoning it's no surprise that a late night talk show host would take a few cheap shots. It was embarrassing but I couldn't stop watching.

LOCAL TALK SHOW:

In recent news, Assistant District Attorney R.F. Sanchez has issued a warrant for the arrest of Caleb Escueta. The professional basketball player has been formerly charged with sexual assault.

I think maybe the judge ought to consider using instant replay in order to make a definitive call ha-ha-ha.

Well, the good news for Caleb Escueta is that he just might end up being the tallest player—on his prison team.

Hey, you know why Caleb Escueta wears goggles during sex? It's to keep the mace out of his eyes ha-ha-ha.

This is a serious charge though. It should be taken seriously. I understand his lawyers are really worried about jury prejudice— should there be a trial. I think his lawyers are worried for a good reason: no one likes a rapist.

This just in, Caleb Escueta has the top-selling basketball jersey—in prison.

In case you haven't heard Caleb Escueta's nickname is Kingmaker; that's got to be so much better than what his new nickname is going to be—Rapist.

But I don't know all the facts. The investigation is still going on. I shouldn't rush to judgment of Caleb Escueta. All I can say for now is that his teammates better hope Kingmaker never gets sexually confused ha-ha-ha.

*

Surrendering at county jail is a novel experience. The episode begins with me emptying all of my pockets into a plastic bowl. I, then, spend the next 9 hours with my left wrist handcuffed to the arm of a metal chair. Sitting under the lights and the constant rush of air from the ceiling ventilation I have plenty of time to wrestle with the idea that, if my wife has her way, I could be sent to the gulag for 10 years.

In county jail, there are different levels for incarceration for different inmates. This is determined by a variety of factors. For instance, my classification is based on my behavior, the criminal charge set against me, my criminal history, my potential for being a victim, my gang affiliation(s), and my programming needs. After exactly 9 hours, I'm finally classified. I would venture to guess that, to the corrections staff, my presence is something of a logistical problem. The deputies transfer me to a place called M-Dorm. This is where the routine of my jail life will begin.

The corrections staff have me put on prison fatigues: green top, green bottom, and brown rubber slippers. I pick out linens and a mattress. My mattress is so worn down that it's more like a pillow.

I'm appalled by the fact that the corrections staff didn't separate me from the violent offenders. I've got my annotated version of *The Constitution* with me. I've got a pencil and even a roll of toilet paper. Perhaps I should use my time to draft a grievance letter to the Supreme Court. Before I do that I should take a moment to collect my thoughts on the matter.

Indulge me.

Let's say a man named "Caesar" has never been convicted of a violent crime. "Caesar" goes to jail. He is housed in M-Dorm with the likes of "Brutus" and "Cassius". Now, "Brutus" is doing time for armed robbery and "Cassius" is doing time for attempted murder. By the time "Caesar" is released form M-Dorm he would've likely been influenced by those around him. Thus, "Caesar" (a non-violent criminal) learns one thing from his time in jail. "Caesar" learns how to be violent.

*

It's been a few hours. I have to admit, that I've always imagined inmates to be this army of dangerous conspirators who were plotting to escape, from bondage, and overthrow the Republic. Looking around M-Dorm, I can tell you that, this just is not the case. "Brutus" and "Cassius" are just guys trying to do their time. They seem nice enough; although, I don't intend to keep in touch with anyone in particular. I'm willing to bet that a majority of these inmates are low-level drug dealers or addicts. From the looks of things they need drug treatment more than they need punishment. M-Dorm has a barracks-style lay-out. The corrections staff has their office in the center and front entrance part. Our bunks [racks or beds] are lined up on either side. There are about 20 to 30 inmates per side. At the far ends of each bunk area, there are two areas: one for game playing and such and the other for television. M-Dorm tends to get really loud because all of the sounds are trapped and they bounce off of the concrete walls. As you already know, I have an annotated version of *The Constitution*, a pencil, and a roll of toilet paper. On my rack I find a plastic spoon/fork or "spork", tiny bars of soap, a disposable razor, a toothbrush, and tooth paste.

As one can imagine M-Dorm is a busy place. Visitation starts at 9:00am and ends at 9:00pm. Due to this, inmates are constantly coming in and going out. There are a few inmates playing the loudest and most physical game of cards I have ever seen. They use chopped up playing cards as chips. Other inmates are playing chess and checkers. Still other inmates are doing calisthenics, grooming, gossiping, writing, reading, and acting out *Julius Caesar*. M-Dorm offers classes, in different subjects, where inmates can pursue their General Education Degree. It's not a country club, but M-Dorm has plenty of activities to help pass the time.

Some of the long-time inmates have jobs. A few of them are secretaries for the corrections staff while a few others prepare and serve meals. The inmate living in the bunk below me holds a janitorial job. His name is Dexter Valez. He also works in the laundry. In the morning he exercises wearing nothing but a t-shirt as shorts. Let me rephrase that, Dexter Valez uses his t-shirt as shorts. All thing being equal I would prefer he did crotchet—fully clothed.

Though I'm a professional athlete my face isn't one people recognize. It comes with little surprise that the other inmates haven't figured out or showed that they cared who I am on the outside. I try to keep to myself but it's not so easy when you're on display in a place like M—Dorm. I'm watching a few of the inmates preparing to pray. The inmates kneel on the tops of their blankets. Their movements appear rehearsed. They stand up. I watch as they raise their hands to their ears and say "*Allah Akbar*." Together they stack their hands and place them on their stomachs. I have to block out the other noises in order to listen to them recite their prayers "*subhanakal-lahumma, wabihamdika watabarakas-muka wataaaala, judduka wala ilaha ghayruk, a'auodu billaahi minash-shaytaanir rajeem, bis-millaahir rahmaanir raheem"*. At this point, the pious group of men do their best to ignore everyone and everything else. Their chanting goes on for a while. It appears to end when they bend forward and repeat *"Allah Akbar."* Their hands go back to their ears, *"Samey—Allahu—leman—Hameda."* There's more bowing and kneeling but the whole thing ends with them turning to their left and saying *"As Salam Alaykum wa Rahmatullahi wa Barakatuhu."*

M-Dorm gets especially loud during last chow. Inmates scream things like "two milks for pudding" or "hot meal for sandwich and milk". It's about this time that I'm beginning to think about my body fat. It's well-known that Coach is a control freak. It's not one of his enduring traits. I imagine Coach would make a satisfactory correctional staff member. At any rate, Coach is serious and even obsessed about what his players put into their bodies. In fact, the first time Coach invited me to his house he explained his body fat program.

> Guards are allowed to have a maximum of 7% body fat.

> Forwards are allowed to have a maximum of 9% body fat.

> Centers are allowed to have a maximum of 11% body fat.

Whenever something doesn't go the teams' way Coach tells us it's because we're out of shape. If we turn the ball over: it's because we're out of shape. If the bus is late: it's because we're out of shape. If the referee makes the wrong call: it's because we're out of shape. The next thing you know we're having a 3 hour long knock-down-drag-out practice. It's as petty as it is ridiculous. Seasons prior to my arrival Coach's teams were in great shape but they were losing teams. A part of me is of the opinion that Coach isn't authorized to talk to down to me. A part of me is aware that, basketball-wise, not only have I accomplished more than Coach but I also accomplished it in less time. That is to say I've obtained every accolade an amateur career has to offer. I already know what it takes to win and it has absolutely nothing to do with guards having 7% body fat, forwards having 9% body fat, and centers having 11% body fat. It's got nothing to do with that.

Case and point: look at Bo. The man is a physical specimen; yet, when you think of the league's top forwards you can't even fit him anywhere on that list. I'm not prescribing laziness as a form of training. All I'm saying is that when you get to a certain level body fat doesn't mean a thing. Basketball is about technique, and desire, and court awareness . . . basketball is about things that have little to do with how much dinner wine you drink or how big your ass is. In fact, I'd say we guards need a little more than 7% body fat in order to absorb the poundings we take during the season. Your body can't handle that type of daily punishment when you're lean to the tune of 7%. I think Coach is out of his depth in saying otherwise. The players all know it is but none of them want to rock the boat. They'd rather eat salad-freaking-salad, defer to Bo, and kiss Coach's ass. Sitting in M-Dorm makes it seem all the more petty and all the more ridiculous.

So there I am. I've got my plastic spork and I'm trying to enjoy my pudding. My bunkmate Dexter Valez sits across the table and offers me a biscuit. "Merry Christmas, Brother." He offers as an opening gambit. I'd have to say that the worst thing about my county jail experience was the lottery I faced on arrival. I wasn't sure what the other inmates were going to be like. Would they be serial killers or psychopaths? Will my bunk mate be some poor guy, who really should be in a hospital, because he's suffering from a mental illness? What if my bunkmate is a big-bull homosexual, on the prowl, for fresh meat? In county jail homophobia isn't so much a prejudice as a survival instinct. It doesn't matter how tolerant a person you like to believe you are. When an inmate stares at you, for more than 20 seconds, without blinking, you think to yourself fight-or-flight. You don't stop to imagine the pillow talk.

"Don't worry. Your secret is safe with me." Dexter Valez tells me. My face tenses up but he continues anyway. "I know who you are. You're the guy from The Kingmaker Case. That's right, I know you. Brother, you're that point guard who got arrested for sex stuff. Now, I read about you in the newspaper. I know all about it. You know, they did a poll asking people if your arrest would change their opinion of you. You want to know what those results are?"

"No." I tell him. "Not really. You must have me mistaken for someone who cares about other people's opinions." Valez tell me the results, anyway:

'Yes it changes my opinion of him' 43%.

'No it doesn't change my opinion of him' 30%.

'I'll wait for the trial' 27%.

I don't say anything to encourage Dexter Valez. "I bet you're wondering why I'm in here?" He asks me.

My subtle attempts to get rid of him have failed. I try to give him a stronger hint "You know what, how about we leave it a mystery?"

"Don't be supercilious. It doesn't suit you." He's waiting for me to respond but I don't. "I'm in here because it's part of His plan" he insists. "You're part of His plan, too, brother."

"His plan?" Oh no. I'm curious. "I take it you're talking about something spiritual?"

"What else is there" he asks though his tone is rhetorical. "What do you know, about it, anyway? Brother, you play a child's game for a living? That's right, but you don't have inkling as to what the *real* game is about." I could walk away. The only thing is that if I walk away from Dexter Valez, now, I'll spend the rest of my time in county jail walking away from him. He needs to walk away from me. "You see, society want you to be a winner. They want you to win for them but do you think they really want you and your family living in their neighborhoods ha—ha-ha? Don't be an idiot."

"Well, that's certainly a theory." I say.

"You and me, brother, we met for a reason. I'm here to tell you that you've got to forgive." I look at him as if to ask he's serious. "Forgiveness is freedom, brother. Your body may be locked in M-Dorm but—what's worse—is that your soul is down in the hole that is in solitary confinement. You'll be lost in limbo until you forgive." He repeats, "Forgiveness is freedom, brother."

"Anything else?" It's just one of those things you ask.

"Look at you all lawyered up. No lawyer in the world can free your soul. Now, tell me something, brother. Does this bother you?"

"Let's say yes." I tell him; offering yet another hint to go somewhere-anywhere else.

He says, "Well you think about what I told you while you're enjoying your Christmas."

It's been my experience that it's near impossible to have an adult conversation with someone who believes in ghosts. "You need god to tell you who to forgive?" I ask but he doesn't respond. "You need Christmas to bring out the spirit of Christmas? That's okay, for you, but I don't need that. You need Santa Clause to make you feel good? That's okay, for you, but I don't need that.

You see, I can appreciate the spirit of Christmas without believing in ghosts?" Oops. I catch myself. "You know what, brother, let's just drop it."

"It's too late for that, now. You break it; you bought it." Valez persists. "So, what are you . . . oh, I see . . . you're an atheist? Boy-oh-boy. There's always one." Fascinating, every time Dexter Valez opens his mouth I dislike him even more.

"Everyone's an atheist?" He seems stunned, so, I elaborate. "Have you ever prayed to Vishnu? When was the last time you lay awake at night contemplating what might happen if you die before making your peace with Quetzalcoatl? When you go to the beach do you pay homage to Poseidon? Every belief is in a minority somewhere—even Santa Claus and even Jesus. Like I said, we're all atheists."

"So what do you believe in?" He pokes.

"What if I told you I was Amish?" I ask. "Would it matter? We'd tell each other that we respect the others beliefs; then—secretly— damn one another on *account* of those conflicting beliefs. It's Christmas, how about we skip that part?"

"You're lost in limbo, brother." He taunts me.

Maybe he's right? How does one truthfully navigate the moral contradictions? [Monologue redacted.]

I accept that, for Dexter Valez, faith is a source of strength. I get that. I truly do. I also get that his sense of strength comes at a very high price. I'll spare you the history lesson. Looking M-Dorm I find it repugnant that mankind is the only species on the planet to claim god(s). Let me ask you this: Is there anything else from the Bronze Age that the human race still clings to?

I digress.

In M-Dorm, last shut down is promptly at 10:00 pm. The inmates appear to respect the shutdown. Out of courtesy and for our own safety we confine ourselves to our racks. My theological conversation with the Dexter Valez continues at a mere whisper.

"God is good, brother." He says trying to lock horns with me. "And He never makes mistakes." Suddenly, four years of college hits me like an avalanche of thoughts: crusades, inquisitions, witch trials . . . . Imagine 3 of Jesus' Apostles are here, in M-Dorm. They have arrived in a time machine. Now, they happen to wander into the bathroom where they stop in front of the toilet bowls. One of the Apostle's gets down on his knees and he starts drinking from the toilet. Another Apostle dips his hands in the toilet and washes his face with the water. I'm not trying to be comic. I'm making a point. Maybe, we've all got it wrong?

"You know what the Bible says about rape?" Dexter Valez asks. "Honestly, I don't really give a rat's ass." With that the conversation ends.

After spending the last 4 days in county jail I think I finally have the routine down. It begins with breakfast at 4:00am. In recent months I've been suffering through some nagging basketball injuries or as Coach would say "a variety of maladies". I must say that the M-Dorm rest has done me some good. Until now I've been sleeping right through breakfast but today I'm scheduled for early morning court. With hopes of being released on my mind I hurriedly eat the cold meal which consists of a bagel, a banana, and milk. The reason they serve breakfast so early is so that the morning court crew will have time to be searched, shackled, and ready for transport. Also, inmates who, for whatever reason(s) were locked in cells for the night are also allowed to enter the day room.

\*

My first impression of a courtroom is that it's a calm and quiet place. There's only one bailiff in here but, with all the protocols, one gets a sense that the room is completely secure. Having read *The Constitution* I can tell you that—at the heart of justice—is the grave responsibility of determining guilt or innocence. The courtroom is where the truth (or the proof of the truth) comes out. There's a wood waist-high gate that horizontally crosses the room. The back-half of the room is a lot like a church with its pew-like seats. The front-half is the court area. There's a large platform for the judge. There are two desks, one on each side of the judge's platform, in which the defense attorney and the prosecutor sit.

The Assistant District Attorney glares at me. He looks as though he'd be more than happy to put me away for the rest of my natural-born life. Adjacent to the judge's platform is a chair with some small walls around it. This is the witness stand. After being bunkmates with Dexter Valez, for the last few days, I'm more than relieved that I finally get my day in court. The judge enters and the bailiff calls the proceedings to order. Then the judge looks directly at me. At this moment it becomes perfectly clear that my life is in someone else's hands. I'm cuffed and shackled. I'm wearing prison issued attire and, unfortunately, there's nothing I can do about any of that.

Physical appearance matters. Whether it should or not doesn't really factor into it, does it? Let's talk about Mrs. Taurasi's make-up. I think a woman who wears just the right amount of war-paint, as she did today, appears more competent. However, it's not her physical attributes that determine how competent I perceive her. It's the fact that she *took the time* to make herself look more presentable. It's more about the effort behind her war-paint than the war-paint itself. Putting an effort into making her appearance appropriate and presentable shows that she wants to be taken seriously and that she cares about how others perceive her. Today, I think she looks professional and attractive and I'm sure she'll be able to use those qualities to charm this judge.

The arraignment . . .

THE COURT:

What's it to be, counselor?

MR. SANCHEZ:

Docket ending 7128: The People versus Caleb Escueta. The charge is spousal rape.

THE COURT:

Q Mr. Escueta, do you understand the charges set against you?

A I do, your Honor.

Q And how do you plead?

A It didn't happen, your Honor. Not on my mother's eyes.

Q Mr. Escueta, a simple answer would do the court just fine.

A Absolutely-positively not guilty.

Q In the future you'll want to avoid absolutes.

A simple declarative 'not guilty' is incredibly sufficient.

MR. SANCHEZ:

Thank you, your Honor.

THE DEFENDANT:

A Not guilty.

THE COURT:

Mr. Sanchez, before I make a ruling, would like to you want to weigh in on the Defense's application for bail?

MR. SANCHEZ:

The prosecution recommends no bail, your Honor. The defendant is financially self—sufficient, has family overseas, and is familiar with types and means of flight. More significantly, your Honor, due to the heinous nature of the crime, we believe freeing the defendant would represent a serious risk to the community. To put it indelicately, the defendant is a sexual predator and because of this we request the he be remanded in custody.

THE DEFENDANT:

Your Honor, I find this charge to be an outrageous assertion; I'll wager with nothing to substantiate it. More importantly, to put it indelicately, your Honor, the pants Mr. Sanchez is wearing don't go with his jacket.

THE COURT:

This is merely an arraignment, Mr. Escueta. We're only here to have the charge read, enter your plea, and talk about bail. Feel free to jump in, any time, Mrs. Taurasi.

MRS. TAURASI:

Your Honor, my client is a father of 2 young children. He has obvious ties to this community. He has no criminal history, no less a major felony. He's been living an exemplary private life.

(Clears throat.)

As I've stated he has no criminal record and no connections to criminal circles. The allegation made against him is blatantly false and is no reason to deprive this man of his liberty. He has no urge to run from this; quite the contrary, he intends to clear his name. Locking him up would greatly hinder his ability to do so. I don't believe this unfounded allegation is worth risking my client's liberty.

MR. SANCHEZ:

Objection you Honor. 'Blatantly false' is a characterization.

MRS. TAURASI:

No more than 'sexual predator'. Perhaps my learned friend would prefer I refer to the allegation as 'groundless'?

MR. SANCHEZ:

The same objection, your Honor.

MRS. TAURASI:

What about 'unwarranted accusation'?

MR. SANCHEZ:

What about the same objection?

MRS. TAURASI:

' . . . an accusation lacking sound basis'?

MR. SANCHEZ:

Characterization, your Honor.

MRS. TAURASI:

'An outright lie'?

MR. SANCHEZ:

Now, I strenuously object to that.

MRS. TAURASI:

Since we're dotting the I's and crossing the T's I strenuously object to my learned friend constantly referring to Mr. Escueta as 'the defendant' as *that* term is a form of characterization all its own.

MR. SANCHEZ:

This is absurd.

THE COURT:

(Gavel raps.)

Fortunately for us we don't have an impressionable jury to worry about. Impressive as that display was it'll have to do. Let's try to avoid emotive language shall we? Goodness, my heart goes out to the judge who is assigned to this trial. As to Mrs. Taurasi's motion for bail the court is not thoroughly convinced.

MRS. TAURASI:

Your Honor, would the court find home confinement to be more convincing?

THE COURT:

> Mr. Sanchez, I assume you want to weigh in on the matter?

MR. SANCHEZ:

> Your Honor, I can see how house arrest may minimize both the risk of flight and the danger to the community but prison would eliminate both those risks. Furthermore, there is a stay away order between Mr. and Mrs. Escueta.

MRS. TAURASI:

> That's why the Defense is suggesting Mr. Escueta be electronically monitored from my private residence.

THE COURT:

> You're up Mr. Sanchez?

MR. SANCHEZ:

> While I'm sure Mr. Escueta is a proper little angel the prosecution would feel better if the Defense were prepared to shoulder the cost of having a police officer posted outside the residence.

THE DEFENDANT:

> Your Honor, wouldn't that be a violation of my attorneys Second Amendment rights?

THE COURT:

> . . . her right to bear arms . . . ?

MR. SANCHEZ:

> Please the court, I think Mr. Escueta is referring to the Third Amendment.

THE COURT:

> Mr. Escueta, the Third Amendment would protect your attorney from having government troops taking up residence in her home.

THE DEFENDANT:

> Oh, my bad.

THE COURT:

> Mrs. Taurasi, is this dialog really necessary?

MRS. TAURASI:

> My apologies your Honor. My client has spending his time in county jail studying *The Constitution*.

THE COURT:

> I'm impressed, Mr. Escueta. In the future, if there are any interruptions to be made I'm sure your very able attorney can make them. Otherwise, if you want to stand out wear pink socks.

THE DEFENSE:

> Thank you, your Honor. And I understand that it's natural to feel sympathy for a perceived victim but that sympathy shouldn't result in punishing an innocent man.

THE COURT:

Counsel, please advise your client that this is only a preliminary hearing. His defense will be heard in due course.

MRS. TAURASI:

My client's been so advised. Please the court, on the matter of house arrest, the Defense is prepared to meet the prosecution's criteria.

THE COURT:

Very well, house arrest it is. Caleb Escueta is ordered to be confined to the residence of his attorney. Communication will be allowed; however, keep in mind the conversations will be closely monitored. Go see the court clerk for the specifics. In addition, Mr. Escueta is ordered by this court to surrender his passport. This is your only warning, Mr. Escueta. Don't give me reason to rescind this order. If I have to lock you up I won't be losing any sleep over it.

(Gavel raps.)

# CHAPTER FOUR

After a few hours of processing a police officer attaches a GPS monitor to my ankle.

They put me in an unmarked police cruiser and begin to transport me over Mrs. Taurasi's private residence. The police officers are listening to my case the radio and I feel inclined to distract them. "You guys mind if we stop and pick up a pizza?" They don't respond. "Hey, it's my treat." I see what's going on. These police officers don't agree with the judge's decision. It's okay. I'll forgive them. "Let me ask you something and don't spare my feelings: Is there such a thing as a penile exam? I'm thinking about filing a motion but I'm not sure if it would go under illegal search and seizure or cruel and unusual punishment . . . ?"

After about a half an hour one of the police officers finally breaks the vow of silence, "In a few hours you could order all the pizza you like."

The officer sounds upset. "You know the judge said the strangest thing. He said 'If you want to stand out wear pink socks.'" I tell them. "What do you guys suppose he meant by that?"

One of the officers turns the volume up. The radio station's legal experts would have us believe that they know more about my case than my lawyers.

LOCAL RADIO STATION:

After a 4 night stay in county jail, basketball player Caleb Escueta was released late this morning and put under house arrest, the police department announced today. The decision was made after 'extensive consultations,' a department spokesman stated. 'This is certainly not unprecedented. Confidentiality laws prevented us from offering any further details,' the spokesman said.

An unnamed source told us that a private psychiatrist visited Escueta in jail and wondered if that person played a role in the decision. According to the law, Escueta will spend the remainder of the trial, at the residence of his attorney Gisele Taurasi, with a tracker attached to an ankle. The ankle bracelet has a range of 3000 to 4000 square feet.

Escueta's high-profile case is already sparking controversy over whether the privileged and well-connected get favorable treatment by law enforcement officials 'We cannot tolerate a two-tiered jail system, where the privileged and well-connected receive special treatment,' said Assistant District Attorney R.F. Sanchez, the prosecutor on the case.

\*

I look out the car's window and see that there's already a press contingent stationed outside the Taurasi's private residence. It's as though the members of the press had been sharpening their spears. Mrs. Taurasi arrives ahead of us and, as she pulls into the driveway, is questioned by a few reporters. She shakes her head and makes gestures that suggest to me that she's declining to comment. A bystander approaches and yells "All in a day's work, aye, counselor? Getting another criminal back on the streets? It's a good thing these criminals have got you to be their champion."

I see a direct correlation between the manner in which the media is covering the case and the bystander's attitude towards it. Nobody dependent on the media for information about the case would have any idea of the facts. For instance, during my time in county jail, I was never visited by a private psychiatrist. If I didn't know any better I'd be asking my own attorney (a) why would the accuser make such a claim if it weren't true and (b) why would the Assistant District Attorney be so confident about getting a conviction if he didn't have proof?

All tangents aside, a phalanx of police officers escorts me into the Taurasi's private residence. I take a seat in the living room. I immediately notice that this is a Victorian style house. The police officers step outside and appear to give my attorney final some instructions. The moment they leave I try to loosen the ankle bracelet.

As this is taking place I hear sound of quick-puny footsteps scurry towards me. It takes only a moment for the creature to begin hopping around the room. It's the little white dog with black patches from outside *The Law Office of Gisele Taurasi.* "Gisele was going to bring her (the dog) to your house, upon your release, but it seems there was a last second change of plans. A bit of a buzzer beater, huh?" The gentleman re-introduces himself as Damian Taurasi, my lawyer's husband-slash-private investigator. "See? You get two for the price of one ha-ha-ha. Anything you say to me is protected under attorney/client privilege because Gisele pays me a dollar a day whether I show up to work or not ha-ha-ha."

I like him, already.

Mr. Taurasi drops a doggy bed next to me then takes a seat on the sofa. He's a tall—slender man who favors his left leg. "I've read the ADA's discovery. I'm not saying this to bring you down but I think this Sanchez fellow is going to continue to prosecute this case regardless of the evidence—or lack thereof. You see the jurisdiction has a 'no drop' policy for all rape charges." All I can think of is whether or not I'm being charged for this legal advice.

I reach down and pet the little dog "Does she seem at all house-trained?"

"I'd hope so seeing as I've been married to her for over 20 years ha-ha-ha. I was a defense lawyer, once upon a time" Mr. Taurasi tells me. "We defense lawyers make for easy targets because we take positions that are in favor of regular citizens—like yourself. This makes us easy to vilify." He uses his hands as he explains. "When folks walk out of a courtroom there is a winner and there is a loser. Oftentimes even the winner isn't completely satisfied with the outcome. Thus, we defense lawyers end up being the targets of controversy. That's what you just saw outside in that man's little outburst."

"Hmm." I add.

"Now, lobbyists and political analysts use terms like frivolous, and ambulance chasers, and jackpot justice." Mr. Taurasi continues in his strong tenor voice. "I take exception to that. Now, when I was practicing, I wasn't out there defending folks with stubbed toes and acne. I was defending folks with brain damage and other devastating injuries brought on by medical malpractice. Try telling someone who went to the hospital and got the wrong limb amputated that her compensation has been capped to whatever menial amount. What people, like the man you saw outside, are really trying to do is limit the ability of defense lawyers to be a political force for regular citizens—like yourself."

Damian Taurasi followed in his father's footsteps. He received a B.S.B., a M.B.A., and a J.D. He began his career as a public defender. As a public defender Damian Taurasi started out handling felony cases/preliminary hearings. This was rare, at the time, because he was fresh out of law school. As Sanchez advised me this morning preliminary hearings are a screening process for the judge to determine whether or not a particular case should go on to trial. Not only did Mr.

Taurasi do bench trials right then and there but he would do about 8 or 10 of those a day. When he got everything he felt he could out of the public defender's office he went on to become a trial lawyer. During a 17 year stretch, as a trial lawyer, Mr. Taurasi secured more in rewards (both in recoveries and aggrieved plaintiffs) than I would ever make as a basketball player. He was a successful man. "Now, I'll ask you to excuse me" he says then goes outside with his wife and the police officers.

I turn on the television and it doesn't take long to find a local news program ridiculing me. I'm okay with that but what I'm not okay with is them questioning my future in professional basketball. I'm upset. It's insulting that they actually believe I give a rat's ass about my career when I'm facing 10 years in the gulag for a crime I did not commit? I change channels. The night I went to jail a talk show host was making jokes at my expense. Four days later I find that same talk show host doing it again.

LOCAL TALK SHOW:

Have any of you been following The Kingmaker Case? You know Escueta's being released from jail, today, after serving only 4 days. I find that both startling and depressing. It's startling because this isn't a slap on the wrist; it's a pat on the back. It's depressing because now he has the local news under siege while he lolls around his attorneys luxurious Victorian home. Scientist announced today that our tap water might be poisoned but thanks to Caleb Escueta we won't be hearing anything about it ha-ha-ha.

So the police department gave him one of those ankle bracelets. It won't allow him to go any further than 4000 feet from the residence, but he'll certainly be enjoying all the comforts of a privileged home for the duration of the trial. You have to wonder how a guy whose nickname is 'Kingmaker' is going to be spending his days under house arrest.

12 noon: He wakes up and buzzes his housekeeper for breakfast in bed.

12:35 p.m.: He screams: "Why am I being punished?"

12:45 p.m.: His housekeep draws him a bath and personally washes his . . . toes.

12:50 p.m.: He complains the bubbles aren't bubbly enough and blames it on the 'prison water'.

12:55 p.m.: He calls his teammates and tells them how harsh house arrest has been.

1:30 p.m.: The judge comes over. They eat lobster and drink champagne.

2:00-4:00 p.m.: They take a nap together.

4:00 p.m.: They watch themselves on television

4:01 p.m.: The judge says 'Let's give them something to talk about'.

6:00 p.m.: Escueta eats dinner and reads his hate mail.

11:00 p.m.: He passes out.

2:20 a.m.: Wakes up and attempts to leave the house.

2:25 a.m.: His attorney reminds him he's on house arrest.

2:30-5:00: He crank calls Assistant District Attorney Sanchez.

5:00 a.m.: He cries himself to sleep on the satin sheets. Oh, the horror ha-ha-ha.

*

The little dog paws at my shin. "I'm Cal, huh." I tell the animal. So begins a relationship. We talk, talk, talk—sharing our likes and dislikes. Surprisingly, we seem to agree on everything from clothing, to cars, to politics. Neither of us is willing to turn the other off by disagreeing. Such topics, such as religion and birth control, are avoided. Now that I think about it the talk show host might be on to something. House arrest is so much better than spending the time in a 7 foot by 10 foot cell.

Shortly, the Taurasi's accompany me in the living room. All the police officers leave—except one. As per the Assistant District Attorney's instructions an officer is going to be stationed outside the house. The Taurasi's take a peek at what I'm watching on the television. The talk show host seems impressed with himself. Mr. Taurasi tells me that he can't blame me if I'm upset; that Assistant District Attorney Sanchez must've leaked the certain details of the case.

Mr. Taurasi tells me that this high profile case is a public relations triumph for Sanchez. Mr. Taurasi also says that it's a shame that we didn't do it first. "We're going to let Sanchez drag us down to his level?" I charge my legal team.

"If we took the initiative we could have framed the issue—not Sanchez. There's much to be gained by winning public opinion." Mrs. Taurasi tells me that this is one of the happy accidents of having me go into house arrest at her place. "The Great R.F. Sanchez made his statement now we have to make ours. And for us to call a press conference all we have to do is stand on the porch." It's difficult, for me, to think of my case in terms of being some kind of game. I admit it might take some time for me to accept the notion; after all, this is—or should be—a private matter. "Public relations matters whether we like it or not." Mrs. Taurasi says handing me today's newspaper. This is the first time my name was printed somewhere *other* than the sports section.

LOCAL NEWS PAPER ARTICLE:

### Kingmaker Charged With Sexual Assault

In an announcement, the professional basketball player Caleb Escueta (also known as Kingmaker) has been charged with sexual assault, prosecutors announced today. Assistant District Attorney R. F. Sanchez announced at a press conference that Escueta was charged with sexual assault and such a charge can carry a prison term of 4 to 10 years in the gulag and a probation period of 20 years to life.

The investigation first became public when the police department announced that an arrest warrant had been issued for Escueta. Escueta quietly surrendered at the local precinct.

The alleged incident occurred December 12th at the Mr. Escueta's residence. Assistant District Attorney Sanchez emphasized that Escueta's popularity did not come into play when deciding whether to press the charge. 'This decision came only after reviewing all the evidence—testimonial evidence and physical evidence—and conferring with prosecutors from around the state,' he said. 'Then and only then did I make my decision.' Assistant District Attorney Sanchez said that he can prove this case 'beyond the shadow of a reasonable doubt.'

Prior to the announcement, Sanchez's office had been reviewing a report from the state crime laboratory analyzing evidence in the case from both Escueta and the victim (whose name has not been revealed). At the press conference, Assistant District Attorney

Sanchez said he could not comment on the facts in the case but he did ask members of the media 'to respect the victim's privacy.'

Various press reports on Caleb Escueta's accuser say she is a familiar figure in the community and media.

Commissioner of the Professional Basketball Association (which Caleb Escueta plays for) also released this statement; 'As with all allegations of a criminal nature, our policy is to await the outcome of a judicial proceeding before taking any action. We do not anticipate making further comments during the pendency of the judicial process.'

\*

Mrs. Taurasi tells me that there was a time when speaking to the press was considered unprofessional. Lawyers used to ignore the press. Today, confronting the media is unavoidable. She calls up a public-relations expert named Willis. I don't know if Willis is his first or last name. The Taurasi's just refer to the man as Willis. With Willis on speakerphone we are treated to the dos-and-don'ts of dealing with the media.

"This is more than a mere public relations problem." Willis tells us. "This is a serious cloud and it'll require concrete measures to dispel it. On my side of the tracks people are calling it The Kingmaker Case. The television stations keep playing old footage of you going after—and slapping—that fan last season. The journalists really have it in for your client. They use the word 'victim' when they ought to be using 'accuser' and they don't even bother to use the word 'alleged'."

The idea of doing a television interview or even a radio talk show interview is thrown on the table. The Taurasi's don't think we're at that point, yet. I squash any inkling Willis might have about leaking Sojey's name as the alleged victim or accuser. I'm standing by my decision to not have the mother of my children dragged through the mud.

After exactly one hour of a discussion, with Willis, we find ourselves in agreement. He gives us the name of a media contact, of his, "should we feel the need to go in that direction". By that I think he means that his contact might come in handy if we want to plant a story of our own.

At least now we have the beginnings of a plan. Mrs. Taurasi feels she has everything she needs to stand on the porch and speak to the other court—the court of public opinion. She puts on her coat and steps onto the porch. "Good evening ladies and gentlemen. As you know my name is Gisele Taurasi and I'm the attorney for Caleb Escueta. First I'd like to say we are confident that a fair and impartial jury will find that my client is innocent. Please hold your questions for the end. At this time I'd like to read a statement on behalf of Caleb Escueta."

> I am innocent of the charges filed against me.
> Nothing that happened December 12th was against
> the will of the unnamed woman who now falsely
> accuses me. This unfounded allegation of assault has
> hurt my family. I will fight against this allegation with
> all my strength. I have so much to live for and by that
> I do not mean the contracts, or the notoriety, or the
> championships. What I mean is that I have my two
> young children to live for. I will fight this fight for
> them. I appreciate all those who are supporting me.
> I want to thank you for believing in me. I'm going to
> need your support, now, more than ever.

After reading the statement Mrs. Taurasi answers exactly 3 questions. I've never seen someone say so much but reveal so little. No matter what the reporters ask her she ends with something to the effect of "I'm confident that a fair and impartial jury will find that my client is innocent."

I've been made aware that it'll take time to change the atmosphere created by this adverse publicity; that, in this case, Sojey's accusation of rape is perceived as big news while my denial of it is perceived as irrelevant news.

Mr. Taurasi hangs up the phone and tells me that the judge assigned to this case is 44-year-old Reena Kosteniuk. Judge Kosteniuk went to a better Law School than Sanchez did and "she's a looker" (Mr. Taurasi's words not mine). "But don't let the judge's good looks fool you. She's a war hero and she spent 5 years putting people like you behind bars ha-ha-ha. Judge Reena Kosteniuk has spent her entire adult life serving society. Now, assignment of judges is *said* to be random. Hmm? The fact that this is a high profile rape case and the judge assigned to it is a woman—and a good looking woman for that matter—is suspicious."

Mrs. Taurasi's press impromptu conference, and the news from Mr. Taurasi's phone call, and the little dog whining at my feet comes at me in such a way that "she's a looker" is all I can offer to the sum of knowledge.

"Sir, yes sir." Mr. Taurasi chimes in. "But our standards for looks are fully subjective, aren't they? Men like to boast that sensitivity, warmth, and intelligence are more important to us. We pride ourselves as so sophisticated a gender that physical attractiveness does not move us; however, we might never learn about other people's personalities if they don't meet our minimal standards (for physical attractiveness). The truth is that looks are the key factor in consideration of partners for dates, for sex, and for marriage."

Mrs. Taurasi looks at her husband and jealously scolds "Now how is *that* supposed to help us do our job?"

# CHAPTER FIVE

Before Honorable Reena M. Kosteniuk, and a jury, the defendant has been indicted for spousal rape.

Appearances:

For the Plaintiff: R.F. Sanchez, Esq. (Assistant District Attorney)
For the Defendant: Gisele Taurasi, Esq. and Damian Taurasi, Esq.

This is the first time I got to see the jury that the Judge, R. F. Sanchez, and the Taurasi's picked out for me. I always imagined a jury of my peers to be a group of young underpaid and mellow-dramatic athletes. Contrary to popular belief not all professional athletes are spoiled millionaires. In fact—after the powers that be get their piece of the action—my take home [income] is comparable to that of a forensic pathologist. Contrary to popular belief I don't have a publicist and I don't have an agent. If I had been playing this game for money I would've complained, a long time ago, *about* the money.

Now, if I read it correctly, the Sixth Amendment guarantees my right to a speedy trial with a lawyer present. It's the Seventh Amendment guarantees my right to a trial by an *impartial* jury. I'd be lying if I said I didn't secretly hope these 12 citizens (and 4 alternates) were all basketball fans. At the moment I'd settle for them to just be fans of the proof of truth.

I found jury selection to be a long-dull, albeit it necessary, process.

I've always heard people speak of trying to get *out* of jury duty. I got out of jury duty once upon a time. Due to the high-profile nature of this case people are actually willing to put their lives on hold and serve. These people did this knowing there was a strong possibility the jury would be sequestered. From my understanding, those selected for jury duty on this case, would have to spend the entire trial away from their normal lives. Judge Kosteniuk would stick the jury in a hotel as if they were being quarantined.

The Taurasi's went through great pains trying to piece together what they would call "the right kind of jury". The courtroom is where truth was going to be brought out. The right kind of jury would get to the bottom of it; yet, 90% of the prospective jurors we found to be other than truthful. These citizens claimed to be open-minded but they proved themselves to be otherwise. They claimed to not have been exposed to the case, through the media, but how likely is that? If Dexter Valez read about the case in county jail—while the case was still in its infancy—then how could these law abiding citizens *not* know about the case now that it's all over the local news? It's an insult to our collective intelligence to believe they don't know anything about the case. If they've been living in isolation would they really mentally be fit to sit on a jury and decide a case as big as this? I don't think so.

I sat and watched as the potential jurors, who did admit to being exposed to the case through the media, claimed to have no preconceived about it. They would have the court believe that their thoughts and knowledge are a pure as that adorable little dog at the Taurasi's private residence. Some of the potential jurors stared at me. In fact, one or two of them stared at me, for greater than 20 seconds, without blinking. Other potential juror members stole glances when they thought wasn't paying attention. Still other made an effort to ignore me, altogether. With members of the press sitting in the public gallery the process was a bit uncomfortable; although, it wasn't as uncomfortable as that penile exam. Here are a few of the questions that got potential jurors disqualified:

*Under the law, a person's religious beliefs (or lack thereof) do not excuse compliance with the criminal laws prohibiting non-consensual sexual intercourse. Are you willing to accept and abide by this rule of law?*

*Do you have any religious beliefs, moral feelings, political views, or philosophical principles that would interfere with your ability to serve as a juror in this particular case?*

*The fact that Caleb Escueta is charged with a crime is not evidence that he is guilty of the crime charged. Are you willing to accept and abide by this rule of law?*

*Do you have any strong feelings about Caleb Escueta simply because he has been charged with a crime?*

*Any person charged with a crime must be proven guilty beyond a reasonable doubt before they can be convicted of that crime. Are you willing to accept and abide by this rule of law?*

*Caleb Escueta does not have any obligation to testify, present evidence, or prove his innocence. The entire burden to prove the defendant is guilty beyond a reasonable doubt is on the complainant. Are you willing to accept and abide by this rule of law?*

*Sexual intercourse without consent is all that is required for spousal rape. Ignoring a person's 'no', standing alone, may be sufficient for a conviction of spousal rape, even without the use of threat or force. Are you willing to accept and abide by this rule of law?*

*The practice of Atheism is not an issue in this case; however, Atheism is a central belief of the defendant Caleb Escueta. Are you comfortable setting aside any feelings you may have regarding Atheism and reaching a verdict based solely on the evidence presented in court?*

*Has anyone ever expressed an opinion to you about whether Caleb Escueta is guilty or not guilty of the charges in this case?*

*Have you personally formed an opinion about Caleb Escueta's guilt or innocence as a result of anything you have heard, read, or seen?*

*Do you have any strong feelings towards Caleb Escueta as a result of what you have heard, read, or seen in the news media about the defendant?*

*If you were convinced, at the conclusion of the trial, that Caleb Escueta is either guilty or not guilty of the crime charged, and a majority of the jurors disagreed with you, would you change your verdict simply because you were in the minority?*

I take a mental inventory of this jury. I see that it's an even split between men and women. Two of the jurors are definitely Asians. I see one or two who can probably pass as Middle Eastern. There are three Caucasians, a few Hispanics, and two African Americans. Their ages ranging anywhere between early-20s to mid-60s.

It's truly a mixed lot. It's the right kind of jury.

It's too bad I can't say the same for the grand jury that Assistant District Attorney Sanchez used to get me here in the first place. The way I understand it, before the prosecution could go to trial against me Sanchez had to seek an indictment from a grand jury. I never met this grand jury. The Taurasi's never met this grand jury. Getting a grand jury to indict is something that goes on behind the scenes but has a huge effect. Sanchez could subpoena whoever he wanted to and present whatever evidence he saw fit to get an indictment.

No one was there to oppose, object, to check him, or to check the jury. For all I know the grand jury was comprised of a group of spousal rape complainants. For all I know the grand jury gave Sanchez a standing ovation. Now the powers that be put the grand jury in place as a shield against the abuse of authority but, from my perspective, not so much. I shudder to think of Sanchez' indict-at-all-cost strategy; let's just say I would've loved to be a fly on that wall with my annotated version of *The Constitution*.

THE BAILIFF:

> All rise. Court is now in session. Give your attention and you shall be heard. The Honorable Judge Reena M. Kosteniuk preceding. You may be seated. (The jury is impaneled and duly sworn in.)

THE COURT:

> Is the prosecution ready?

MR. SANCHEZ:

> Yes, Judge Kosteniuk. The prosecution is definitely ready.

THE COURT:

> Very well, Mr. Sanchez, please proceed with your opening statement.

MR. SANCHEZ:

Thank you, your Honor. Members of the court, my name is R.F. Sanchez and I appear on behalf of the People. The defendant is represented by my learned associate Mrs. Gisele Taurasi. May I begin by asking you to look, again, at the indictment? It's a very formal document written in very brief legal language. Perhaps, with your permission, I can help fill in the blanks.

On December 12th, at approximately 11:00am, the defendant Caleb Escueta put his two children to sleep. He then entered a room in which his wife Sojey Escueta was sleeping. He woke her up, took off her clothes, and raped her. I am obliged, in due course, to expose you to evidence of the heinous nature of the crime.

Rest assured that there will be nothing we will claim that we will not prove.

Over the next few weeks the people will prove that Caleb Escueta's marriage had been strained for some time and there are documented marital issues—including but not limited to issues of a sexual nature. Furthermore, we will show you that the defendant Caleb Escueta is a violent man by nature, by nurture, by habit, and by profession. We will even provide evidence that the defendant confessed to the crime. Let me say that again: We will even provide evidence that the defendant confessed to the crime.

Members of the jury, let me tell you about the victim Sojey Escueta. This is a young—pious woman of 23 years, a kind, friendly and intelligent young woman. She comes from a warm, tight-knit, loving and god-fearing family. It's a family which enjoys much respect and popularity among the community. These are qualities the defendant—a man known for beating his chest on the basketball court—decided to ignore on December the 12<sup>th</sup>. Perhaps it was his ego that couldn't accept the fact that his wife was rejecting his advances. "How dare she say 'no' to me? I'm her husband. Who is she to deny me?"

Finally, when the defendant had finished what he entered that room to do he fled the scene of the crime. Ladies and gentleman, make no mistake, spousal rape is a crime.

You will hear and you will learn, members of the jury, how Caleb Escueta has an unusually aggressive and violent nature—even by the standards of his profession. You will also hear evidence of his confession of the crime. And when you have heard all this I am convinced that you will reach the only reasonable conclusion.

Ladies and gentlemen, let me make one thing perfectly clear from the onset. The person on trial—the person whose actions you are to judge—is Caleb Escueta. By the time the judge sends you away to deliberate there will be no doubt—reasonable or otherwise—that we have proved that on the December 12<sup>th</sup> Caleb Escueta raped his wife Sojey Escueta.

Your Honor, that concludes the opening for the prosecution.

THE COURT:

Does the Defense wish to make their opening statement now or wait until the close of the prosecution's case?

MRS. TAURASI:

With your permission, your Honor?

THE COURT:

By all means.

MRS. TAURASI:

She who consents to an act is not wronged by it.

Ladies and gentlemen, that is a legal truism. It's as true as the sun rising in the east and setting in the west. The allegation brought before you today is unfounded; however, when the state brings a charge of spousal rape—however blatantly false it may me—it must be defended with earnestness and vigor. By the time all the evidence has been revealed you'll know exactly what I know; that Caleb Escueta is an innocent man; that he is being falsely accused of a very serious crime.

This is an emotionally charged allegation that we have painstakingly investigated. In the course of our investigation we found that the true motive behind it, bitter-sweet as it is, is rooted in infidelity on the part accuser. I'll say *that* again, the motive behind this unfounded allegation is rooted in infidelity on the part of Mrs. Escueta. The Defense will prove that during the course of a long affair Mrs. Escueta fell in love with a man named Lucas Kyle Ayers. She and Ayers had one big obstacle, the one thing standing in the way of their love, was my client Caleb Escueta. As a result, he has to now sit here in fear that he's going to spend time in the gulag for a crime his wife concocted in her head.

Now, as to the events of December 12th, my client concedes that sex had occurred—*consensual* sex. My learned colleague will provide no evidence to prove that the sex the Escueta's had on December 12th was anything but consensual. Mr. Sanchez will offer that Mrs. Escueta said she *never* consented or she *initially* consented but later changed her mind but that all adds up to one thing—reasonable doubt.

The prosecution can't do much more, for you, than establish the *probability* of a crime. Now, probability may be enough for a meteorologist to give a weather report but probability won't cut it here in the court of law. When all the smoke has cleared there will be no physical evidence or material witnesses to corroborate this unfounded allegation.

So what are we all doing here, folks? We're here because of a 'he said, she said' accusation. All the prosecution is coming to this trial with is the word of a woman who cheated on her husband while she was pregnant with his child. It was an affair that lasted two years. The truth is my client can rest his case and you'd have to come back 'not guilty' because a jury cannot convict if there is any reasonable doubt about who is telling the truth and who is lying.

Instead, I'm going to stick around and tell you a little about Caleb Escueta. Nowhere in his criminal record is there evidence of him assaulting anyone: women, men, sexually, or otherwise. He has a clean psychological profile. His Rape Kit came back negative, and he passed a voluntary polygraph test. Regarding our evidence there is no doubt—reasonable or otherwise.

Since the moment this unfounded allegation reared its ugly head my client—despite whatever the prosecution's jailhouse snitch is going to say—has done nothing but protest his innocence. This entire trial comes down to the accusation of an unfaithful wife against the undeniable truth.

Members of the court, I talked to you a little while ago about reasonable doubt and, now, I'm going to make you a promise. By the time this trial is over you'll be knee-deep in reasonable doubt. You'll doubt whether this crime even occurred . . . because it didn't.

# Chapter Six

This morning, in an anteroom, Mrs. Taurasi gives me her version of a pep talk. "When I was a prosecutor the testimony of the complainant, alone, wasn't enough. In order to put a rapist away you needed external evidence. Complainants didn't have rape shields in those days, either. You see laws change all the time and laws, concerning rape, changed more than the rest. As a society, we decided that enough was enough. It was all happening right in front of us. After all those years, prosecutors finally had the ability to put those rapists behind bars and keep them there. The more rapists we locked up the more the number of rapes claims declined. I believe that one day the world will be free of this crime. It may take time but I believe we'll stop it. But, you see, the thing is there's no free lunch. I can tell you now that I've seen some honest defendants get hurt in the transition. The price of our progress—our good cause—was that sometimes a defendant would get convicted of a crime he didn't commit. As terrible as it is to see a rapist get a free pass; it's even worse to see an innocent man be convicted of a sex crime. This was one of the reasons, actually it was the *main* reason, I joined Damian (her husband) on the other side. See, my husband and I believe defense is an invaluable part of the legal process. In our system every citizen deserves the best possible defense."

There are two kinds of people in this world and I'll take a fool over a fraud any day. "Mrs. Taurasi, do you think I raped my wife?" I ask her rather bluntly.

"I don't think I've seen *all* the evidence but based on what I've seen . . ." "Don't be my lawyer, right now." I say. "Do you think I did it?"

"If I did," she smiles, "do you think I'd chase down that dog and give it to you ha-ha-ha? I know you don't want to hear this but, Mr. Escueta, I think your wife's calculated behavior is criminal." Funny she should mention the dog. Last night she (the dog) peed in my bed. So, to teach her a lesson, I peed in her little doggie bed. I know. It's cruel and unusual, right?

\*

Sitting behind my young and pious wife is a priest. Prior to this trial I knew the clergyman by face only. Of course my wife's mother and father are here. Also joining them, and flown in from the Philippines, is my wife's grandmother. The four of them have already gone on the record saying Sojey Escueta is a rare and delicate snowflake who would never lie, and never cheat, and never leave the rice cooker on. Sanchez even paraded our neighbors in to help paint the picture of an angelic-wife. I'm not going to bore you with the testimonies of these character witnesses.

According to the Sixth Amendment I have the right to be confronted with witnesses against me. Apparently the rape shield law supersedes due process because Mrs. Taurasi couldn't cross-examine Sanchez' witnesses the way she wanted (and I needed her) to. My attorney wasn't allowed to thoroughly impeach Sojey's priest or family or friends and determine whether or not they were credible. Mrs. Taurasi wasn't even allowed to show that these witnesses are biased against me.

At any rate, I am afforded the right to see these people. In doing so I exchange uncomfortable glances with my in-laws as Judge Kosteniuk tries to keep the jury awake. Sitting behind me is my best-est friend and teammate Javaman. I'm sure the entire team would just love to give up their day-of-rest and spend that free time in a criminal court proceeding. However, I don't think having what amounts to a boys' club sit behind me would win me any points with this jury.

In due time, Sojey is called, by Sanchez, as a witness for the People. She's the last person to be testi-lying this morning. It's probably an appropriate time for me to mention that my wife's big dream is to become a top Filipina actress. She's *that* dramatic. I've often found her sending audition footage of herself to *Tagalog* movie producers. We were hoping that one day she would get a call-back from one of those international studios. So far, all Sojey's done is a crazy commercial for Slush Laundry Detergent.

I remember, she had no speaking lines but it still took 2 days to shoot the thing. They had her squat down on this little stool and act like she was hand scrubbing a piece of cloth. Really all she was doing was rubbing her hands together. The friction sounds were later added and so was the sound of a *Tagalog* drama that was supposedly playing from an old radio. The idea was that this woman got so into the broadcast that she lost track of what she was doing. The camera backs up to reveal the soap suds she created were over 6 feet tall. In amazement, my wife gazes up at this tree-like formation. There's a slight pause, for dramatic effect, then text is inserted on the screen *Merry Christmas from Slush*. Then, the commercial fades to black.

My wife Sojey Escueta is duly sworn in and states as follows:

BY THE COURT:

Q What is your name, please?

A Sojey Escueta.

Q I understand this might be difficult for you but I think I'm the only one who can hear you. Would you mind repeating your response a bit louder?

A My name is Sojey Escueta.

Q Very good. And how old are you, Mrs. Escueta?

A I'm 28-years-old, your Honor.

DIRECT EXAMINATION BY MR. SANCHEZ:

Q How long have you been married to the defendant?

A Three going on four years.

Q Describe what happened on the day of December 12th.

A I was taking a nap. Cal came into the room and he raped me.

Q When you say 'Cal' you mean your husband Caleb Escueta? (Indicating the defendant.)

A I'm sorry, yes, my husband.

Q Where did the rape occur?

MRS. TAURASI:

Objection your Honor. The prosecution is clearly drawing a conclusion with that question.

THE COURT:

Sustained. Mr. Sanchez, perhaps you could modify your question and achieve a response?

MR. SANCHEZ:

Q You say you were taking a nap. Where?

A I was sleeping in the kid's room.

Q In the kid's room of your house?

A That's right.

Q At the time of the incident you and your husband lived at the same address: *Willow Pond.* Is that correct?

A Yes, that's correct. We lived at *Willow Pond.*

Q And where were your children at this time?

A They were sleeping in the bedroom . . . that's the room right next to the kid's room.

Q Whose bedroom?

A Our bedroom. Our old bedroom, Caleb and mine.

THE COURT:

Q The master bedroom, then?

A Yes, your Honor. The master bedroom.

MR. SANCHEZ:

Q The two rooms—the kid's room and the master bedroom—you say they're next to one another. Do the two rooms share a wall?

A Yes they do.

Q Sojey, on the day of December 12<sup>th</sup>, was there anyone else home at the time?

A No. I don't think so. It was me, Cal, and the kids.

Q About what time did the incident occur?

A I don't know exactly.

Q Morning? Noon? Night?

A It was daytime. I'm not sure exactly. Like I said; I was sleeping.

Q Take a guess. About what time did it happen?

A I'd say about noon if I had to guess.

Q Do you normally take naps at around noon?

A I try to. I'm a nurse. It's not uncommon for me to work grave shift.

Q Perhaps you can clarify for the court. When is grave shift?

A About 11:00 to 7:00.

Q 11:00 at night until 7:00 in the morning?

A Yes, that's correct.

Q How long have you been working as a nurse?

A I've been a nurse for about four years. These last two years I've been working part-time.

Q At which Hospital?

MRS. TAURASI:

Objection. This line of questioning is *incompetent* and immaterial.

THE COURT:

I'll allow it, for now, but I'll be keeping an eye on it.

MR. SANCHEZ:

Q And you say you worked on December 12$^{th}$, is that correct?

A Yes, that's correct. I worked later that night—grave.

Q For the record did anyone see you at work?

A Yes, the entire grave staff.

MRS. TAURASI:

I renew my objection. This is *incompetent* and immaterial.

THE COURT:

Same ruling, Mrs. Escueta. I'm allowing this.

MR. SANCHEZ:

Q What type of nurse are you?

MRS. TAURASI:

Objection. Your Honor is this *really* material?

THE COURT:

Okay. Sustained. Mr. Sanchez, I thought it might be, but this line of questioning doesn't seem germane to the case.

MR. SANCHEZ:

Q Let's go back to before you went to work. When you were asleep in the kid's room was the door closed?

A Yes, I know closed it.

Q Did you invite the defendant into the room where you were sleeping?

A No, I didn't invite him.

Q Prior to the defendant entering the room, did you ever say anything on the lines of 'Hey, let's meet later in the kid's room.'?

A No. I never said anything like that, to him. I went into the kid's room just to sleep.

Q Was it routine for this type of thing—namely sex—to occur in the kid's room?

A Routine? No, it certainly wasn't routine.

Q Prior to the incident have you and your husband ever had sex in the kid's room?

A No. Not that I recall.

Q So, there was no reason for the defendant to expect that you went into the kid's room to have sex?

MRS. TAURASI:

Objection. The question calls for a conclusion. I move to strike that out.

THE COURT:

Strike it out and the jury are to disregard it.

MR. SANCHEZ:

Q Did you invite the defendant into the room where you were sleeping?

MRS. TAURASI:

Asked and answered.

MR. SANCHEZ:

Withdrawn.

Q Did the defendant knock on the door prior to his entering the kid's room?

A No, not that I recall. Cal just came in.

Q I see. 'Cal just came in.' When the defendant came into the room did he say anything?

A He told me that the kids were sleeping.

Q Do you remember his exact words, Sojey?

A He said, 'The kids are asleep.'

Q What happened after he said 'The kids are asleep.'?

A He came in, he said 'the kids are asleep' and then . . . then that's when he raped me.

Q Did you invite the defendant to lay down with you?

A Not to the best of my recollection.

Q Sojey, to the best of your recollection, did you do anything that might suggest that you wanted to have sex with the defendant, in the kid's room, on the day of December 12th?

(At this point the witness begins to weep.)

(After a lapse of several minutes.)

THE COURT:

Mrs. Escueta, are you sufficiently composed to go on?

(No response.)

MR. SANCHEZ:

Please the court, if it would help the witness to calm down I would be willing to adjourn.

THE COURT:

Are you sufficiently composed to go on, Mrs. Escueta?

THE WITNESS:

I don't want to go on.

THE COURT:

I'm going to give the witness all the time she needs to compose herself. I want to give her complete time for composure.

(At this point the court takes a recess.)

(After recess.)

Mrs. Escueta, if you feel you need to stop or you need help with anything you please let me know; having said that, I'll now remind you that you are still under oath.

DIRECT EXAMINATION BY MR. SANCHEZ:

Q I know this is difficult, Sojey, but we need to know the details of how it happen?

A He got on top of me. I never said anything to him.

Q Sojey, did the defendant penetrate your vagina?

A Yes . . . yes he did.

(Public gallery whispers.)

Q What were you doing while the defendant was assaulting you?

A Nothing. There's nothing I could do. All I could do is wait for it to end. Ever since then my body doesn't feel like my own.

Q I know this is difficult. Try to bear with me, Sojey. How long did this go on before it was over?

A I don't know how long, exactly.

Q Was it closer to 10 minutes or closer to 1 hour? *Approximately* how long did it take place?

A I don't. Closer to 10 minutes. I can't remember. I'd say it was closer to 10 minutes.

Q Did the defendant ejaculate?

A Yes, I think so.

Q Where did the defendant ejaculate?

A Inside me.

Q I'm sorry, by 'inside me' you mean your vagina?

(No response.)

I apologize for the crudeness of the question, Sojey, but this is necessary.

A Yes, he did.

Q And what happened afterwards?

A He just left.

Q The defendant raped you then left the kid's room or he left Willow Pond?

A I don't know. He just left.

Q Who was monitoring your children?

A He was.

Q Do you think the defendant left the children at home while he was supposed to be monitoring them?

A No. He probably stayed home. I remember. He was there when I left for work.

Q Mrs. Escueta, have you and your husband ever participated in a role playing game such as a rape fantasy?

A No. Never. That's absurd. We never did that.

Q No one ever said you did, Sojey, but I do have to ask. Now, what time did you leave for work?

A It must've been a little after 10pm.

Q At what point did you notify the police?

A Later that night. I went to the precinct . . . the police station.

Q And what time was that?

A It went there after work. So, it must've been around 7:30.

Q At about 7:30 in the morning? So, it was actually the next morning that you notified the police.

A Yes, that's correct. I went to the police station about 7:30 the next morning.

Q Sojey, why did you wait so long?

A I was debating whether or not to go to them because Cal is my husband and I was afraid no one would believe me.

Q But you went down to the precinct anyway?

A Yes, I did, because I couldn't live with him getting away with it.

Q I appreciate how difficult it must have been for you to do that. Sojey what happened after you went to the police station?

A Well, I didn't want to go back to Willow Pond if he was there.

Q You mean you didn't want to go back to Willow Pond if the defendant was there? Why not?

A I didn't want to go back there because he just raped me.

Q Yes, of course. Did the police take a statement from you?

A Yes, they took down my statement.

Q And what did you tell the police?

A I told them that my husband raped me.

MR. SANCHEZ:

Thank you, Sojey. That's all. Please stay there. Mrs. Taurasi is going to have some questions for you, now. You did great.

CROSS-EXAMINATION BY MRS. TAURASI:

Q Mrs. Escueta, do you know a man by the name of Lucas Kyle Ayers?

(No response.)

Q Did you not hear my question, Mrs. Escueta? (Question repeated by stenographer.)

A Yes. I know Lucas.

Q Please *do* speak up. I couldn't help but notice you were accompanied by Father Duncan, this morning. I assume Father Duncan is your priest?

A Yes he is. He's here for support.

Q Did you ever confide in Father Duncan?

A Yes I confide in him regularly.

Q What drugs are you on?

A No. Never. I don't do that.

Q 'Never'? Surely you've tried; everyone has at some point.

THE COURT:

Speak for yourself, counselor.

MRS TAURASI:

Q Not so much as an Aspirin?

A Well, yes, I thought . . .

Q How much you drink?

A Not often.

Q Were you under the influence of alcohol, on December 12<sup>th</sup>?

A No. I wasn't.

Q Do you take any prescription medication?

A No I don't.

Q On December 12<sup>th</sup> did you take any over the counter medication; maybe something to help you sleep?

A No I did not.

MRS. TAURASI:

I'll refer the court to Defense Exhibit Alpha. It's the results of a toxicology test administered to the witness. Please note the date of December 13<sup>th</sup>: the day after the alleged incident. The witness tested negative.

Q Mrs. Escueta, how long have you known your husband?

A About 5 years.

Q In those 5 years has your husband ever hit you?

A No, he hasn't.

Q Has your husband ever grabbed you or pushed you?

A No, he hasn't.

Q Has your husband ever hit his children?

A Well, not that I can remember . . . .

Q Yes or no, Mrs. Escueta. Has my client Caleb Escueta ever hit either of his children?

(No response.)

Perhaps you'd prefer we bring your children in and ask them?

A No, he hasn't.

MR. SANCHEZ:

Objection.

THE COURT:

She already answered, Mr. Sanchez.

MRS. TAURASI:

Q Prior to this alleged incident have you ever had to call the police on your husband?

A No. I never called the police on my husband, before.

Q I'm confused and maybe you can help me clarify this; in your testimony you stated you were asleep in the kid's room. But then you testified that you (a) didn't hear him knock and (b) heard him say 'The kids are asleep'. Which one of those statements is untrue?

(No response.)

Mrs. Escueta, I'm finding your lack of response to be a problem and I do hope that it's not going to be a recurring one. Now, please answer the question.

(Question repeated by stenographer.)

THE COURT:

> Q Do you understand the question?

> A No, I'm sorry, I don't know what she's asking me.

MRS. TAURASI:

> A I'll modify the question, then. If you were asleep, in the kid's room, then how could you know whether or not my client knocked? If you were asleep in the kid's room then how could you have heard your husband say 'The kids are asleep'?

> Q I was trying to sleep but I wasn't asleep. It's hard to sleep in the daytime.

> A So, am I to understand that the testimony you gave earlier is *blatantly* false—unfounded?

MR. SANCHEZ:

> Your Honor, I object to this line of questioning as it's clearly argumentative.

THE COURT:

> Objection sustained. Let's tone it down, Mrs. Taurasi.

MRS. TAURASI:

> Q With your leave, your Honor, I'm just trying to clarify this for the court. So, first you said you were asleep but now you're saying you were awake. Which statement is unfounded?

A Yes, I was awake or *half*-asleep. When he came into the room he woke me up.

Q And you're sure about your story, this time?

MR. SANCHEZ:

I object to that.

THE COURT:

Objection sustained. I'll exclude that. You have a right to show that she gave responses that differ from the ones she's giving now, that would be proper cross-examination, but this is menial.

MRS. TAURASI:

Exception. Considering the allegation Mrs. Escueta is making whether or not she was awake during the incident seems very relevant.

THE COURT:

Your exception is noted. Now, let's move on.

MRS. TAURASI:

Q Where were your children when this was happening?

A They were probably in the next room; the *master* bedroom.

Q Was the door to the kid's room—the room you were half-awake in—locked?

A No, it wasn't. The door to the kids' room doesn't have a lock.

Q Where exactly was your husband when he told you the kids were asleep?

A He was by the door of the kid's room.

Q About how far is that door from where you were laying half-awake?

A I don't know. About 8 feet, I guess.

Q Did your husband holler at the top of his lungs, 'The kids are asleep.'?

A No. The kids would've woke up. He just put them to sleep.

Q Did your husband close the door behind him?

A I think so.

Q I'm sorry, Mrs. Escueta, you're responses giving me mixed signals. Is that a yes or a no? I can't tell.

A I don't remember but I think he did.

Q Did your husband slam the door shut?

A No, I don't think so.

Q Was he carrying anything when he walked into the room?

A I don't think so.

Q Do you recall what your husband was wearing?

A Shorts and a T-shirt.

Q Do you remember the color of those clothes?

A No, I don't.

Q So were you awake enough to notice certain details by the time your husband made his way to you?

A Yes, I was half-asleep.

Q 'Half-asleep'. And, depending on your life view, you were also half-awake

MR. SANCHEZ:

Objection characterization.

THE COURT:

Sustained. Be careful, Mrs. Taurasi.

MRS. TAURASI:

Q I must say, Mrs. Escueta, you're recollection of the event is a bit sketchy.

MR. SANCHEZ:

Objection.

MRS. TAURASI:

Q I'll withdraw my last statement. Were you under the covers, Mrs. Escueta?

A Yes. I was under a blanket.

Q Did my client yank that blanket off of you and throw it across the room?

A No, he didn't.

Q Did he try to restrain or smother you with the blanket?

A No. He just got in.

Q Let me see if I understand this correctly. Your husband calmly came into the room, calmly closed the door behind him, calmly told you the kids were asleep, and then calmly got under the blanket with you. Okay. What were you wearing on the day of December 12th?

A I was wearing shorts, panties, and a shirt.

Q Do you remember which shorts, panties, and shirt you were wearing? A No, I don't remember.

Q Were those clothes ever taken as evidence?

A I don't think so, no.

Q Do you own a pair of black spandex shorts, panties, and brown shirt that says "Will Work for Chocolate"?

A Yes I do.

Q Would you recognize them as the clothes you wore on the day of December 12th?

MR. SANCHEZ:

Objected to as hypothetical.

THE COURT:

Now, that is immaterial, if she would recognize those clothes. They would be her clothes, so of course she'd recognize them, but she said she doesn't remember what she was wearing on December 12th.

MRS. TAURASI:

Q Between the time your husband entered the room to the time you say he penetrated you how did your clothes come off?

A He took them off.

Q 'He took them off.' Can you please explain to the court? (No response.)

What you mean by that? Did your husband tear your clothes off in a fit of rage? A Not really.

Q Once again, I'm confused by your response. Is that a yes or a no? Did your husband . . .

A No, he didn't.

Q Where are those clothes, now?

A I don't know. I moved out of Willow Pond. Things were misplaced. You know how it is when you move. I don't know where those clothes are, now.

Q You don't know?

MR. SANCHEZ:

Objection, asked and answered. With respect, it does appear my learned friend is flogging a dead horse.

THE COURT:

I tend to agree. Mrs. Taurasi, the witness has already answered that. She said she doesn't know and she further stated that the clothes got lost when she moved out of Willow Pond.

MRS. TAURASI:

Q You didn't think to submit them to the police when you made your statement?

A No. I didn't think of that.

Q The police who took your statement didn't ask for those clothes?

A Yes, they did, but it was too late. I was just off of work and those other clothes were still at Willow Pond. I didn't think to bring those clothes with me.

Q Did you take a shower before you went to work?

A Yes, I did.

Q Mrs. Escueta, while your husband was undressing you did you resist?

(No response.)

Am I talking too fast for you? I'll, slowly, repeat the question and the court will await a response.

(Question slowly repeated.)

A No, I didn't. I was scared.

Q Scared of what? You *have* had sex with your husband before, correct?

A Yes . . . but . . . I don't know. This time it was different. I can't explain it.

Q What were you scared of?

A I don't know. I was just scared.

Q Did you communicate to your husband that you were scared?

A I couldn't do that.

Q 'You couldn't do that'. Why couldn't you do that? Mrs. Escueta, was your husband covering your mouth?

(No response.)

I'm sorry, this time I'm puzzled by your lack of response. I'll have the question repeated and the court will await a response.

(Question repeated by stenographer.)

A No, he didn't.

Q So you were free to have spoken if you chose to? You could've told him the secret to the meaning of life.

A Yes, but like I said I was scared.

Q Yes, we've all heard you say that, Mrs. Escueta. Now, where were your hands during the alleged incident?

A What do you mean?

Q What were you doing with your hands during the alleged incident? Were you pushing your husband off of you?

(No response.)

I'm finding your lack of response ambiguous. You testified that you were being raped by your husband. You claimed your husband was raping you. If it were me I would be slapping him and punching him and gouging his eyes out. Do you mean to say, in open court, that you made no attempt to physically resist your husband?

THE WITNESS:

Do I have to answer that, Judge?

THE COURT:

Yes you do, Mrs. Escueta, and we'll wait for an answer.

A No, I didn't.

MRS. TAURASI:

Q Did you scratch this man you say was raping you? Did you try to choke him?

A It's impossible to know unless you're in that situation.

Q Please the court, the witness is non-responsive. (Question repeated by stenographer.)

A No. I said I was scared.

Q Too scared to kick or anything?

MR. SANCHEZ:

Objection, asked and answered.

THE COURT:

Objection denied. The witness was never asked about the kicking.

THE WITNESS:

No. I didn't kick him. I'm not an aggressive person—Cal is. My husband is a professional athlete. You don't get to the level he is at by being passive.

MRS. TAURASI:

Q So, while all this aggression was happening did you ever say the word 'no.'?

A Maybe, I can't remember.

THE COURT:

You can't remember?

A No, you Honor. I'm sorry. I can't remember.

MRS. TAURASI:

Q You can't remember whether or not you said the word 'no.'? No means no Mrs. Escueta. Did you ever tell the man you claim was raping you 'no'?

A Maybe, like I said, I can't remember.

Q 'Maybe'. Well, I'm sure confused. You can't remember?

A No, I can't.

Q Is that the best answer you can give me?

A It happened so fast and I was scared.

Q About 10 minutes, Mrs. Escueta. You testified that the alleged incident lasted for about 10 minutes. Wouldn't you say that's long enough for you to make some kind of attempt to resist?

MR. SANCHEZ:

Objection, your Honor. That's argumentative.

MRS. TAURASI:

Q I'll withdraw the question, your Honor. While this alleged incident was happening did either of your children wake up?

A I don't know. They were in the next room.

Q Did you hear your children crying out?

A No, I don't think so.

Q So your recollection of the event is all kind of grey, huh? If they were to cry out, from the master bedroom, could you hear those cries from the kid's room?

A Probably. Yes I could.

Q You stated that if your husband were to slam the door shut the kids would hear it and wake up. Is it safe to assume that if you screamed, from the kid's room, your children would hear it in the master bedroom?

MR. SANCHEZ:

Objection your Honor this calls for speculative.

THE COURT:

I'll allow it. The question will be answered.

A Yes, they'd probably hear it.

Q You also stated that if your husband were to say 'The kids are asleep', in a firm tone, the children would hear it and wake up. Is it safe to assume that if you screamed, from the next room, your children would hear it?

MR. SANCHEZ:

The same objection, your Honor.

THE COURT:

Motion denied. Let's proceed.

MRS. TAURASI:

Q Mrs. Escueta, if you had cried out, would it have woke the kids?

A Yes, it probably would.

Q But they didn't cry out, did they? They were probably sound asleep, weren't they?

A I don't know.

Q Did you say anything to your husband afterwards?

A No, I didn't

Q Did your husband say anything to you?

A No, he just left.

Q You testified that he left the room but probably not Willow Pond because he wouldn't leave his children during his watch. Is that correct?

A Yes. I think that's correct.

Q In fact, when you say he said 'The kids are asleep' your husband was acknowledging that his children were absolutely safe.

MR. SANCHEZ:

Objection, calls for speculative.

THE COURT:

Objection sustained.

MRS. TAURASI:

Q Let me see if I understand this. You claimed that your husband just raped you. Is it your testimony here today that, after the alleged event, you didn't feel the urge to go after him physically or verbally?

MR. SANCHEZ:

Objection, that question has already been asked and answered.

THE COURT:

Objection overruled. Let her answer.

(No response.)

The witness will answer the question.

THE WITNESS:

I told you I'm not the aggressive one. He's the aggressive one. He raped me. I didn't know what to do. This never happened to me before.

MRS. TAURASI:

Yes, because your husband is not a rapist.

MR. SANCHEZ:

> You Honor . . .

THE WITNESS:

> He raped me and I want justice.

MRS. TAURASI:

> I'm sorry did you say vengeance?

THE WITNESS:

> I said . . .

MR. SANCHEZ:

> I move to strike that out.

THE COURT:

> (Gavel raps.)
>
> Strike it out. The jury will be advised not to consider that
> last exchange. You shouldn't have heard it but you did. It
> will be stricken from the record and you must strike it from
> your minds.

MRS. TAURASI:

> Q I'll rephrase the question. Mrs. Escueta, why would you
> let a man who you claim violated you in the worst possible
> way—an 'aggressive' man—walk out of the kid's room and
> take care of your children?

A I didn't think he'd do anything to them?

Q To clarify, you mean you didn't think this aggressive man, who you claim just finished raping you, would do anything aggressive to your children?

A No. I didn't.

Q Prior to December 12<sup>th</sup> did you ever think your husband was capable of such a thing?

A I don't know?

Q Mrs. Escueta, if you *did* believe your husband was capable of such a thing would you still let him take care of your children?

MR. SANCHEZ:

Objected to as hypothetical.

THE COURT:

Sustained. You don't have to answer that.

MRS. TAURASI:

Exception your Honor.

THE COURT:

Exception noted. Let's move on.

MRS. TAURASI:

Q You still went to work—grave shift—is that correct?

A Yes it is.

Q You left an aggressive man, alone at Willow Pond, with your small children?

MR. SANCHEZ:

I object to the form of the question, if your Honor pleases.

MRS. TAURASI:

Okay, I'll withdraw it.

Q So, when you claim this rape occurred you didn't do anything before, during, or immediately after it?

A I went to the police station.

Q Yes, you did, after you showered and went to work and entire shift, as you usually do. Mrs. Escueta, do you recall getting any sleep before you went to work?

A I don't remember.

Q Besides taking a shower, what did you do between the time your husband left the kid's room and the time you went to work?

A I don't remember.

Q You don't even remember what you did for all that time?

MR. SANCHEZ:

Objection, asked and answered.

THE COURT:

Objection to that will be sustained.

MRS. TAURASI:

Q You can recall—with certainty—what your husband said when he entered the kid's room but you can't recall—with that same certainty—whether or not you told him to stop having sex with you?

A That doesn't even deserve a response.

Q Your husband—the father of your children—is on trial because of accusations you made. Don't you think *he* deserves a response?

(No response.)

You didn't say anything to your husband afterwards. You just let him leave the kid's room and go about tending to your children? You didn't fear for their safety?

(No response.)

I'm sorry, Mrs. Escueta, your lack of communication is giving me mixed signals. I'm going to ask you a question and I want you to take your time before you respond. How was your husband supposed to know that the sex was anything *other* than consensual? How was your husband supposed to know that it was *not* what you wanted?

A I didn't. He raped me and you have to believe that.

Q Mrs. Escueta, I'm sorry but how do you expect this court to believe that this was not consensual sex between a husband and a wife?

MR. SANCHEZ:

I object to that. That's for the jury to determine.

THE COURT:

I agree. That'll be excluded from evidence.

MRS. TAURASI:

Q Mrs. Escueta, look at my client. Is it your testimony today that the man you have known for 5 years, and have been married to for 2 years—the father of your children—raped you?

MR. SANCHEZ:

Objection.

THE COURT:

Sustained. We've been over this.

MRS. TAURASI:

Q Speaking in the hypothetical, I'm walking down the street. I see a woman running at me with a gun. The woman is screaming. I see her point the gun at me. I see that this screaming woman is about to pull the trigger. I make a decision. I reach into my purse and pull out my *own* gun. I decide to kill this woman before she kills me. The police arrive. It turns out the gun she had was just prop. The screaming lady was an actor in a movie that was being shot. Now, I have just made a huge error that caused the death of another human being. My question to you is am I guilty of a crime?

A Well, you didn't know . . .

Q I think we could save the court so much time if you just told us yes or no?

A I would say no.

Q Then you'd be correct. According to our legal system if a person makes a reasonable mistake of fact which leads to the commission of a crime that person is generally not guilty. That is to say, if you failed to communicate to your husband that you *didn't* want to have sex, and sex occurred, then he didn't rape you.

MR. SANCHEZ:

Objection. My learned friend is making a closing argument.

THE COURT:

Overruled. I'll allow it but I'll ask counsel to get to her question.

MRS. TAURASI:

Q Mrs. Escueta, you also testified that my client penetrated your vagina, is that correct?

A Yes it is.

Q Did he penetrate your vagina with his penis?

THE WITNESS:

Do I have to answer that?

MRS. TAURASI:

You accused your husband of rape; a sentence that carries with it a maximum penalty of 10 years in the gulag. Forgive me if these questions are making you at all uncomfortable. Judge?

THE COURT:

Mrs. Escueta, I can't prevent counsel from asking questions on the grounds of delicacy.

You will have to answer the question.

THE WITNESS:

(Stammers.)

A Yes, he did.

MRS. TAURASI:

Q Oh please do speak up, Mrs. Escueta.

A I said yes.

Q How did his penis penetrate your vagina and by that I mean who put it in?

A I don't remember.

Q I'm sorry, what?

A I said I don't remember.

Q Mrs. Escueta, during intercourse, who *usually* puts the penis in your vagina: is it you or your husband?

A I do.

(Public gallery murmurs.)

Q Oh, do please speak up.

MR. SANCHEZ:

Objection.

THE COURT:

Objection sustained.

MRS. TAURASI:

I'm done, your Honor.

RE-DIRECT EXAMINATION BY MR. SANCHEZ:

Q Sojey, can you point to the man who raped you?

A Yes I can.

(Gesturing.)

Q Let the record reflect that the witness has identified the defendant Caleb Escueta.

THE COURT:

The record shall so reflect.

MR. SANCHEZ:

Thank you, Sojey.

RE-EXAMINATION BY MRS. TAURASI:

Q Mrs. Escueta, do you think *claiming* rape proves that rape occurred?

A No, but I think . . .

Your Honor, I have no further questions for this witness.

# CHAPTER SEVEN

LOCAL RADIO STATION:

MRS. TAURASI:

Although my client has been accused of committing a heinous crime, he is no less human than you or I. It does no good to anyone to vilify Caleb Escueta. It's the dark part of our nature that's chooses to objectify others. There are many reasons why we do this. Maybe we need to feel superior to someone? Maybe we need a scapegoat for our own problems? It's reflected in the language, used by the protestors, in front of the courthouse. You can see it in their description of my client. I don't care to repeat the words of these protesters because I feel that type of prejudicial speech is unacceptable.

However, even among decent people, it's still socially acceptable to call an innocent man such vial things. The fact that decent people buy into this mob-mentality is appalling. One day you hear about a young girl being gang-raped and murdered. The people want blood and don't get it. A few weeks later, we hear about a basketball player being charged with sexual assault and we immediately want his blood as some kind of compensation.

The extent of male predation and female victimization has gone so far that we believe that no women (or a mere 2% of women) lie about rape. In today's world, men accused of rape often face a de *facto* presumption of guilt despite undeniable exculpatory evidence. It's unfair to presume my client is guilty simply because you feel it's not right to question the accuser. Somehow we need to get the pendulum to swing back to the center. There's nothing wrong with making a legitimate inquiry about an allegation.

An innocent man should not have his life destroyed because of an unfounded allegation. I'll remind you, that our justice system is not a retributive justice system. It is not a system based on exile and hatred. We ought to be pushing our justice system to try to restore and bring these people back into the community rather than closing him/her out; especially, if that person is not guilty.

There are those who want my client's order of house arrest rescinded. They want him back in county jail for the duration of the trial. It's as though there are those who want to make sure this man is miserable every second of the day. Caleb Escueta is innocent until proven otherwise and there are those who want nothing more than to see him suffer. There's a difference between punishment and suffering. Prison ought to be the last resort after all other measures have failed.

As a society we should not legitimize this type of cruelty and callousness. This lack of compassion not only has detrimental effects on the mental state of my client—who hasn't been convicted of anything—but it teaches our children that it is acceptable to be uncaring to people we do not like or do not fit into a perceived mold. Our children are watching the way we treat men like Caleb Escueta. Right now, what they're seeing, is neither compassion nor reconciliation. heard.

All we ask at this time is that you reserve your judgment until *all* the evidence has been

\*

Dexter Valez called by the People as a witness, is duly sworn in, states as follows:

DIRECT EXAMINATION BY MR. SANCHEZ:

Q Please state your complete name for the record.

A My name is Dexter Junior Valez.

Q Mr. Valez, I noticed earlier that you have a black eye. Could you please, now, tell this court what you told me?

A A few nights ago a couple of Caleb Escueta fans gave me a beating.

MRS. TAURASI:

Objection, your Honor. Prosecution is out of line.

THE COURT:

Sustained. Please strike that last exchange from the record.

MR. SANCHEZ:

Q Now, Mr. Valez, you recently served time in county jail with the defendant Caleb Escueta. Is that correct?

A Escueta was my bunk mate, sure. By that I mean he had the top bunk and I had the bottom bunk.

Q Did you know who he was at the time?

A I thought he looked familiar, you know, the point guard from *The Kingmaker Case*—sex stuff. Then when the CO called roll he confirmed my suspicion. I knew he was the guy, alright.

Q So you knew him to be Caleb Escueta?

A Yes, I most certainly did. I knew who he was.

Q You say the CO—to use the more popular jargon—confirmed your suspicion, how so?

A In M-Dorm, privacy is non-existent. COs do headcounts six times a day. During headcount everyone has to shut up and stay on their racks. The CO [corrections officer] goes to everybody's rack and identifies the guy. Everyone has to be accounted for or all hell is going to break loose. You know what I mean?

Q Go on.

A Right. The CO looks at a picture of you, calls your last name out, and you have tell him your first name. The CO said 'Escueta' and the defendant answered 'Caleb'. That's how I knew he was the guy.

Q You had a discussion with the defendant in county jail, is that correct?

A Oh yes. That's correct.

MR. SANCHEZ:

Please the court, I have a letter from the witness to the office of the District Attorney. It's been previously marked as the People's Exhibit Alpha.

THE COURT:

That's correct.

THE PEOPLE'S EXHIBIT ALPHA:

> *To Whom it May Concern,*
>
> *My name is Dexter Valez. I'm currently in county jail. I think we need to have a long discussion. Caleb Escueta has just confessed to me that he raped his wife. He also told me that he has a plan to beat the rap. I'd like to speak with the District Attorney if at all possible. Thank you and God bless.*
>
> *P.S. Have a Merry Christmas*

MR. SANCHEZ:

Permission to approach the witness?

THE COURT:

Very well, counselor.

MR. SANCHEZ:

Q Mr. Valez, is this your handwriting?

A That's my handwriting. I wrote that while I was in county.

Q So, you had a discussion with the defendant?

A I absolutely did.

Q Well, what did you talk about?

A Caleb Escueta told me that there is no such thing as spousal rape.

(Public gallery whispers.)

THE COURT:

(Gavel raps repeatedly.)

Order.

MR. SANCHEZ:

Q Please do continue, Mr. Valez.

A He started lecturing *me* . . .

Q I'm sorry you mean Caleb Escueta?

A Yes, he defendant started lecturing me. He said once consent is formally given in public ceremony, it can't be revoked.

(Chatter from the gallery.)

He told me that the only means to revoke consent is through divorce.

THE COURT:

Settle down.

(Gavel raps repeatedly.)

(Chatter subsides.)

THE WITNESS:

He said the attempt to create a legal concept of spousal rape is no less than an attempt to destroy the basic concept

117

of marriage. If the husband has no more claims to his wife's body, than anyone else, then the marital vows are meaningless and the marriage is a charade. Caleb Escueta told me that once consent is withdrawn the marriage has ended.

MR. SANCHEZ:

Q Thank you. Did the two of you discuss anything else while in county jail?

A Oh, we talked a lot. He said the only difference between rape and domination—which is what he did to his wife on the day in question—is consent. Then he started bragging about he and his Jew-lawyers were going to beat the rap.

THE COURT:

(Gavel raps.)

Mr. Valez, we'll not have that in my court. If you mean Mrs. Taurasi then you'll refer to her by her name. Listen to me closely because I will not warn you, again.

MR. SANCHEZ:

Thank you, Mr. Valez. I have no more questions. Please stay there as Mrs. Taurasi is going to ask you some questions, now.

THE COURT:

Your witness, Mrs. Taurasi.

CROSS-EXAMINATION BY MRS. TAURASI:

Q Good day, Dexter.

A And a good day to you, counselor.

Q You've been busy, haven't you?

A As have you.

Q I suppose, we've *both* been busy. I understand that after your testimony you're going to tell your story to a local tabloid and appear on a talk show. Can that be true?

A It most certainly *is* true, you know, people want to hear the truth.

Q The people want to hear the truth? Well, it's hard to argue with that. I bet you're going to get a pretty penny for your efforts, as well.

A It's not about the money.

Q But you are getting paid to tell your story to the tabloid, and the television show, aren't you?

A Like I said. It's not about the money.

Q About how much money are we talking about, Dexter?

MR. SANCHEZ:

Objection. Immaterial. What does this have to do with the issues?

THE COURT:

It may have something to do with it. I don't know, yet.

MRS. TAURASI:

Oh, it is material but I will withdraw the question. Now, the Assistant District Attorney asked about an *alleged* discussion between you and my client. You claim that it took place while he was in pre-trial detention. Is that true?

A That's right, and I told this court *exactly* what your client told me.

Q Yes, we all heard but a discussion—even an *alleged* discussion—goes both ways, doesn't it?

A Now, what do you mean by that?

Q Many of us are surprised by your testimony here, today. It's been my experience that when a client 'lawyers up' he knows better than to talk about his case with anyone; especially, other inmates. It's one of the first thing defense attorneys advise their clients to *not* do. In fact, as lead counsel in Mr. Escueta's case I can assure you that he was so advised. Surely, a man of Caleb Escueta's intelligence would know to *not* discuss his case with you because you could do exactly what you did. He knew you could turn state's evidence. Why do you think my client would risk that?

MR. SANCHEZ:

Object, the witness is not a psychologist.

THE COURT:

Overruled.

THE WITNESS:

A I don't rightly know. It's a crazy world, counselor. People do crazy things.

Q I can certainly appreciate that, Dexter. I took a glance at the Assistant District Attorney's witness list and didn't see anyone else from M-Dorm. Are you the only inmate he talked to in M-Dorm?

A Well, you got Escueta his pass. You did that, as lead counsel, right? You saw to it that he wasn't in M-Dorm for very long.

Q So, he was only there long enough to talk to you and *only* you. Were you surprised by the *alleged* discussion you *claim* took place between you and my client?

A No. I wasn't surprised at all. This type of thing happens more than you big shot defense attorneys would like them to. Everything happens for a reason.

Q Well, it's hard to argue with that. And in this *alleged* discussion did you have anything to say in return?

A I told him what I thought.

Q Of course you did, Dexter. Please clarify for the court what your thoughts, on the matter, are?

A I told Escueta what I thought. I told him that my concern for level of pain of rape would be greater if it weren't for the fact that most women deserve to raped.

(Public gallery murmurs.)

THE COURT:

(Gavel raps.)

I'll ask the public gallery to show restraint. You ought to know better.

THE WITNESS:

That's right. Society opposes prostitution as a sexual outlet for men. Since women deserve to be raped, I can't concern myself with the pain rape causes them. The very first human intercourse was a rape. Women have a hymen. Every intercourse after that is still a rape because women still have hymens. All men are women first when they develop in the womb, they just have overgrown . . . you know. Female ejaculation contains trace amounts of semen and that's how the ancient female reproductive system reproduced before men raped them.

Q I find myself intrigued. Please, do continue.

A The book says not to covet your neighbor's wife. The book doesn't say not to rape. A married woman can't have sex with anyone but her husband but a married man can have sex with a single woman. If a man rapes a single woman— according to scripture—he has to pay the father off and marry the girl.

Q Thank you for sharing, Dexter. If I can ask you this: Do you think my client committed the crime he's being accused of?

A No, he didn't.

Q And would you please share with the court why you don't think he did?

A Because it's not a crime to have sex with your wife. Now, if the law would do the right thing and force rapists to marry their victims—like the book says—then the number of rapes will decline to near zero, wouldn't it?

(All murmuring.)

THE COURT:

(Gavel striking.)

I won't warn the gallery again. This is a public hearing but I will not tolerate these constant disruptions.

MRS. TAURASI:

Q Dexter, isn't it true that you made a deal with the Assistant District Attorney to avoid jail time for your testimony here today?

A Yes, but it hasn't affected my memory and that's not why I'm testifying.

Q I understand. I also understand that you made an oath before god to tell the truth here, today. Is an oath with god important to you? How import . . .

A Counselor, god is the precondition for all logic and morality. If we presuppose anything other than god as our starting point, we end up with absurd and contradictory affirmations. The tri-unity of god—the father, the son, and the holy spirit—is inescapable if we want to make sense out of our world. To reject the triune god is to end up asserting your own philosophical demise. Deny god and you commit logical suicide.

Q Fair enough. We certainly can't have that, can we?

MR. SANCHEZ:

Objection. This is preposterous, your Honor. Counsel has spent the last 10 minutes taunting the witness.

THE COURT:

Sustained. I'm going to keep a very close eye on this.

MRS. TAURASI:

Q Let me see if I understand this, you're *not* testifying to save yourself: you're testifying to, I don't know, *save* my client?

A That's absolutely correct, counselor.

Q Dexter, I want you to think about this next question really hard. Was the alleged conversation you had with my client a complete lie?

THE COURT:

You don't have to answer that.

THE WITNESS:

A The answer is no. You see my atheist brother has gone too far and I really think he's damned to hell. Right now I'm disgusted, although I know I'll become sad. Jesus Christ, my Lord and Savior, died for Escueta's sins and mine. People like you and your client spit in his face. I'm so disgusted I want to vomit.

Q Dexter. You put your hand on a Bible and swore to tell the truth, the whole truth, and nothing but the truth . . .

A That's right I did. While Escueta may be my brother; while we are all sinners I say he's the only one of us happily breaking Commandments right and left. I'm beside myself. Brother, if god doesn't matter to you, do you think you matter to him?

THE COURT:

> I'll ask the witness to not direct his responses to the defendant. Mr. Valez, one more outburst like that and I'll hold you in contempt.

MRS. TAURASI:

> Q Dexter, are you prepared to tell the truth now?

MR. SANCHEZ:

> Move to strike.

MRS. TAURASI:

> Withdrawn. I'll rephrase.
>
> Q Dexter, are you telling the truth now?
>
> (No response.)
>
> Dexter, would you like a lawyer?
>
> A I don't need a lawyer. Escueta's the one who needs a lawyer. Why would I need a lawyer?
>
> Q Because at this moment I am certain, to a moral certainty, that you are not being truthful with this court. I strongly advise you get a lawyer because, right now, you're looking at a perjury charge.
>
> A I already told you, counselor. I don't need a lawyer— Escueta does.

Q As you wish. Mr. Valez, when you learned of my client's religious views it really upset you, isn't that true?

A I think all atheists should have some of their rights ripped from them. They shouldn't have freedom of speech like good Christians do. All atheists do is tell lies like the Earth is billions of years old. It has been proven that it is about six thousand years old. Dinosaur tracks with human tracks . . . hello Escueta, got a brain in there?

THE COURT:

Mr. Valez. You've been warned . . .

THE WITNESS:

Where did the big bang come from, your Honor? Then where did that come from? And that, and that, and that? Stop telling lies, Judge. You have no right. Judge, god's penis is not a biological organ. God's penis is not the same as man's penis. Obviously it wouldn't be [unintelligible monologue].

THE COURT:

(Gavel raps.)

Dexter Junior Valez, I'm holding you in contempt of this court. Bailiff, if you would please secure the witness. Yes, take him into custody.

THE WITNESS:

This is why I pointed out god has a holy-righteous penis. That is to say, it's not the same as man's corrupted-fleshy one. Your Honor, penises are not just for sex and peeing.

It is only because man is evil that he thinks of penises exclusively in those terms. Man is made in the image of god the father. That is the primary reason why man has a penis. You cannot insert your evil prejudicial ideas of man's penis onto god—which is exactly what you are doing. God's penis is not equal to man's penis. It's really not hard to understand.

MRS. TAURASI:

Your Honor, the Defense moves to dismiss the indictment upon the ground of prosecutorial misconduct.

THE COURT:

I'll see counsel in my chambers. I mean now.

(Gavel bangs.)

*

LOCAL NEWS REPORT:

Defense Attorney in The Kingmaker Case Alleges Prosecutor Misconduct

Gisele Taurasi the defense attorney in The Kingmaker Case filed a motion today, arguing that the case should be dismissed due to prosecutorial misconduct. 'This motion will prove that the prosecution abused a plea bargain by seeking testimony in exchange for leniency. This lent itself to perjury and falsified evidence.' Taurasi said today. Her client denies any wrongdoing.

'We can only hope that when this is over Mr. Caleb's life and reputation will be restored.'

*H. Valencia*

Assistant District Attorney R.F. Sanchez declined to comment. 'As always, we continue to be confident in the facts of this case' the ADA's spokesman said in a statement. 'We also continue to maintain that in order to protect the integrity of the case and the defendant's right to a fair trial, it would be inappropriate to comment any further.'

# CHAPTER EIGHT

Mrs. Taurasi said that I shouldn't hate R.F. Sanchez. When she said it I couldn't believe my ears. I mean Sanchez is probably throwing darts, at a voodoo doll of me, in his basement. How am I *not* supposed to hate R.F. Sanchez? She sat me down and went on to explain to me how the Assistant District Attorney somehow wants the same thing we want. Somehow we are *all* after the same exact thing. Well, I for one don't want to go to the gulag for the next 10 years of my life. Mr. Sanchez wants me to go to the gulag for *more* than the next ten years of my life. Was I missing something? My lawyer sure thought I was.

"Above all," as she put it. "the Assistant District Attorney wants justice to be done. As a prosecutor he doesn't necessarily want to send you to the gulag because—as a prosecutor—*winning* is not synonymous with *conviction*. You may not like him and vice versa but, in the end, the two of you want the same thing. When you see him thundering away at you just remember that the duty of a prosecutor is not to convict you but to seek justice. Surely, you can appreciate that?"

She went on to tell me that R.F. Sanchez was an actor. I thought that was special because his client, my wife, wants to be an actor. At Sanchez' apex he played the lead in a Tennessee William's play called *A Streetcar Named Desire*. I find that ironic because I remember that as the play where the main character rapes his wife's sister.

Sanchez's father was a respected prosecuting attorney. When his old man died Sanchez set off on something of a personal crusade. He quit acting and went to Law School. Compared to Mrs. Taurasi he's a novice but he's got that crusader thing going for him. The juries eat it up. It also helps that Sanchez could pass as a male-model. Whether or not he's the kind of prosecutor Mrs. Taurasi described [a seeker of the truth] is yet to be seen. Personally, I think the Sanchez would do anything to win—anything. Putting Dexter Valez on the witness stand proves the point. I just hope that, before this trial is over, R.F. Sanchez has an attack of conscience.


Trial continued . . .


Joseph Bo called by the People as a witness, duly sworn in, states as follows:

DIRECT EXAMINATION BY MR. SANCHEZ:

Q Please give the court your full name.

A My full name is Reginald Joseph Bo.

Q And Mr. Bo what is your occupation?

A I'm a professional basketball player.

Q Thank you. And you are the defendant's teammate. Is that correct?

A That's correct. I'm his teammate.

Q Mr. Bo, please do speak up. You've been playing for your team for 8 seasons. Is that also correct?

A Yes, you got that right.

Q You are, by some margin then, their longest serving member?

A Yes, but there's been coaching staff that's been there a bit longer. Compared to the other players I've been there the longest.

Q I see. And how long have you known the defendant Caleb Escueta?

A I've known Kingmaker for about a year and a half.

Q You met him through basketball. Is that correct?

A That's correct.

Q On a given week, during a basketball season, how much time would you say you spend with the defendant?

A I'd say I spend about 40 hours a week with him. Professional basketball is a full-time job.

Q Are you friends with the defendant?

A No, we're not friends ha-ha-ha. We're just teammates.

Q Is the defendant a good teammate?

A Kingmaker's about average.

Q Thank you. Your Honor, these are two videos from last season. The videos have been previously marked as Defense Exhibits Bravo and Charlie. With your permission I'd like to play them for the court.

THE COURT:

Very well. Bailiff would you mind playing the videos?

DEFENSE EXHIBIT DELTA:

A player and a fan exchanged words and more in the stands near the end of a game Friday night in one of the worst brawls in league history. In the mayhem several people were injured. This prompted a police investigation. Professional basketball players Joseph Bo and others charged into the stands and fought with fans in the final minute of their game. The brawl forced an early and ugly end to their loss.

Officials stopped the game with less than a minute remaining after pushing and shoving between the teams spilled into the stands and fans began throwing things at the players near the scorer's table. About three hours after the startling finish, police officers walked out of a television trailer with videotapes gathered from media outlets. Police officers interviewed witnesses at the arena and planned to talk to the players involved. One of the half-dozen people treated for injuries was taken to a hospital by ambulance and another sought treatment, police said. A local television reporter interviewed Joseph Bo afterwards.

REPORTER:

What happened that led up to this brawl?

JOSEPH BO:

I thought it was a regular foul. The referees told me it wasn't a technical and it wasn't a flagrant. I think the reaction was too much. It was an over-reaction. I don't mind him pushing me. But he also caught me in my nose. I'm not sure what will happen regarding that. I was sitting on the scorer's table when he threw a towel at me. I got up and then was sitting down again when I got hit with a liquid, ice, and glass container on my chest and on my face. After that it was all about defending myself.

REPORTER:

Bo, did anyone from security or police talk to you?

JOSEPH BO:

They came in to ask me if I needed medical help. I just thanked them for helping me get out of the building. I'm sorry. I can't say anything else on the advice of The Forces of Reaction [team ownership].

After several minutes of players fighting with fans in the stands, a chair, beer, ice and popcorn were thrown at them as they made their way to the locker room. The public address announcer said the game was being stopped and pleaded with fans not to throw things. The melee started when a player went in for a layup and was fouled hard by Bo from behind. After being fouled, he wheeled around and pushed Bo in the face. The benches emptied and punches were thrown. As the players continued shoving each other near center court and coaches tried to restore order, Bo sat down on the scorer's table, looking relaxed.

Just when it appeared tempers had died down, Bo was struck by a full cup thrown from the stands. He jumped up and charged into the stands. After Bo charged into the stands, Caleb Escueta joined him in the melee and had a few choice words for them. The fans in turn had a few choice words for Escueta. Security personnel and ushers tried to break it up. Later, a man in a fan approached Escueta on the court, shouting at him. Escueta knocked the man to the floor before leaving the court. Escueta was escorted away by teammates and the fan charged back. Teammate Joseph Bo stepped in and pushed another man who joined the scrum. Players from both teams left the arena without comment. Police officers prevented reporters from crossing the loading dock to get to the locker room or the area where their bus was located.

DEFENSE EXHIBIT ECHO:

Professional basketball player Caleb Escueta [also known as Kingmaker] was suspended, for the rest of the month, on Sunday. Joseph Bo must miss a total of five games for fighting with fans during a melee that broke out at the end of their last game. Escueta's suspension is the strongest ever levied for a fight during a game. 'The line is drawn, and my guess is that won't happen again—certainly not by anybody who wants to be associated with our league.' The league commissioner said. Both of the suspensions are without pay. The Player's Union director, calling the penalties excessive, said an appeal would be filed Monday.

The Player's Union can expedite an arbitration hearing three times during any given season and will request a hearing on behalf of the two players as soon as possible. 'We have to make the point that there are boundaries in our games,' the league commissioner said. 'One of our boundaries, that have always been immutable, is the boundary that separates the fans from the court. Players cannot lose control and move into the stands.' Caleb Escueta's penalty was the most severe because of his checkered history. Escueta being provoked into running into knocking down a fan who yelled at him did not appear to be a mitigating factor in the decision.

'The league has singled out Caleb Escueta in an arbitrary and capricious way,' A spokesman from the Player's Union said, faulting the league for not considering the players' fear for their own safety.

The Team owner issued a statement saying 'We believe that there was a rush to judgment and not enough opportunity for all sides to be heard. We will vigorously support our players in any available appeal process.'

All appeals of disciplinary penalties for on-court disturbances are heard by the commissioner, making it highly unlikely any of the suspensions will be reduced. 'It was unanimous, one to nothing,' the commissioner said. 'I did not strike from my mind the fact that Escueta and Bo have been reprimanded on previous conditions for loss of self-control. To watch the out-of-control fans in the stands was disgusting, but it doesn't excuse our players going after those fans. We have to do everything possible to redefine the covenant between players and fans, and between fans and fans, and make sure we can play our games in very welcoming and peaceful settings. We also have to redefine the bounds of acceptable conduct for fans attending our games and resolve to permanently exclude those who overstep those bounds.'

The altercation was particularly violent, with Bo bolting into the stands near center court and yelling and pushing at fans after debris was tossed at the players. Later, a fan that came onto the court was knocked to the floor by Caleb Escueta. Players who entered the stands and tried to act as peacemakers were not penalized.

The initial skirmish wasn't all that bad. But when a fan tossed a cup at Joseph Bo, he stormed into the stands. Authorities talked to a man by telephone who acknowledged he was the fan seen throwing a cup. The man failed to show up for an in-person interview, but police said Monday that they expect to talk to him once he has an attorney. 'He, I think, precipitated the whole event that transpired in the spectator section,' said a court-side reporter. 'I have no doubt that that man is going to be facing some criminal charges.'

Bo joined Escueta and at one point, a chair was tossed into the fray. 'Joseph Bo was well into the stands, and certainly anyone who watched any television this weekend understood he wasn't going in as a peacemaker,' the commissioner said. 'Escueta, I think it's fair to say, exceeded any bounds of peacemaking with the altercation with the fan in which he was involved.'

MR. SANCHEZ:

> Q Mr. Bo, remind us, how long have you been in the league?
>
> A I've been in the league for eight seasons.
>
> Q How long have you been playing basketball?
>
> A I've been playing basketball my entire life.
>
> Q Have you ever, before, seen anything like what you've seen in these two exhibits?
>
> A No. I've never seen anything like that. That was a fluke.
>
> Q I have one final question: Based on the videos we just watched would you say the defendant Caleb Escueta has a propensity for violence?
>
> A I would say yes but . . .

MR. SANCHEZ:

> Thank you. That'll do. I have no more questions.

CROSS-EXAMINATION BY MRS. TAURASI:

> Q Mr. Bo, you went into the stands to defend yourself, is that correct?
>
> A Yes, I was defending myself.
>
> Q In fact, that's why the commissioner of the league only suspended you for only five games, is that correct?
>
> A That's right.

Q After you came back from the stands we saw you making your way to the locker room, right?

A Yes, I just wanted to get out of there.

Q But, then, we saw you coming back *onto* the court. Why did you do that?

A I was sticking up for my teammate.

Q You were sticking up for my client?

A That's right.

Q Is one of your duties to stick up for Mr. Escueta after the game has already ended? Is it your job to protect him from fans?

A It's not exactly in the job description.

Q Have you ever done anything like that before?

A Not like that. I never had to.

Q Why did you think he needed extra protection?

A Those fans were going at him for the entire game.

Q But you could've saved yourself the trouble. We saw the video. You were already off the court and on your way to the locker room. You said my client isn't your friend. Why didn't you just keep walking away?

A I don't know, counselor, I guess I was in a crazy mood. (Laughter heard from the jury.)

THE COURT:

Amusing but not acceptable, Mr. Bo.

(Gavel raps.)

MRS. TAURASI:

Q To your knowledge has the defendant ever done something like this before? I mean had an altercation with a fan?

A No. It was a crazy situation. Like I said it was a fluke.

Q Explain that.

A Fans are tough on him.

Q They're tough on Caleb Escueta the defendant?

A Yes. Fans are extra tough on 'the defendant'.

Q Please do go on.

A I'd go as far to say that Kingmaker's the most disliked player in the league. Look at him. He's like six-foot-nothing. He's not athletic by professional basketball's high standards. Yet opposing fans hate him because he's a lock down defender.

Q Would you mind explaining that for the court?

A He's in your face, beating you to the spot you want, and if you stop to complain about it he takes the ball from you ha-ha-ha. You have to understand that your average fan wants to see their favorite players dunking and draining jump shots. Kingmaker stops all that with his pestering defense. It's like your client thrives on making his opponents look bad. His *modus operandi* ha-ha-ha is to make the game ugly. Fans hate that.

Q So, you're saying fans have an animosity towards my client?

A Well, it's a love/hate relationship. Kingmaker is an easy target: not just for opposing teams but opposing fans. The arenas are filled with hecklers who tell him he sucks and he should be taken out of the game . . . whatever. When there's no accountability hecklers will say anything— anything. It's not just the typical punks who disrespect him; it's also those punks' parents and grandparents. The type of people you would expect to have a little more, I don't know, character. They'll say *anything* to get him to start thinking and acting unproductively. And that's what you saw in those two videos. You couldn't hear it in the videos but I heard it because I was right there. The fan called him a—pardon my French—a [redacted].

(Public gallery chattering.)

(Gavel raps.)

In Kingmaker's defense any other guy on the team would've probably done the same exact thing. That fan crossed the line.

MR. SANCHEZ:

Objection, your Honor. The witness cannot possibly testify to what 15 other men would do in this unique situation.

THE COURT:

The jury will disregard the witness' last statement. Is there anything else, Mr. Bo?

THE WITNESS:

> If a man called me a [redacted] I would've went after him.
> I can say that. That much I do know. See? There's always
> someone who thinks he/she could do better than you. As
> much as you'd love to see those people try they're in no
> position to. They haven't earned it.

MRS. TAURASI:

> Q Mr. Bo you have 8 years of experience playing
> professional basketball. Is it your testimony here today that
> my client was provoked by the man in the video?
>
> A Absolutely. It was obvious. Those fans were drunk and
> heckling him the entire game. Coach told security but they
> couldn't or wouldn't do anything but give those guys dirty
> looks. When the called him Kingmaker a [redacted] *and*
> threw his beer at him that was it. He *had* to do something.
> He had to respond. If word got around the league that the
> heckler got a pass it'd be open season on Kingmaker.

MR. SANCHEZ:

> I object to this. The witness is speculating, at this point.

THE COURT:

> I going to sustained the objection. Strike that last comment
> from the record.

MRS. TAURASI:

> Q Mr. Bo, are you aware of your win-to-loss record of
> games played *without* my client? A Well, counselor, I'm not
> real big on statistics.

Q 34 wins and 29 losses. Is it safe to assume that you're not aware of your win-to-loss record of games played *with* my client?

A Sorry ma'am. Numbers were never my strong suit ha-ha-ha.

Q 45 wins and 10 losses. Mr. Bo, my client is more than an 'average' teammate, isn't he? Isn't it right that my client makes you a better player?

MR. SANCHEZ:

If your Honor pleases, I object. I can't see how this is material.

THE COURT:

I understand, of course, that this is technically objectionable I'm going to let this happen.

Q Mr. Bo, does the defendant make you a better player?

A I should plead the Fifth but since you both asked me so nicely: Yes, when he's on the court he makes me a better player. He may not have Solomon-ic wisdom but Kingmaker knows basketball.

MRS. TAURASI:

Q Thank you Mr. Bo. It looks like it hurt you a little to admit that ha-ha-ha. Now, you've been referring to my client as 'Kingmaker'. Would you now, please, explain that nickname to the court?

A The guys gave him that name because he could either make you a King (with his playmaking) or he could take your crown from you (with his defense). It's really up to him. That's why he's the Kingmaker.

MRS. TAURASI:

Thank you Mr. Bo. I have no more questions.

\*

Outside the courthouse, Assistant District Attorney Sanchez had a lot to say to the media. "Spousal Rape is hard to prosecute and often doesn't carry a tough enough punishment. This is why we've been pushing to change the law. Cases of spousal rape are severely under-reported out of fear. Across the board the penalties for spousal rape are less than those for stranger rape:

10 years versus 30 years. In this jurisdiction, a spousal rapist can be eligible for probation while every other type of rapist is *not* eligible for probation."

He went on to say. "I want people to be aware of this differential before they walk into courtroom. I also want women to know that there is a way to get justice. This emotive case is even more delicate because the accused is a semi-celebrity. Your colleagues in the media that now follow Caleb Escueta to and from the courthouse have polarized the public. For starters, the public is outraged at the fact that the judge put the accused under house arrest. This is yet another case of celebrity justice. There should *not* be one very lenient law for the privileged and a second set of strict laws that Jo Public must adhere to."

# CHAPTER NINE

Trial continued . . . Alexandra Bernardo is duly sworn in and states as follows:

DIRECT EXAMINATION BY MR. SANCHEZ:

Q Please state your name for the record.

A Alexandra Ligaya Bernardo.

Q Ms. Bernardo, you are a clinical psychologist, duly licensed to practice in the state?

A Yes, sir, I am.

Q Thank you, and for how many years have you been a couple's therapist?

A I've been practicing for two years.

Q And as such a therapist how many couples have you worked with?

A Over the course of two years there have been six.

Q Did you work with the complaining witness in this case Sojey Escueta and her husband the defendant Caleb Escueta?

A Yes sir. I worked with the Escueta's.

Q How many times did you meet with the Escueta's either one at a time or together?

A Over the course of six months we had total of 21 sessions.

Q Who was it who first came to you seeking your services?

A I first received a call from Mrs. Escueta.

Q And then?

A And then we had an initial meeting; where she and her husband were both present. From there we all agreed to meet about once a week time permitting.

Q And what were your findings of those sessions?

A Do to various stressors the Escueta's—particularly Mrs. Escueta—was experiencing a disconnect.

Q Please explain that the 'disconnect'.

A People have a deep need to feel closely connected to others, especially, their spouses. When that connection is compromised the relationship—in this case their marriage— was in danger. Sojey admitted to feeling lonely, and feeling as though Mr. Escueta didn't care about her, and feeling as though she were living with a stranger.

Q And Mr. Escueta?

A Well, Mr. Escueta conveyed a loss of passion. He stated, in several sessions, that they were living like siblings or roommates. He missed a sense passion and romance in his marriage.

Q Ms. Bernardo, did they ever discuss their sexual relationship?

A Yes. They, mainly Mrs. Escueta, discussed at great length sexual difficulties.

Q Would you please elaborate for the court.

A When they came to see me they were unable to talk about their sexual problems, which—on the part of Sojey—included difficulties with arousal and orgasm, significant differences in sexual interest and preferences, sexual avoidance. Basically, Mrs. Escueta described their sexual encounters as routine and unsatisfying.

Q And Mr. Escueta? Did you get his take on their sex life?

A Unfortunately no. As I recall, he would differ to his wife during those discussions.

Q So the defendant was not cooperative during those sessions?

MRS. TAURASI:

If your Honor pleases, I object to that as leading.

THE COURT:

Objection sustained. That last question will be stricken from the record.

MR. SANCHEZ:

Q Ms. Bernardo, are you still employed by the Escueta's.

A I'm not. No.

Q And why not?

A Mr. Escueta informed me that my services would no longer be required.

Q So it was the defendant who ended the couple's therapy sessions?

A Yes he did. I never knew why?

Q To your knowledge was this a decision reached by both Mr. and Mrs. Escueta?

MRS. TAURASI:

I object to that as hearsay.

THE COURT:

The objection to that will be sustained.

MR. SANCHEZ:

Q You are a clinical psychiatrist who examined the defendant over the course of over one year. Did you reach any conclusion about him?

A Mr. Escueta is intelligent, articulate, capable of grasping abstract concepts, opinionated, and very neurotic.

Unfortunately, he is also a man who hasn't overcome the incapacitating traumas of his childhood.

Q Would you mind elaborating as to which childhood traumas are you referring?

A Mr. Escueta never knew his biological father and his mother was a known . . .

MRS. TAURASI:

Objection your Honor. You've already made a ruling on this and the prosecution has been made well aware. I move to strike the witness' last statement from the record.

THE COURT:

Objection sustained. Strike out that last statement. Mr. Sanchez, I've already ruled on this in chambers.

MR. SANCHEZ:

Q Ms. Bernardo, you stated the defendant is 'very neurotic' would you please elaborate on that?

A As a prey species we've all been primed, by evolution, to be neurotic. It is my opinion that Mr. Escueta has a higher-than-normal level of neuroticism; with its trademark fear, anxiety, hyper-vigilance, and feelings of stress and inadequacy.

Q I see. Ms. Bernardo, were you surprised when you found out Mr. Escueta was charged with the rape of his wife?

A No, I wasn't surprised at all.

Thank you, Ms. Bernardo. No further questions. Please remain seated.

CROSS-EXAMINATION BY MRS. TAURASI:

Q Ms. Bernardo, where were you on December 12th?

MR. SANCHEZ:

Objection you Honor. This isn't proper cross-examination. I'd like to know exactly what my learned friend is implying.

THE COURT:

Objection sustained. Mrs. Taurasi, that is not admissible.

MRS. TAURASI:

Q Are you a medical doctor?

A No, I'm not.

Q Do you have any specialized training in forensics?

A No, I don't.

Q Do you have any specialized training in criminology?

A No, I do not.

Q Do you have any experience and/or training that would qualify you to give the court an *objective* forensic evaluation?

A No, I don't.

Q So, you're far an expert.

MR. SANCHEZ:

Objection.

MRS. TAURASI:

Withdrawn.

Q You're not objective, are you. Ms. Bernardo. In fact, you're a bit cross with him. The truth is you don't like Mr. Escueta, isn't it?

A I wouldn't say that's true. Mr. Escueta is my client. We have a professional relationship.

Q You mean he *used* to be your client. He fired you. With your leave, your Honor. I'd like to call the court's attention to Defense Exhibit Zulu. Ms. Bernardo, are these your hand written notes?

A Yes they are my notes. Those are confidential.

THE COURT:

I've ruled on this, Ms. Bernardo. We'll have the evidence.

MRS. ESCUETA:

Q I couldn't help but notice you dated this particular entry December 14ᵗʰ; the day *after* the police investigation of my client was made public. Is that correct?

A Yes, but that didn't . . .

Q Yes then. Mr. Escueta wasn't even your client anymore. Did you think he was coming back?

(No response.)

Would you mind reading the highlighted portion of your notes dated December 14<sup>th</sup>?

A ' . . . Mr. Escueta is an arrogant egoist who always has to have the last word . . . '

(All murmuring.)

It's true I wrote that but that's how he is; always using his sense of humor to embarrass me in sessions. He does do that.

Q Isn't it true that your personalities put Mr. Escueta and you on a dangerous collision course?

A I think Mr. Escueta uses his sense of humor to mask the pain he's feeling. It's an incapacitating pain that goes back to his childhood.

Q Was he ever comfortable enough with you to talk about the pain, you allege, he was feeling?

A Not really, no. I think it was too deeply guarded by his defense mechanisms.

Q Could it be . . . Is it possible that Caleb Escueta worked through the alleged neurosis and overcame it?

A I don't think so, no. The pain merely manifested itself into this Kingmaker character.

Q Caleb Escueta is a man who—despite his allegedly high and dangerous level of neurosis—graduated college, married, had two children, and became a professional athlete. Is this indicative of a man who hasn't overcome the incapacitating traumas of his childhood?

A It doesn't mean overcame them. He could still be harboring the feelings.

Q Allow me to venture into the hypothetical. Let's say I'm self-critical (which is a form of pessimism). Is it possible that-that can be a healthy thing? Is it possible that my being self-critical could make me strive to be better?

A It could, of course it's possible.

Q So, wouldn't it follow that even traits considered negative have behavioral value?

A Yes, that follows.

Q So, is it possible that the very traits you charge my client of having—traits you would hope to alter or expunge through your treatment—may in fact help Caleb Escueta overachieve?

(No response.)

Q Ms. Bernardo, isn't it possible that a mix of discontent can be a healthy thing?

A Yes, it's possible.

JUROR NUMBER THREE:

Q May I ask how the witness felt when the Escueta's broke the news to her?

A I don't recall what I felt on that day.

MRS. TAURASI:

> With your leave, your Honor, I'd like to ask the witness plainly. I believe the juror wants to know if being fired by my client made you mad?

MR. SANCHEZ:

> I object to the form of the question.

THE COURT:

> The juror wants to know how the witness felt about being fired. Is that correct?

JUROR NUMBER THREE:

> It is, your Honor.

MR. SANCHEZ:

> Well, I don't object to the question per say but the witness already answered the question. She said she doesn't remember. I'm not asking for anything to be excluded I simply want to leave it at that.

THE COURT:

> Ms. Bernardo doesn't remember. We'll have to accept that answer. Let's move on.

MRS. TAURASI:

> Q Okay, Ms. Bernardo, when Mr. Escueta fired you did he give you a reason as to why?

A I left a message for Mrs. Escueta but I never received a reply.

Q So, you wanted to know why you were fired?

A Well, there's that and it's not uncommon for clients to choose to avoid facing certain parts of treatment.

Q I see, it's not uncommon for you to be fired by your clients.

MR. SANCHEZ:

Objection. This is argumentative and immaterial.

THE COURT:

Mrs. Taurasi, would you care to rephrase your statement?

MRS. TAURASI:

No. I don't think I would.

THE COURT:

I would like the jury to disregard Mrs. Taurasi's last statement. It is incumbent upon counsel to *ask* questions of witnesses and not make statements *about* them. Let's proceed with caution, shall we?

MRS. TAURASI:

Q Ms. Bernardo, of those 21 sessions how many did Caleb Escueta attend?

A I believe he attended all of them.

Q Am I to understand that you are unsure of whether or not my client was physically present at your sessions?

A He attended all of them.

Q In your opinion was Caleb Escueta trying to repair the damage in his marriage?

A Yes, he was.

Q Do you think he's capable of raping his wife?

MR. SANCHEZ:

Objection, your Honor, the question asks for an opinion rather than facts.

MRS. TAURASI:

I thought we already established that everything this witness has to say is only her opinion.

THE COURT:

I'm going to allow this line of questioning.

MR. SANCHEZ:

Exception.

MRS. TAURASI:

Q Isn't it true that if you felt my client was a threat to anyone, by law, you would be required to report it. In fact, you would be derelict in duty to *not* report it.

(No response.)

Q Ms. Bernardo, did you not understand the question?
(Question repeated by stenographer.)

Q Is it true?

A Yes, that's true.

Q But you made no such report because in your professional
opinion, and from all the time you spent with Caleb Escueta,
you believed he wasn't a threat to anyone. Isn't *that* true?

A Well, that's true. Yes.

Q Was there anything in those 21 sessions that could in any
way have predicted Caleb Escueta could be capable of the
heinous crime he is being accused of?

A No, there wasn't. Of course there wasn't.

Q So, it was reasonable to assume that in your professional
opinion my client was *not* capable of raping his wife?

(No response.)

Mr. Bernardo, did you not understand the question? Is that
a reasonable assumption? If Caleb Escueta were a threat to
his wife you'd have to report it. You never reported anything
because in your professional opinion he was never a threat.

A Yes, that follows.

Q Let's back up a bit. During Direct Examination my learned
friend asked 'Ms.

Bernardo, were you surprised when you found out Mr. Escueta was charged with the rape of his wife?' Do you remember him asking that?

A Yes, but . . .

Q To which you responded 'No, I wasn't surprised at all.' Ms. Bernardo, do you assume all men are rapists?

A Of course not.

Q Do you assume all husbands are rapists?

A No. That's absurd.

Q Do you assume all professional athletes are rapists?

A Absolutely not.

Q Maybe it's just basketball players you hate then?

A No. That's not true.

Q So are we to conclude that you harbor this prejudice of my client alone?

A I don't.

Q Then why weren't you surprised at all when . . .

A I misspoke.

Q I see. You misspoke. It's unusual how your mistakes always seem to the detriment of my client.

MR. SANCHEZ:

Objection.

THE COURT:

Sustained.

MRS. TAURASI:

So, now you're saying that you *were* surprised to learn Caleb Escueta was being accused of this crime. Is that correct?

A Yes it is.

Q I'm glad we were able to clear that up, Ms. Bernardo. Now, during those 21 sessions did you ask either of the Escueta's if they were having an extramarital affair?

A No. The subject never came up.

Q I don't understand, you testified earlier that and I'll quote: 'When they came to see me they were unable to talk about their sexual problems, which—on the part of Sojey—included difficulties with arousal and orgasm, significant differences in sexual interest and preferences, sexual avoidance. Basically, Mrs. Escueta described their sexual encounters as routine and unsatisfying.' You didn't think to explore that in terms of her having an extramarital affair?

A Perhaps if they continued their treatment we might have explored that avenue further but, like I said, the subject never came up.

MR. SANCHEZ:

> I object to the entire cross-examination, of this witness, your Honor. The last time I checked Mr. Escueta was on trial—not Ms. Bernardo.

THE COURT:

> Now, the witness' competence is not in question and if it were it wouldn't matter here. The law doesn't require her to explore whether or not an affair took place. She said they never mentioned it to her and that is conceded. Whether or not the therapist asked about it doesn't affect this case one way or the other.

MRS. TAURASI:

> With respect, your Honor, my client trusted this couple's therapist to repair some of the damage in his marriage. If the witness was doing her job correctly then maybe we wouldn't be sitting here today. Furthermore, the witness says she wants to know why she was fired. My client told me why he fired her and I'm, now, prepared to relay that information to the witness. She wants to know.

MR. SANCHEZ:

> Judge Kosteniuk, may we have a sidebar, please?

THE COURT:

> Very well. Counsel approach the bench.
>
> [Inaudible dialogue.]
>
> [After conference.]

MRS. TAURASI:

Q Let me see if I understand this. The Escueta's had 21 couple's therapy sessions with you and you never once talked about extramarital affairs?

A No, we didn't.

And that's not uncommon.

Q Did the name Lucas Kyle Ayers ever come up in those sessions?

A Not to the best of my recollection.

Q Is it possible, in your therapy sessions, for your clients to be completely objective?

A It's impossible to be *completely* objective.

Q Is it possible, in your therapy sessions, for your clients to be mistaken?

A Yes, of course.

Q Is it possible, in your therapy sessions, for your clients to withhold information?

A Yes, though, I encouraged my clients to be forthright.

Q Would you say there is even a greater possibility that your clients withhold information that they might perceive to be *damaging*?

A Yes, it's possible.

Q And the possibility is greater, correct?

A It is.

Q Can your clients even be dishonest?

A Yes, I admit they can be.

Q So, as a couple's therapist, you only know what your clients tell you and even that information is suspect.

MR. SANCHEZ:

I object, if you Honor pleases.

MRS. TAURASI:

I'll withdraw it. I have no further questions for this witness.

THE COURT:

Now, madam, you may take a seat back there in the courtroom, but you must not talk to anyone, because you may be recalled as a witness.

# CHAPTER TEN

I'm sitting in an anteroom watching Dexter Valez do what he does best—talk. He's on television, again. This time he's on a talk show giving a post-contempt of court interview. I understand Judge Kosteniuk kept him locked up until he made a sincere apology to the court. I would've loved to see that.

Eventually, most inmates are going to be released back into society. You'd think that our society would help give them education and job skills. This could help them to be successful instead of resorting to committing more crimes to get by. Ex-cons need resources and support to help them stay on track. I offer Dexter Valez as Exhibit Tango.

LOCAL TALK SHOW:

Former deacon Dexter Valez entered jail out of shape, depressed and anxious. He has since has emerged physically unrecognizable from his pre-incarceration life. Incarceration appears to have shaved years off his looks. He has broad shoulders from a daily regimen of exercise. He has a goatee and his head, formerly covered with black hair, is completely shaved and tan. He says his blood pressure and cholesterol are lower than when he entered county jail and his body fat has dropped dramatically. County jail also offered the former clergyman a new set of peers: Drug offenders Sir Real, and White Mamba, as well as a bunkmate known as Kingmaker.

'I trust Sir Real and White Mamba with my back.' said Mr. Valez, in his first interview since he was fully released from custody. Mr. Valez is among the first white-collar criminals to be set free after aggressive crackdowns designed to rein in shenanigans at public companies. He remains as combative as ever, insisting he never committed a crime, while describing his experience in county jail as something akin to "40 days and 40 nights."

A grand jury indicted Mr. Valez of illegally making investment decisions based on information that was not available to the general public. The information allowed the clergyman to not only profit but also avoid losses.

'Valez was right down to earth,' said White Mamba, who asked that his real name not be used because of the stigma his drug-conspiracy conviction carries. White Mamba, said other offenders were 'just all full of themselves . . . we're brothers now,' he said, adding that if Mr. Valez' 'ever needs a lung or a bone, I'm there.'

Some former shareholders remain unmoved. Mr. Valez made lots of enemies, some of whose retirement accounts were drained when their stocks took a dive. 'There is no sympathy and there will never be forgiveness for Dexter Valez,' said a shareholder who asked to remain anonymous. She said she has been approached at retiree meetings by people who told her that when Mr. Valez is released 'there's going to be a hit out on him.' She said, 'I don't think these retirees would do it, but that's how strongly they felt'.

Dexter Valez has since filed legal claims against his criminal defense lawyers accusing them of malpractice and overbilling, allegations the firm has disputed in court filings. Mr. Valez is also seeking a rather large tax refund, saying his forfeiture is tax deductible. He contended the indictment was illegal. 'I feel vindicated,' he said. 'I never broke the law, and I never will.'

For now, Valez is focusing on shopping two books to publishers. One will be about his controversial encounter with basketball player Caleb Escueta. Another will be based on his religious beliefs. In a recent publicity stunt Valez is responded to a recent challenging made by the Atheist community:

And now these godless people all have their snouts in my troth. I refuse to debate with an atheist. I would rather leave an empty chair than share a platform with one of them. For the past few days, I've been asked to go publically debate with one of those savages. I have consistently refused. In fact, I take pleasure in refusing. And if any of my colleagues find themselves browbeaten or inveigled into a debate with an atheist, my advice to them would be to stand up, walk out and leave him talking not just to an empty chair but, one would hope, to a rapidly emptying hall as well. My advice to my followers is to join me in making an emphatic statement that we're willing to inconvenience ourselves by occupying the most obvious machinery of injustice—the county courthouse.

\*

Twice already I've been stopped by someone from the non-sports media. One of them stuck a recorder in my face and asked me to respond to Dexter Valez. What did he expect me to say? As far as I'm concerned Valez can do whatever he pleases. He should be out enjoying his freedom. I think Valez wants me to come back at him and I think the media does, too. This way Valez can get publicity and the media can sell their advertisements. Do I want to sue Dexter Valez? Of course I do. Am I going to sue Dexter Valez? Of course I won't. I'd rather let him have his 15 minutes of fame then watch him fade into oblivion like all the other tabloid freaks.

I've got my ammunition. I smiled and told both reporters the same exact thing, "Since the matter is now the subject of a legal proceeding, my lawyer has advised me to make no public comment about it. I'm sure you understand." It's a question of finesse. I have no intention of dignifying the ramblings of a crazy man with a response.

Not all people are against me. In fact, not all Christians are against me. Man on the street to a reporter:

"This gentleman has been standing alone. Now, he doesn't say that doesn't believe in god. He just says he isn't sure. Well, it's not easy to stand alone against the ridicule of others. I respect his motives. I believe in god but I want to hear more. I think there ought to be more conversations. Regardless of the outcome of his trial Escueta may never recover from the damage that's been done to his reputation. The law affords the plaintiff anonymity: irregardless of the outcome. The law does not afford the defendant that same anonymity. No matter what he has done in his life he should never have to deal with being falsely accused of a crime."

\*

Trial continued . . .

The next witness called by the People is Dr. Johnson. Dr. Johnson was an autocrat, like Mr. Sanchez, and a man of size. He carries with him a ponderous bulk and a hidden depth of spirit. The doctor has a dignity and assurance about him that one would expect from a man of high station. Dressed in a brown three-piece suite, with gold cuff links, the grey-haired gentleman is duly sworn in. After settling in the doctor and I get a good look at one another. He leans forward a bit and his left hand slightly rises. His eyes squint and his eyebrows tense up forming a set of wrinkles on his forehead.

DIRECT EXAMINATION BY MR. SANCHEZ:

Q Doctor, you are a physician, duly licensed to practice in the state?

A Yes, I'm a doctor.

Q Thank you, and for how many years have you been engaged in that practice?

A I've been practicing medicine for over 8 years.

Q You are the physician for the Society of Prevention of Cruelty to Women?

A I concur.

Q And as such a physician how many women have you examined the private parts of?

A I have examined women for the purpose of ascertaining whether any injury had occurred. Is that what you mean?

Q Yes, that's correct.

A Well, I don't exactly keep score but over the course of 8 years there has been considerably over 2000.

Q Did you examine the complaining witness in this case, Mrs. Sojey Escueta?

A Yes, I did examine the complaining witness.

Q Did you examine her private parts?

A Yes I did.

Q Please state for the record what the examination disclosed.

A I examined her private parts and found her hymen had recently been ruptured, indicating complete and recent penetration of her genital organs by some blunt body.

Q Please explain that, Dr. Johnson, the hymen?

A The hymen is a membrane partially covering the opening of the vagina, the opening to the internal private parts. The hymen is thin and the penetration of any blunt body large enough to tear or stretch that membrane causes complete rupture.

Q Would the entrance of a man's penis produce the condition found in Mrs. Escueta?

A Yes it would.

MR. SANCHEZ:

That is all.

CROSS-EXAMINATION BY MRS. TAURASI:

Q Dr. Johnson, are you able to tell this jury about Mrs. Escueta's degree of mentality when you examined her?

A No. I didn't have sufficient time to form an opinion?

Q Take your time and think, now, you couldn't tell us whether or not the complainant was malingering?

MR. SANCHEZ:

Objection.

THE COURT:

> This is cross-examination. I'll allow an *acceptable* intuitive leap. Doctor you've dealt with a lot of this did you think she was 'faking' to use a slang term or vernacular?

MR. SANCHEZ:

> Exception, if your Honor pleases. I submit my client has rights.

THE COURT:

> Yes; your client has some right, the right to have the truth brought out. If you have an objection or motion to make— make it. We know that your client has rights and they will be meticulously observed. And the people have some right, also, and that is to bring out the facts, and there is nothing at all improper in the question. Your exception is noted.

MRS. TAURASI:

> Dr. Johnson—keeping in mind your response to my *previous* question—let's address Judge Kosteniuk's question. Could you tell if Mrs. Escueta was 'faking'? A I'm sorry but I couldn't tell you either way.

> Q Now, could the entrance of any blunt instrument or any other blunt object produce the same result?

> A Yes. Any blunt object large enough to produce a tear.

> Q Doctor is it true that you can't tell—beyond a reasonable doubt—that it was my client who penetrated the vagina of Sojey Escueta and produced that rupture?

A That's correct. The examination couldn't tell us that. Q So it could have been something else?

A It's possible.

Q So it could have been *someone* else? Someone else who had sex with Sojey Escueta before your examination?

A Yes, it *is* possible.

Q Yes or no, please, Dr. Johnson. Could it have been something or someone else who produced the rupture?

A Yes.

Q Doctor earlier you said the rupture was 'recent'; can you express any opinion as to the length of time that had passed between your examination and the rupture you speak of?

A The parts had not yet healed and that usually takes 3 to 10 days.

Q So it was at least within 3 days.

A Yes, ma'am.

Q It was very recent?

A Oh, yes, it was very recent.

Q But you can't say—beyond a reasonable doubt— *precisely* when the rupture took place?

A No. It doesn't work that way.

Q So the rupture could have been produced anywhere up to three days prior to your examination of her.

A That's correct.

Q Doctor—to be perfectly clear—you're testifying that it is possible that someone other than my client could've ruptured the complainant's hymen?

A Of course, it's possible.

Q Were there any other abrasions on the complainant's body?

A There was an abrasion on the edge of her hymen.

Q Dr. Johnson, it was on the raw surface?

A Yes ma'am.

Q The raw surface where some unknown blunt object tore the hymen.

MR. SANCHEZ:

Object. Asked and answered.

THE COURT:

Sustained. Counselor, we're going in circles with this.

MRS. TAURASI:

Q Dr. Johnson, you stated that you're the physician for the Society of Prevention of Cruelty to Women?

A Yes, that's correct.

Q As an expert in sexual assault what are some situations that might increase the likelihood of a woman to make a false claim of rape?

A Well, before we get to that I'd be remiss to not state that the vast majority of women would *never* tell a rape lie under any circumstance. In fact, only a mere 2% of reports of forcible rape were later determined to be unfounded upon investigation.

Q Doctor isn't it true that-that 2% doesn't include instances where the accuser has failed, refuses to cooperate, or drops the charges?

(No response.)

Couldn't it be also said that the vast majority of men would never rape under any circumstance?

A I suppose you can say that.

Q So, having made your obligatory exception-rather-than-the-rule statements, why would a woman lie about being raped?

A It's difficult to list . . .

Q Dr. Johnson, you're an expert and you've had 10 days to prepare.

A I can't even begin to speculate . . .

Q Well, let me help you. Doctor what if the accuser felt a need to deny her consensual tryst to someone important in her life: someone as important as say a 'true love'. Would that reason a woman would lie about being raped?

(No response.)

'Lucas I love you and I would *never* have sex with someone other than you. I'm telling you Cal raped me.' Doctor does it follow?

(No response.)

Or how about this, maybe the accuser is setting the table for a divorce or custody dispute.

'You Honor, my husband is in prison for raping me. I filing for full custody of the children and I might as well have Willow Pond, as well. Doctor is it possible that a woman would lie for her kids . . . and a house?

(No response.)

Doctor what if the accuser is unstable or in some type of distress. Isn't it likely that someone close to her stands a greater chance of being smeared by an accusation? (No response.)

Doctor, isn't it possible that an unfounded allegation may simply be a cry for attention or sympathy?

(No response.)

And what if, Doctor, the accuser has absolutely no compunction about lying? Isn't it true that if a person has no difficulty lying, to extricate herself from trouble, then she may not even *need* a reason to make a false claim?

(No response.)

Doctor, isn't it true that there are certain people in our society who don't even need a reason to lie?

(No response.)

Your Honor . . . ?

THE COURT:

Dr. Johnson, answer the questions.

MRS. TAURASI:

Q They're all reasons a woman would lie about being raped, aren't they, doctor?

A Yes, I concede that they are. Well done.

MRS. TAURASI:

I have no further questions for this witness.

THE COURT:

Dr. Johnson, you're excused.

JUROR NUMBER SIX:

Your Honor, the last witness is currently my private physician. I don't know . . . that is I'm not sure whether that makes any difference.

THE COURT:

No, that doesn't make any difference, but you will not be influenced in your decision one way or the other?

JUROR NUMBER SIX:

> No. No your Honor. I won't.

THE COURT:

> What light that throws on the case you may determine independently of any other consideration.

MRS. TAURASI:

> You Honor, I move to dismiss the indictment upon the ground the People failed to prove a case against my client.

THE COURT:

> Motion denied, Mrs. Taurasi.

MRS. TAURASI:

> Further upon the ground that under the statute it is necessary that corroborative testimony be given of a crime of this character. There is no evidence adduced on the part of the prosecution that there was any rape committed on the person of the accusing witness nor is there any corroborative proof which is absolutely essential under the statute before the defendant is called upon to prove his innocence.

THE COURT:

> I will submit that matter to the jury as to what they think happened in that room from the stories told to them. They must determine how much weight they will give the testimony. So far as the law is concerned all the requirements of the law have been met with. It is up to the jury to determine what weight if any to give this testimony.

MRS. TAURASI:

> Exception.

THE COURT:

> Ladies and gentlemen of the jury, be very careful not to discuss this case among yourselves, or with anyone else. You must not come to any conclusion as to the guilt or innocence of the defendant until you have heard all the evidence on both sides. You must keep your minds open until the case is submitted to you by the court for your decision. That is the time to make up your mind and not before that. We will now take a recess.

> (The court takes a recess.)

# CHAPTER ELEVEN

I think I might be suffering from Cabin Fever; so much so, that this morning I received a call from my pharmacist. Oddly enough it doesn't take much to start a conversation with a pharmacist. She and I spoke for about half-an-hour.

CALEB:

So, how's work?

PHARMACIST:

Well, my day started with a call from a drunk who kept asking me about the relationship status of one of the checkout girls. Then he told me that his doctor phoned in his prescription. Of course the doctor didn't and the drunk didn't want to wait.

CALEB:

And that's when you called security, right?

PHARMACIST:

No, I called his doctor's office. They put me on hold for 10 minutes to tell me that his prescription was phoned into another pharmacy. I told the drunk and he kept cutting me off in the middle of my sentences.

CALEB:

Then you called security?

PHARMACIST:

No, I informed the drunk that I'm the type of person who prefers to speak in *complete* sentences.

CALEB:

[Laughter.]

That's amusing. You actually said that to him?

PHARMACIST:

You're damn right I did. Then I called the other pharmacy to get the drunk's prescription transferred to us. They immediately put me on hold for another 5 minutes. While this is going on I return to the counter and ask the drunk if we've ever filled prescriptions for him before. For some reason, he thought that 'for you' meant 'for your ex-girlfriend' and he answered my question with a 'yes'. Of course the drunk wasn't on our files.

CALEB:

Maybe, I'm half-awake but you're talking really fast right now.

PHARMACIST:

Then the drunk took off to gawk at girly magazines. I had to do three PA announcements requesting that he return to the pharmacy. I needed to add his address, phone number, date of birth, ask him if he had any allergies and what his insurance coverage was. We spent the next 5 minutes failing to find his insurance card. I call the other pharmacy and am immediately put on hold, again. I get the insurance information and file his claim, but then it gets rejected because the drunk changed jobs 6 months ago. To make things worse he kept asking me for my phone number.

CALEB:

So you called for an exorcist?

PHARMACIST:

No. I told him that the insurance the other pharmacy has on file for him wasn't working. He produced his *new* insurance card in less than 10 seconds. So, I file his claim with but it gets rejected because he had a 30 day supply of Vicodin filled 15 days ago at another pharmacy. I called the insurance company and was immediately placed on hold. They informed me that the Vicodin prescription was indeed filled at another pharmacy.

CALEB:

Well, that's unfortunate. I say you take a mental health day.

PHARMACIST:

After going back and forth between the drunk's doctor's office and his insurance company and getting an override and all that you know the thanks I got?

CALEB:

A date with a drunk who exhibits drug seeking behavior?

PHARMACIST:

That would be a no. He had the nerve to ask me why it took so long to fill his prescription.

*

I'm learning more about trial law than I want to. I took a voluntarily polygraph test but Sanchez has been desperately trying to have it excluded. Mrs. Taurasi thinks Judge Kosteniuk is on the fence about it and just needs a little push. Unfortunately, Mrs. Taurasi is the only one on my legal team with such a sunny disposition. If you've never had the pleasure of taking a polygraph test I can tell you, first hand, that you're really not missing much. My examiner's name is Geoffrey something . . . we have the paperwork with his full name on it here somewhere. I remember he wore an argyle bow tie. I focused on his bow tie that day because the only times I ever wore a bow tie were (1) Senior Prom and (2) my wedding.

Geoffrey lead me to the polygraph room and, despite the images presented in popular culture, it's not a dark room with a single beam of light aimed at your forehead. It was just a regular-looking office: not a dungeon. He read something and I had to initial and sign everything we went over. He asked for my pedigree asked for identification then asked me about my health and non-existent drug habit(s). I told him that if he didn't believe me he could ask me again when I was all hooked up. Then he asked me about Sojey and the allegation of rape. It was a huge relief for me to be able to tell Geoffrey what did and didn't happen on December 12th.

Then it was strange because Geoffrey told me the questions he was going to ask me during the test. It was the first time I ever got the questions to a test *before* the test.

An hour later it was time to hook me up to the polygraph machine. Geoffrey attached leads to my chest, my stomach, my fingers, and the palm of my hand. Then he put on the blood pressure cuff. We went over the questions he gave me earlier. He did this a couple of times. I wasn't worried. Like I said it was sort of relieving. A polygraph test is no big deal if you have nothing to hide. After Geoffrey analyzed all the data he came back into the room and announced that "my physiological responses are consistent with the usual indicators of truthfulness." I remember thinking *just be sure you remember that if we call you onto the witness stand.*

It would be a shame if Judge Kosteniuk didn't allow my polygraph test into evidence. I mean this is information the jury should be privy to. More and more I'm hearing about cases that are brought to light *after* it's discovered that prosecutors or police officers failed to do their jobs properly. Key evidence—like my polygraph test—and eyewitness testimony is too often lost or withheld. No one forced me to take that test. Legally, I don't think anyone could've. I took it voluntarily; knowing full-well that if my responses came up deceptive Sanchez would be all over it. I took the test knowing full-well that the polygraph test has been wrong in the past.

Mrs. Taurasi said that, even if the test isn't allowed into evidence, it will be valuable should we decide to make a deal with Sanchez. This tells me two things (1) she doesn't care that I don't want to make a deal and (2) she has doubts about the strength of our case.

I'm waiting in an anteroom. Every now and then I see jury members walking around the courthouse. According to the rules I'm not allowed to talk to them. Mrs. Taurasi is in the judge's chambers. She's trying to find a way to convince Judge Kosteniuk to allow my polygraph test into evidence. I can hear the media circus outside the courthouse. Due to recent testimony, it's not just the women's rights people protesting outside the courthouse. I have to say that these people sound more upset that the hecklers at our basketball games:

*"This is a Christian nation. If you don't like it then maybe you should leave."*

*"To not believe is a sin against the virtue of religion".*

*"No means no". "Regret is not rape."*

*"The fool has said in his heart, There is no god. They are corrupt, they have done abominable works, there is none that does good."*

*"You have a choice, Escueta, and you can choose not to be an atheist." "You're nothing but an elitist-sellout. All atheists are elitists."*

*"False accusations of abuse are abuse."*

Mr. Taurasi tells me he read a study that revealed that respondents were less likely to support a kidney transplant for hypothetical atheists needing it, than for religious patients with similar medical needs; that not too long ago, atheists weren't even allowed to testify in court because it was believed that an atheist would have no reason to tell the truth. I ask him to keep those little factoids to himself.

Then I distract myself by beginning from the premise that my polygraph test will *not* be allowed. What can I say? At least it's more productive than venting about Dexter Valez. Let's say the judge rules in favor of Sojey and my test is thrown out. What then? It's basically her word against mine. She says I did it. I say I didn't. We can't *both* be right. I know this sounds simplistic but I'm going somewhere with this.

What if Sojey and I took the same exact polygraph test? What if we went question by question, line by line, and one by one? For example:

GEOFFREY:

Q Did Caleb Escueta rape you?

SOJEY:

A Yes.

GEOFFREY:

Q Did you rape Sojey Escueta?

ME:

A No.

Let say the Geoffrey reveals, in regards to that single question, Sojey lied and I told the truth. If you like we can even switch the test results around. Let's say, the polygraph reveal that Sojey told the truth for that one question. Let's say, the polygraph revealed I lied for that question. Given the construct of that hypothetical situation I think *my* version should be excluded from evidence.

Even if my version of the story were not excluded from evidence— so what? Knowing the result of the pair of tests I would be less likely to take the stand and commit perjury. I'm not going to lie, in this given hypothetical situation, because Sanchez would know I was going to lie. If he knew the results of the pair of tests he would tear me apart during cross-examination. It would be Dexter Valez all over again.

The jury would never even have to see the polygraph results because *ipso facto* there would be no false testimony being given. This way would save everybody time.

If I took the test alone (like I actually did) and it came back that I was truthful in all my responses (like it did) then I can see how there *might* be room for reasonable doubt. Maybe I got lucky? Maybe I paid Geoffrey off? Maybe the test was inaccurate? Whatever.

However, if Sojey and I *both* took the test (as in my hypothetical) and she came back "golden" and I came back a "lying ass dog" then *that* would leave very little room for reasonable doubt. A single polygraph test alone is 90-95%accurate. How accurate would *paired* polygraph tests be?

Do you see what I'm saying?

What are the chances of the test being wrong on two different occasions and for two different people? I say strap Sojey in and ask her if on December 12th—or any other time for that matter—I raped her. Then, strap me in and ask me. It's too easy. Game over. Roll credits.

While we're on the subject, of "lying ass dogs", why couldn't we have done the same thing for Dexter Valez? I think if Sanchez made polygraph a prerequisite or if Dexter Valez volunteered to take a polygraph test *before* he was put on the witness list then we would've never heard of Dexter Valez. The man wouldn't be out there, right now, giving interviews and going on about "god's holy righteous penis". He'd be right where he belongs, sitting in county jail waiting for his sentence.

How do you give a man like Dexter Valez a free pass? How does he get a free pass? He can sit on Judge Kosteniuk's witness stand, wasting all of our time, tell his lies, and walk away with a free pass. It's not right. I'm trying really hard to have faith in the legal system but it's very difficult to do that when I see it being abused.

*

Trial continued . . .

Moira del Rosario re-called as a witness on behalf of the People states as follows:

DIRECT EXAMINATION BY MR. SANCHEZ:

> Q Good afternoon, Mrs. del Rosario. I'm sorry to have to call you back up to the stand but there are things that maybe you can help us with. One more time, for the record, what is your relationship to Sojey Escueta?
>
> A I'm Sojey's grandmother.
>
> Q Thank you. You understand you're still under oath, Mrs. del Rosario?
>
> A Yes, I do.
>
> Q Now, no matter what happens in this trial you understand what you're here to do—to tell the truth?
>
> A Of course I am.
>
> Q When you were raising Sojey did the two of you ever attend church?

MRS. TAURASI:

> At this time, we would like our objection to go on the record.

THE COURT:

> Your objection is noted. Mr. Sanchez, please continue with your examination.

*H. Valencia*

MR. SANCHEZ:

You may respond, Mrs. del Rosario.

(Question repeated by stenographer.)

A The answer is yes.

THE COURT:

Is the interpreter present? With respect, I don't understand this witness. Mr. Sanchez, you may understand her but I don't.

[The interpreter is present.]

MR. SANCHEZ:

I object. The witness has been on the stand before *without* the use of an interpreter.

THE COURT:

Well, the interpreter is here. Mrs. del Rosario, do your best to answer the questions in English. If it becomes difficult to do that then you can answer in *Tagalog* and the interpreter will translate.

THE WITNESS:

Yes, your Honor.

MR. SANCHEZ:

Q You testified on this case before did you not? You were on the stand?

(No response.)

If I say anything, Mrs. del Rosario, that you don't understand just let me know and I'll repeat it.

A All right. I will.

Q So, to your knowledge, Sojey was raised to be a pious person?

A Yes, and she still is.

Q Did Sojey often attend catechism classes?

A Of course.

Q Did she go to Sunday school?

A Yes, she did.

Q In that upbringing did you witness her pray?

A She said her prayers nearly every night, yes.

Q To whom did she pray?

A To our Lord.

Q In this upbringing did was it impressed upon her that it is wrong to lie?

A Yes, it's a falsehood 'Though shall not bear false witness against thy neighbor.'

Q And where is that from?

A It's from 'The Ten Commandments'.

Q And where are 'The Ten Commandments' from?

A They came from Moses.

Q And where did Moses get 'The Ten Commandments'?

A He got them from god.

Q Thank you, Mrs. del Rosario. So, according to your beliefs why is it wrong . . . I'm sorry.

(Clears throat.)

What did Sojey learn would happen if she told a falsehood? That is what does your religion teach you is wrong about lying?

A Well, as young girls we are taught that if we tell a falsehood we would suffer in purgatory when we die.

MR. SANCHEZ:

Thank you, again, Mrs. del Rosario.

THE COURT:

Justice delayed is justice denied, Mr. Sanchez, and perhaps we shouldn't be so cavalier with the court's time. I do think I can shorten this case a great deal. Ask the witness this, Interpreter. What is the character of Mrs. Sojey Escueta? And Interpreter, I want you to translate the witness' response exactly as if she were saying it in English. I don't want you to add to or take away anything from it.

THE INTERPRETER:

Yes, your Honor. I simply do it to make the evidence clearer.

THE COURT:

I understand, but as neither I nor either of the counselor's understand *Tagalog* we would just as soon have it translated as it is said.

THE INTERPRETER:

Of course, your Honor.

THE COURT:

And the court understands that what you are doing is a compliment, Interpreter. We are grateful for your services here, today.

(The question is repeated through the official interpreter.)

THE INTERPRETER:

I know my granddaughter to be of good character. I raised her to be an honest woman. She says this crime happened. She says her husband assaulted her. If that's what Sojey says then I believe it to be true.

MR. SANCHEZ:

I object to my witness having to go through an interpreter.

THE COURT:

This is your interpreter, Mr. Sanchez.

(Sighs.)

Anyway, the witness has already answered the question. Do you have anything further for this witness?

MR. SANCHEZ:

Not at this time.

THE COURT:

Does the Defense wish to cross-examine this witness?

MRS. TAURASI:

I take exception to the religious tone of this examination and ask that this testimony be stricken from the record . . . I ask to strike out her entire testimony.

THE COURT:

You motion is denied and your exception noted. Now, do you have any questions for this witness?

MRS. TAURASI:

Do I have any questions about religion? No. Religion is not germane to this trial.

THE COURT:

You've made your point, Mrs. Taurasi. I caution you. You're on dangerous ground. Now, do you have any questions for this witness?

(No response.)

So, is it understood that cross-examination is closed?

MRS. TAURASI:

I do have one point to make, your Honor.

CROSS-EXAMINATION BY MRS. TAURASI:

Q Mrs. del Rosario, besides from the suffering you believe you would endure for lying . . . that is do you-*yourself* believe it is wrong to tell a lie?

A Yes, I do.

Q So, it's possible to believe lying is wrong without the threat of purgatory . . . that is without religion?

MR. SANCHEZ:

Objection. The witness is not a theologian.

THE COURT:

The Defense is asking only for an opinion, is that correct?

MRS. TAURASI:

That's correct, your Honor.

(Question repeated by stenographer.)

A Yes, it's possible.

No further questions.

*H. Valencia*

THE COURT:

The witness may step down.

MR. SANCHEZ:

The People rest, your Honor.

THE COURT:

Then I think this is a good point. Ladies and gentlemen of the jury, you are admonished that you are not allowed to discuss any matter connected to this case, nor to permit anyone to speak to you about it, until it's finally submitted to you. We'll take a recess until tomorrow morning when, in such time, the Defense will call their first witness.

(Gavel raps.)

# CHAPTER TWELVE

Not surprisingly the journalists covering the case don't seem too concerned with searching for the truth. An anonymous source leaked an old video of Bo and me having a heated debate. Underneath the video there is a scroll that reads *When Elephants Wage War against Elephants.* I have no proof that Sanchez leaked this video; however, it doesn't take much of an imaginative leap to arrive at that conclusion. Never underestimate the persistence of paranoia. If you see the mail in the mailbox (circumstantial evidence) you might assume it was the mailman who put it there.

I'm coming to understand that any information that can't be tested in court is less than reliable. Sanchez can't get the video admitted into the court of law so he admits it into the court of public opinion. I vaguely remembered that argument I had with Bo but the video certainly helped refresh my memory. What happened was we were at practice when Bo went up for a shot and got fouled. He, then, turns to me and yelled "Get me the ball."

"I am getting you the ball." I hollered back. "Get it to me— sooner." He orders.

"It doesn't get any sooner than that."

As the video so clearly depicts, I proceed to then throw the basketball at Bo's face. Then I said, "Was *that* soon enough?" Bo comes after me swinging his fists and the guys break it up. The video shows Coach going all "Old Testament" on us before stomping off the court. I know it looks bad but these things happen. It may seem unprofessional and even childish but we're like a family. To some of these guys we're their *only* family. Families squabble. The difference is that our squabble was leaked to the press. People are eating their dinners and watching Bo and I fight—over and over again.

Mr. Taurasi says we need to talk. This can't be good. Somehow don't think he wants to talk to me about letting the dog sleep on the bed. In case you're wondering the dog's very cuddly in the morning. I have to admit, she brings out my paternal instincts.

"There are two types of clients." I'm a bit surprised that Mr. Escueta says there are only two. "As a lawyer, you can tell the first type of client what he needs to do but he won't listen. He'll keep doing it his way until he loses the case. Only in failure will that type of client adjust. And then there's you. You *do* know that your wife is protected by rape shield laws?" Mr. Taurasi asks.

I don't even know really remember what that means." Mr. Taurasi caught me off guard.

I'm still thinking about the two types of clients. "Remind me, again, what's the rape shield law?"

He hands me the legal dictionary and says, "Her name? Her face? The public hasn't even seen her. Sanchez and his character witnesses are portraying your wife as a shy, young, pious, mother, who is interested in nothing more than securing justice. There is a difference between the way the law is written and the way the law is practiced. Sanchez is *using* the rape shield law to present a one-sided portrait of his client."

"We talked about this, right? I already told you guys," I feel the need repeat. "We're not dragging Sojey through the mud. I don't even want you guys to investigate her. That's it."

"Don't you want to know?" We're both speaking loudly at this point. "Don't you want to know if your wife has done this before? Aren't you the least bit curious? If she's falsely accused before, and she's doing it now, what's to stop her from doing it again?"

"Don't even try it. I've been around you two long enough to know better. Even if what you say is true the judge wouldn't let it in—rape shield law. That's how you started this conversation so don't try to play me." I slam the law dictionary down.

"We don't know what we don't know." "What, the hell, does that mean?" I charge.

"Now, I understand that she's the mother of your children. I hear you on this." At this point, I'm starting to get a bit annoyed that he's agreeing with me while *not* agreeing with me. I make a "keep talking" gesture with my hands. "Okay." Mr. Taurasi continues. "This case is one of those cases that don't necessarily require corroborating evidence." I open the dictionary and quickly look up the term /corroborating/. "Now, what that means is Sanchez might not necessarily need a witnesses or physical evidence to convict you. There doesn't have to be a smoking gun, here. There doesn't even need to be a corpse. In all likelihood, this case is going to come down to her credibility against your credibility and, right now," he points to the television, "she's kicking your ass. It's the good and pious wife verses the anti-Christ. You're giving this jury every reason to believe the poor complainant who's putting herself through the agony of a rape trial."

"Look, I told you . . ."

"I know." He interrupts. "You don't want us dragging your wife through the mud. We couldn't properly cross-examine Sanchez' character witnesses because of the rape shield law.

We wouldn't be doing our job if we didn't offer you all legal options. Now, that being said, what we're proposing is that you allow us to show this jury that (a) your wife is being untruthful and (b) Lucas Kyle Ayers is no saint."

"So, what does that mean? 'Members of the court, the Defense can't show you that Mr. Escueta's wife is a whore but we're prepared to prove to you that she's a lying ass dog'"? I ask rhetorically.

"Well, not in those words." Mr. Taurasi says. "She and her friends are not being straight with this jury. It's something that we cannot allow to be side-stepped or explained away. The prosecution has spent the entire trial painting your wife as the victim. We can use that to our advantage. Our defense can be that the circumstances didn't *allow* her to tell the truth about what happened on December 12th."

"Lucas Ayers?" I ask.

"You never said we couldn't go after him." Mr. Taurasi responds.

"Ha-ha-ha, and what happens when that shoe doesn't fit, huh? We say Sojey's doing it all for attention? We say she's doing it all for a settlement? I suppose you want to bring in shrink to say she's crazy, too?"

"I know this is a lot, Cal."

"Spare me the Cal-patronizing . . ."

"You have the will to win this case but the way hasn't been made clear to you—until now. This is the way." He says in a firm tone. "You no longer have the luxury of being chivalrous. You're on trial for spousal rape and right now I'm telling you that we are losing . . ."

This time I cut him off, "I can't believe this."

"I know it's a fine line. I know it. We're trying to defend you and right now you need to explore this option. Think about it for one second. Think about it. If it were you advising me what would you tell me? You'd tell me to do what I have to do and call this accuser on her unfounded allegation. Now, there are inconsistencies in your wife's testimony that need to be addressed. We can try to do this gently and respectfully but we need to shine a light on it." The phone rings as if on cue. "I think that [the caller] would be for you."

As I pick up the phone Mr. Taurasi leaves the room. An machine says "You have a collect call, from a correctional facility, from 'Vincent'. If you would like to accept the charges please say 'yes' or press one". I get the strange feeling I'm being served a poison chalice. I press one and the machine patches me through. The caller and I sit in silence for about a minute.

"Yet each man kills the thing he loves; By each let this be heard; Some do it with a bitter look; Some with a flattering word; The coward does it with a kiss; The brave man with a sword" the convict recites. "Aristotle." I'm nonresponsive. "Disrupted." He groans. "If not destroyed. You been arrested?"

"Hmm." I'm reluctant because the last inmate I spoke to was the infallible Dexter Valez.

"They questioned you?" myself.

"Uh-huh." My theory is that if I don't use intelligible words then I'm not incriminating clink?"

"I see you hired yourself an expensive attorney?" I don't respond. "Spend any time in the

"Sheesh." I tell him. "Grr."

"Did you get fired from your job?"

I'm running out of noises to make at this man. This would've helped if I went with an insanity defense ha-ha-ha. "You do know they record your telephone calls, right?"

"Look at you, Mr. jailhouse lawyer ha-ha-ha. Okay, then I'll talk and you listen. They can't do anything to me." This is all the more reason for me to *not* talk to this man. I grunt. "Listen real because it's like this, even if the DA drops the case, your rep is gone. It's gone. If it isn't gone now it will be by the time this is over—irreparably damaged. They're going to say you pressured the victim to change her story. You lawyered up and the lawyer got you off; that's all people are going to think. Settle if you can because if it goes to trial, like me . . . . You really your ass is going to get the presumption of innocence?"

"My 'ass'"?

"Come on, now. We're talking about rape, here. It isn't 'No means no.' It's 'You Honor, I was *thinking* no.' Ha-ha-ha. Say a unicorn comes down and hands you the big NG; that don't mean your ass is innocent. All an acquittal means—to the public—is that DA didn't have enough to find your ass guilty. Even if you get the big NG from a criminal trial, like I did, they're going to walk your ass through a civil trial. You're going to need to get lawyered up all over again. A prosecutor is going to be all on your ass all over again. Even though you know she's lying, your ass could end up in here with me ha-ha-ha. Hey man. I don't know you but if you've got Taurasi's ear then that's one good thing. Taurasi said, 'talk to the kid' so I'm talking to you. It's nothing to me but if you can fight it—fight it. Maybe, you can stop the beast . . . just don't let it turn you into one."

"Hmm."

It's curious how the truth sometimes comes from the mouths of those we are least inclined to trust.

\*

Trial continued . . .

Dr. Guy Bueno-Moreno called as a witness on behalf of the Defense, duly sworn in, states as follows:

DIRECT EXAMINATION BY MRS. TAURASI:

Q You're a doctor of general and forensic psychiatry, is that correct?

A Yes I am.

Q And what is your expertise?

A I specialize in applications of clinical psychiatry to legal issues in civil and criminal matters at the interface of psychiatry and the law.

Q How many times have you served as an expert witness in matters relating to sexual assault?

A 103.

Q Wow. You wrote the book on unfounded rape allegations, haven't you? Let me rephrase that you *literally* wrote the book on unfounded rape allegations. Is that correct?

A It is among a larger body of work, yes.

Q Would you now explain to the jury what an unfounded rape allegation is?

A It is the designation used exclusively for cases in which it is determined that the accuser *intentionally* fabricated the allegation of rape. In general, the accuser claims an incident of forced sexual contact took place when no such incident occurred, or the contact that did occur was consensual.

Q In your books you discredit the standard assertion that 2% of rape cases are unfounded. In your expert opinion what is the actual percentage?

A Depending on the region it is low as 9% and as high as 41%.

(All gasp.)

Furthermore, because there is no reason to believe that all false accusers recanted that percentage may very well be higher.

Q In your book you state 'Interviews with veteran sex assault investigators verify that rape is one of the most falsely reported crimes . . . In the course of one year as many as 1 in 4 rape reports were unfounded.' Please explain to the jury what are some *specific* criteria for a rape allegation to be classified unfounded?

A That is, a report can be classified as unfounded if the complainant did not try to fight off the suspect, the alleged perpetrator did not use physical force or a weapon of some sort, the complainant did not sustain any physical injury, or the complainant and the accused had a prior sexual relationship.

Q To your knowledge of the events on December 12th did Mrs. Escueta try to fight off her husband?

A No, there was not any evidence that would suggest that.

Q To your knowledge did Caleb Escueta use physical force or a weapon of some sort? A No such evidence was found during my examination.

Q Is there compelling evidence to suggest Caleb Escueta physically injured the complainant?

A No, there wasn't of that either.

Q To your knowledge, did Mr. and Mrs. Escueta have a prior sexual relationship?

A Yes, I think that's obvious.

Q So, Doctor, by previously stated criteria is the complainant's allegation unfounded?

A By that criteria, yes it is.

Q Now, the judicial system, mental health practitioners, and the public at large are reticent to accept that some women lie about rape. However, there is ample evidence that adults lie about virtually anything, including . . . .

MR. SANCHEZ:

Objection. Is my learned friend asking a question or beginning her closing argument?

THE COURT:

I agree, Mr. Prosecutor. Mrs. Taurasi, please, ask your question.

MRS. TAURASI:

> Q Doctor, according to your research, how many cases in this state—last year alone—have you determined to be unfounded?
>
> A Last year, I determined 15% of all forcible rape cases to be unfounded.
>
> Q And what about this year?
>
> A This year, 16% of all forcible rape cases have determined to be unfounded.
>
> Q I'm sure there are numerous reasons why a woman would lie about being raped.

MR. SANCHEZ:

> Objection.

MRS. TAURASI:

> I'll modify the question.
>
> Q Doctor, having done such extensive research, what did you find to be the most frequent context and motive for an unfounded allegation of rape?
>
> A In my study over half of the accusers fabricated the rape to serve as a cover story or alibi.
>
> Q A cover story or alibi for what?
>
> A Of course the specifics vary but it was typically *consensual* sex that led to some sort of problem for the accuser.

Q Could the accuser's problem be something that caused a feeling of shame?

A Yes, it is possible.

Q Could the accuser's problem be something that caused a feeling of guilt?

A Yes, it is possible.

Q Is it common for the . . . . Doctor, from your studies, how common is it for a woman making an unfounded allegation of rape to identify the alleged rapist?

A Approximately half of the accusers identified the alleged rapist. Though their goal was not to harm or cause problems for the acquaintance, but to protect *themselves* in what they perceived to be a desperate situation.

Q So, essentially, the unfounded allegation allows the accuser to deny responsibility for having consensual sex?

MR. SANCHEZ:

Objection. Leading.

THE COURT:

The objection to that will be sustained. Mrs. Taurasi, I hardly think your expert witness needs any leading.

MRS. TAURASI:

Q Doctor, in your expert opinion what does the accuser get out of all this?

A For the vast majority of accusers the unfounded allegation of rape solved a perceived problem the accuser was, or anticipated, facing.

Q Doctor, one final question, how many defendants have been convicted of rape on the basis of an unfounded allegation?

A Well, there's no way of knowing.

MRS. TAURASI:

Hopefully someday, in the near future, we'll know.

MR. SANCHEZ:

Objection.

MRS. TAURASI:

Withdrawn. Thank you, Doctor.

THE COURT:

Your witness, Mr. Sanchez.

CROSS-EXAMINATION BY MR. SANCHEZ:

Q How many times have you served as an evaluator or expert witness?

A About 300 times.

Q Does 370 sound about right?

A Yes, it sounds about right.

Q Other than sexual assault what other matters did you testify to as an expert?

A There are many.

Q 21 to be exact. Does that sound about right?

A Yes, it sounds about right.

Q A man could a living from giving testimony. Isn't that right?

A Yes, I suppose so.

Q Doctor, isn't it true that you're being paid to appear hear as an expert witness?

A The same as you are being paid to appear hear as the prosecutor of this case.

Q Fair enough. Now, isn't it true that this state uses neither the definition nor the criteria of 'unfounded allegations of rape' as you testified to?

A Yes, but the . . .

Q Thank you. So, the statistics you offered today as evidence are meaningless?

MRS. TAURASI:

The Defense requests a sidebar, your Honor?

THE COURT:

Approach the bench.

[Inaudible dialogue.]

[After sidebar.]

MR. SANCHEZ:

Q Doctor, does your designation, of false accusations, include situations in which the victim was raped but unintentionally identified the wrong person as the alleged perpetrator?

A There are some situations in which the complainant . . .

Q Yes or no?

A Yes.

Q Doctor, does your designation, of false accusations, include situations in which the victim was really raped but—for any number of reasons—choose to recant.

A There are some situations in which the complainant . . .

Q I'm sorry to interrupt again, doctor, yes or no?

A Yes.

Q Let me see if I understand this correctly. A victim could be telling the truth and be determined—by you—to have made a false claim?

A Do I have to answer that, your Honor?

THE COURT:

This is cross-examination, doctor. I'll have to ask you to answer the question.

THE WITNESS:

A Given the restrictions of the question the answer is yes.

MR. SANCHEZ:

Q Doctor, does your research take into account rapes that are *not* reported?

MRS. TAURASI:

Objection. How would it be possible to take into account incidences that are *not* reported?

MR. SANCHEZ:

You Honor, the witness testified to the percentage of rapes reports that were determined to be intentionally false. It is the People's contention that it is extremely difficult, if not impossible to do this due to (a) jurisdictional variation in definition, criteria, and reporting practices and (b) not all rapes are reported.

THE COURT:

I'll allow it.

(Question repeated by stenographer.)

THE WITNESS:

A No.

MR. SANCHEZ:

Q Doctor, is it possible for a true victim to not remember the specifics of the rape out of embarrassment or shame?

A Yes, it is.

Q Doctor, if I were to file a false report of rape would it be *easier* for me to say I couldn't identify the assailant?

A Claiming an unknown perpetrator would make the rape appear random and—more importantly—make the case unsolvable.

Q 'Yes' then?

A Yes.

Q It would also free the *false* accuser from the need to fabricate additional lies and the demands of being confronted by the alleged assailant. Is this also true?

A Yes, it is.

Q What percentage of actual rape victims identified their rapists?

A 75% of proven rape survivors knew and were able to identify their rapist.

Q To your knowledge did Mrs. Escueta identify her assailant?

A Yes, I believe that's why we're all here.

Q Doctor, according to your research, do true victims tend to go to law enforcement to file a report?

A Yes.

Q To your knowledge did Mrs. Escueta go to law enforcement to file a report?

A Yes, I believe she did.

Q One final question, doctor, when Mrs. Escueta went to law enforcement and filed a report who did she identify as the man who raped her?

A The complainant identified her husband Caleb Escueta as the assailant.

MR. SANCHEZ:

No further questions.

RE-DIRECT EXAMINATION BY MRS. TAURASI:

Q Doctor, isn't it true that there currently is *not* a formalized, accepted definition of false rape allegations?

A Yes, that's true. This is why we the term 'unfounded'.

Q And you stated that your designation of unfounded accusations include situations in which the complainant was raped but choose to recant?

A Yes, I remember Mr. Sanchez asking me that during cross-examination.

Q That's correct. Now, aren't there far more recorded situations in which the complaint was *not* raped and did *not* recant the accusation?

A Yes, there are far more.

Q As an expert in the field, why do you think that's the case . . . that is why would a liar stick to the lie?

A Quite simply, there are no real *formal* negative consequences for a complainant to make an unfounded allegation of rape. Whatever consequence there is it would not outweigh the benefit gained from the false allegation's initial purpose.

Q So, the lie serves a purpose with no real consequence.

A Exactly. The person making the unfounded allegation never actually has to admit to themselves, to their family, or to their friends that the whole thing was a lie.

MR. SANCHEZ:

Objection. There are grounds for bringing legal action against those who make false accusations.

THE COURT:

Motion denied.

MR. SANCHEZ:

Exception.

MRS. TAURASI:

Doctor?

THE WITNESS:

Well, I don't like to say 'never' but I have to say the prospects of someone being convicted of making unfounded allegations are virtually nonexistent.

MR. TAURASI:

Do they exist in *any* form?

THE WITNESS:

Yes, there are legal actions but statistically those actions are seldom taken. In fact, in this state, filing an unfounded allegation of rape report is only a misdemeanor.

MRS. TAURASI:

Q I have one final question. Dr. Bueno-Moreno, as the country's foremost expert in the field of sexual assault, is Sojey Escueta's allegation of rape unfounded?

MR. SANCHEZ:

Objection asked and answered.

THE COURT:

Objection sustained.

MRS. TAURASI:

Thank you, Doctor.

# CHAPTER THIRTEEN

I've been thinking about a few things the convict told me over the phone. One thing in particular is that Sojey can bring a civil claim even if there is no criminal prosecution. She can actually still sue me—the perpetrator—in *civil* court. She can do this even if I've not been convicted or sentenced in *criminal* court. Sojey can still file a civil claim for damages. Moreover, as a perceived sincere, brave, and credible survivor she'll have an enormous advantage over me— the abuser.

\*

Trial continued . . .

Lucas Kyle Ayers called as a witness on behalf of the Defense, duly sworn in, states as follows:

DIRECT EXAMINATION BY MRS. TAURASI:

Q Do you know Father Duncan?

A Yes, he's my priest.

Q So, you confide in him.

A Yes, sometimes I do.

Q Do you know a woman by the name of Soledad del Rio?

A Yes, I know her.

Q Mr. Ayers, have you ever been arrested?

A I was arrested, once, but I was never convicted of a crime.
Q What was charge?

THE COURT:

That will do Mrs. Taurasi.

MRS. TAURASI:

Your Honor, I'm merely looking for a reference point for this
witness' character.

THE COURT:

Well, he said he was never convicted of any crime. That
ends that. An arrest means nothing. It's only a charge—not
a conviction. I'll exclude the rest.

MRS. TAURASI:

I take exception to the exclusion of testimony without
objection having been raised.

THE COURT:

It is the duty of the court to exclude any testimony that is
irrelevant and immaterial. Your exception is noted. Now, let's
move on.

MRS. TAURASI:

You Honor, a sidebar, please.

THE COURT:

Step up to the bench.

(Inaudible dialogue.)

(At the conclusion of the discussion.)

MRS. TAURASI:

Shall I continue with my examination?

THE COURT:

Please do, counselor.

MRS. TAURASI:

Q Mr. Ayers, what do you do for a living?

A I'm a trainer.

Q And what does that job entail?

A I train players to master basketball fundamentals, with an emphasis on shooting, as well as individual skill development in all areas of the game.

MR. SANCHEZ:

Objection. Is this really material?

THE COURT:

Objection sustained. It is entirely immaterial as to the details of their jobs, as I mentioned before.

MRS. TAURASI:

Exception.

Q Mr. Ayers, how many players do you train to master basketball fundamentals, with an emphasis on shooting, as well as individual skill development in all areas of the game?

MR. SANCHEZ:

I object to that as, irrelevant, incompetent, and immaterial.

THE COURT:

Objection overruled. How many clients the witness has is a different proposition, altogether. Proceed.

(Question repeated by stenographer.)

A I have five clients.

Q Is one of your clients Caleb Escueta?

A Yes. I was his shooting coach.

Q How did you two meet?

A Cal called me up and said he was ready to become a better shooter. I offered him one—on-one private training.

Q And when did that call take place?

A Next month would have been three years.

Q How often did the two of you meet?

A Depending on his schedule a few times a week.

Q Where did the two of you meet?

A He and I, usually, met at the arena.

Q You say 'usually'. Did you two meet anywhere else?

A We also met at his house.

Q You met him at Willow Pond where he and Sojey Escueta lived?

A That's right.

Q Go on.

A I also offered him individual game film analysis. We would watch his most recent game footage and I would give him feedback on where he could improve as a player. I provided him written notes that he could review at any time. Those notes pinpointed specific areas that needed work. He preferred we do this at his house.

Q Is it normal for you to meet clients at their private residence?

A Yes, it is.

Q Mr. Ayers, where you on the morning of December 13th?

A I was at the hospital. Sojey called me up and . . .

THE COURT:

Now, wait until she asks you questions. You'll have sufficient time to tell everything.

MRS. TAURASI:

Q Have you ever been at the hospital—where Sojey Escueta works as a part-time nurse—before the morning of December 13th?

A Yes, I've been there a time or two.

Q 'A time or two'? Would that be closer to 2 or 10?

A Closer to 10.

Q Closer to 10 or 15?

A 15.

(Public gallery whispers.)

THE COURT:

(Gavel bangs.)

Quiet down.

MRS. TAURASI:

Q So, you've been to Mrs. Escueta's place of work a little more than 'a time or two', haven't you?

(No response.)

Mr. Ayers, did you go to the hospital for medical services?

(No response.)

Mr. Ayers, isn't it true that you have *never* been seen at that hospital for medical reasons?

(No response.)

The court will wait for . . .

A That's true.

Q Isn't it true that you went to the hospital to see Sojey Escueta?

A Yes, I admit it's true.

Q So, what exactly brought you to the hospital on the morning of December 13th?

A I got a distressing call from Sojey.

Q Sojey Escueta the defendant's wife?

A Yes.

Q Did the defendant's wife often call you?

(No response.)

Your Honor I'd like to admit the witness' phone records, going back as far as two years, as Defense Exhibit Charlie. May I approach the witness?

THE COURT:

>Yes you may.

MRS. TAURASI:

>Q Now, Mr. Ayers, a telephone number has been highlighted could you read it?

>A Well, if you have the phone record then why do you have to ask me to read it?

>(No response.)

MRS. TAURASI:

>(Sighs.)

>We ask that the record reflect the witness is not cooperating with the court.

THE COURT:

>The record shall so reflect.

MRS. TAURASI:

>Q Mr. Ayers, do you recognize the telephone number that has been highlighted?

>A Of course I do.

>Q And whose telephone number is that?

>A It's Sojey's.

Q Sojey Escueta the defendant's wife?

A That's right.

Q Based on those phone records when was the first time she called you?

A It started two years ago. I don't need the phone records . . .

Q Based on the *evidence* when was the first time you called my client's wife?

A Two years ago.

Q So, you knew Cal longer than Sojey?

A Yes.

Q And you began calling Sojey Escueta while she was pregnant with Caleb Escueta's child. Is that correct?

(Public gallery whispers.)

(Question repeated by stenographer.)

A It's true but . . .

MRS. TAURASI:

With your leave your Honor I would like the witness to respond to this question with either a yes or a no.

THE COURT:

The witness will do so. Please refrain from making any commentary.

MRS. TAURASI:

> Q Isn't it true that you began calling Mrs. Escueta while she was pregnant with her husband's child?
>
> A Yes.
>
> (Public gallery gasps.)
>
> Q Do you usually have such a dialog with your clients' wives?
>
> A If you think I'm the kind of guy . . .

THE COURT:

> Now please just answer the questions. You'll be given the chance, as I told you before, to tell anything but, before you do that, you have to answer Mrs. Taurasi's questions without adding anything, where possible.

MRS. TAURASI:

> Q Mr. Ayers you did have such a dialog with my client's wife, didn't you? In fact, the evidence suggests you spoke to Mrs. Escueta more than Mr. Escueta. Isn't that right?
>
> A Well, you have the phone records . . .
>
> I, again, ask that the witness be instructed to answer that 'yes' or 'no'.

THE COURT:

> I'll allow it.

MRS. TAURASI:

(Question repeated by stenographer.)

Q Yes or no?

A Yes.

Q Based on the *evidence* did she call you on the morning of December 13th?

A Yes, she did.

Q Was this the 'distressing phone call' that motivated you to go to the hospital that morning?

A Yes, I'm sure it was.

Q You were going there to meet with Mrs. Escueta?

A Yes, I was.

Q To your knowledge was her husband going to be at this meeting?

A No, he most certainly was not.

Q Prior to December 13th, did you ever meet with Mrs. Escueta when her husband 'most certainly was not' there?

(No response.)

Your Honor I'd like to admit Lucas Ayers' and Sojey Escueta's bank records, going back as far as two years, as Defense Exhibit Tango. May I approach the witness?

**THE COURT:**

Yes you may.

**MRS. TAURASI:**

Q Mr. Ayers, before I have you read the highlighted portions of those documents I'm going to give you the opportunity to save the court some time. Before I ask you the next question I'm going to remind you that you are under oath. Now, were you having an affair with Sojey Escueta?

(No response.)

Would you prefer I put Mrs. Escueta back on the stand and ask her?

(Question repeated by stenographer.)

A Yes, I admit we were having an affair. And to tell you the truth I'm glad it's out in the open because we're sick of having to hide it.

Q Did the two of you have sex during this affair?

A Yes we did.

Q So we can clarify for the court, did this meeting of December the 13th take place before or after Mrs. Escueta went to the police?

A Before.

Q So, Mrs. Escueta met with you and *then* she went to the police?

A Yes.

Q To your knowledge, was Mrs. Escueta having sex with anyone besides you and Mr. Escueta?

THE DEFENDANT:

Objection.

(Standing.)

Your Honor, I would like my objection noted.

THE COURT:

Consider your objection—to your own attorney's line of questioning—noted. Mrs. Taurasi, please advise your client to remain . . .

THE DEFENDANT:

Damn it Gisele.

THE COURT:

(Gavels raps.)

Mr. Escueta, as sympathetic as I am to your distress I simply cannot allow this type of interruption in my court. Now, take your seat or I'll hold you in contempt.

MRS. TAURASI:

Mr. Escueta . . . please. My apologies your Honor. I'm confident this won't happen, again.

Q Mr. Ayers, to your knowledge, was Mrs. Escueta having sex with anyone besides my client and you?

A Not to my knowledge. No, she wasn't.

Q How could you be so sure?

A I don't know . . . I guess I can't . . . I don't know?

Q Mr. Ayers, before we refer back to the evidence, were you having a sexual relationship with anyone *besides* Mrs. Escueta?

A You would have to define that?

Q Really? You want the court to define what a 'sexual relationship' is? May I have a sidebar, your Honor?

[After conference.]

THE COURT:

For the purposes of this examination, a person engages in 'sexual relations' when the person knowingly engages or causes contact with the genitalia, anus, groin, breast, inner thigh, or buttocks of any person with an intent to arouse or gratify the sexual desire of any person. Furthermore, 'contact' means intentional touching, either directly or through clothing.

(Question repeated by stenographer.)

THE WITNESS:

A Yes, we were having a sexual relationship.

(Chatter from the public gallery.)

THE COURT:

(Gavel raps.)

That's enough of that.

(Chatter subsides.)

MRS. TAURASI:

Q Did you have sex with Sojey Escueta anytime between December 10ᵗʰ and December 14ᵗʰ?

A I'm taking the Fifth.

Q As you wish. To your knowledge, did Sojey have sex with anyone else on December . . .

A No. She was just raped. She wouldn't . . .

Q Oh but the alleged incident occurred on December 12th. Isn't it biologically possible that something or someone could've ruptured Sojey Escueta's hymen on the 10ᵗʰ or 11ᵗʰ?

A I don't know.

Q You don't know if it's biologically possible?

MR. SANCHEZ:

Objection calls for speculation.

MRS. TAURASI:

I'll withdraw it.

Q Mr. Ayers, to your knowledge, was Caleb Escueta aware that you were having a sexual relationship with his wife?

A He didn't care what she was doing.

Q Yes or no, Mr. Ayers, did my client know his wife was cheating on him?

A No, Cal didn't have a clue.

Q Did my client ever ask you, directly or indirectly, if you were having an affair with his wife?

A Never. He never cared enough to ask.

Q Did *you* care enough to tell him you were having an affair with his wife?

MR. SANCHEZ:

I object to the form of the question, if your Honor pleases.

THE COURT:

Objection to that will be sustained.

MRS. TAURASI:

Q Mr. Ayers, did you ever tell Mr. Escueta?

A No, Sojey didn't let me. She said she wasn't ready for that.

Q By that response I assume you *wanted* to tell my client?

A That's right, I hated having to lie to him about it.

Q I see, so you admit you lied about it. So, you consider withholding important facts, like this affair, to be lying?

A I guess so. Yes.

Q So, Mrs. Escueta was asking you to *mislead* her husband? She was asking you to lie?

A No. Sojey wanted to tell Cal, too, but the time wasn't right.

Q Did the two of you ever discuss when the time—to tell the truth—might be right?

(No response.)

Mr. Ayers, if you and Mrs. Escueta lied about an affair for two years then how can this court—to a reasonable and moral certainty—know that the two of you are being honest about your testimony?

(No response.)

Q Let's, maybe, circle back to that one. You just testified that my client 'didn't care'. How do you know that he 'didn't care'?

A Sojey told me. She would confide in me.

Q In a word, Mr. Ayers, how did the complainant describe her marriage?

A Bad. It was a bad marriage.

Q Your saying her marriage to my client was 'bad'?

A If I had to narrow it down to a single word, yes. It was a bad marriage.

Q Let me see if I understand this correctly: The marriage was 'bad' enough for her to hide affair but it wasn't 'bad' enough to end amicably. Did Sojey ever tell you that she and her husband were attending couple's therapy in an attempt to *save* their marriage?

A No, I never knew that.

Q I see. She was *misleading* you, too?

MR. SANCHEZ:

Objection. Among other things that's prejudicial against my client.

MRS. TAURASI:

Would you prefer I said lying?

THE COURT:

I sustain the objection. Let's be careful, here.

MRS. TAURASI:

Look at my client. He is Sojey's husband. They have two children. Cal has been nice enough to keep you as his trainer despite the fact that his team has an army of their own trainers. You've been working with the man for two years. Would it have made any difference to you at all if you knew Cal and Sojey were trying to save their marriage?

(No response.)

MR. SANCHEZ:

Objection. Your Honor . . .

MRS. TAURASI:

Withdrawn. I have no further questions.

CROSS-EXAMINATION BY MR, SANCHEZ:

Q Lucas, do you know what the penalties for committing perjury are?

A Yes, I do.

Q So, you're aware of the consequences of being dishonest here today?

A Yes, I am.

Q In fact, you took an oath just before all this started?

A Yes, I most certainly did.

Q Thank you. When you met with Sojey, on the morning of December 13th, what did she tell you?

A She told me she was raped.

Q At that point did Sojey tell you who raped her?

A Yes, she said it was Cal. I'm sorry, Caleb Escueta the defendant.

Q Did you have any reason to doubt her?

A No, why would she lie?

Q And what happened after Sojey told you she was raped by the defendant?

A We went to the police station.

Q What happened then?

A She told the police what happened. No further questions.

RE-DIRECT EXAMINATION BY MRS. TAURASI:

Q Mr. Ayers, I don't understand what you mean when you asked 'Why would she lie'? A I don't see how that sentence can possibly confuse you, counselor. It's a simple question. Why would she lie about being raped by her husband?

Q Do you love Sojey Escueta?

A Yes, I do.

Q Is it *true* love?

A Yes, and I want the record show to that.

Q Oh I'm sure the record will show that you *said* that. Yet, you admit to sleeping with *other* women. How would you explain that phenomenon?

MR. SANCHEZ:

Objection. Mrs. Taurasi is clearly taunting my witness.

THE COURT:

Objection sustained.

MRS. TAURASI:

Q Do you believe Sojey was in a position to love you back?

A Yes, she was and she is.

Q The same manner in which you love her, *true* love?

A Yes, I suppose.

Q With all the passion that comes from love?

A I'd like to think so.

Q With that same commitment?

A That's not fair.

Q Well, with intimacy then?

A Of course.

MR. SANCHEZ:

Objection. Again, this is taunting, your Honor.

THE COURT:

Well, what does the Defense wish to bring out; that these two people are in love? I think it's already been established that the witness loves her. We'd have to ask Mrs. Escueta the rest.

MRS. TAURASI:

Your Honor, there's a point to this. If I may continue my examination . . .

THE COURT:

Okay. Okay. Objection overruled. I'm going to allow this line of questioning, for now, but I hope you get to your point soon.

MRS. TAURASI:

Q So you love Sojey and she in turn loves you. Is it possible that either of you would be dishonest to get Caleb Escueta—who you testified to as not caring anymore—out of the way of your *true* love?

MR. SANCHEZ:

I move to strike that out. The Defense is clearly on a fishing expedition.

THE COURT:

Yes, I tend to agree but I'm going to allow this. I will remain alert to make sure it doesn't stray beyond what is permissible.

MR. SANCHEZ:

Thank you, your Honor.

THE COURT:

The witness will answer the question.

THE WITNESS:

I'm sorry but I don't really understand the question, Judge.

THE COURT:

It's nothing to be sorry about. I believe what Mrs. Taurasi is asking is if true love would be a motive for lying.

THE WITNESS:

No then. My answer is no. I don't think it is.

MRS. TAURASI:

Well, that answer is self-serving, isn't it? It sounds like a lot like love triangle, Mr. Ayers. It must've been difficult to have passion, commitment, and intimacy with that damn husband always getting in the way.

MR. SANCHEZ:

Objection. Is my learned colleague examining the witness or giving a speech. I can't tell.

MRS. TAURASI:

I'll withdraw my last statement. I think we all see what's going on here. Your honor, at this time, the Defense will have to ask for an adjournment.

THE COURT:

> Very well. If you have no further witnesses here, today, and wish an adjournment for the purpose of producing them I will give an adjournment for that purpose.

MRS. TAURASI:

> I do.

THE COURT:

> Very well, then, counselor. I will give you the adjournment.

# CHAPTER FOURTEEN

Most guys will tell you that they aren't prepared for life after basketball. Oh, I can hear the lawyer's objecting to that one. "Out of the scope of the witness, your Honor". How can I possibly know what "most guys" are and aren't prepared for? I've been spending too much time in the courtroom. What I do know is that we all have a passion for the game. You don't get to the professional level and make a career for yourself without that passion. The people outside the courtroom hold signs that say I don't believe in anything. I never said that. Of course there are things I believe in. I believe love is something strong. If my wife and Lucas are in love then it's no wonder why I'm so beat. You don't want to get in the way of love. It'll burn you. I also believe in positive reinforcement. I believe that we have a duty to help one another. Those last few sentences were beside the point.

Coach has a quote from Aristotle posted in the locker room: "We are what we repeatedly do. Excellence then, is not an act, but a habit." When I had basketball as a part of my life I had structure. I would go to the arena then go to the gym, go to the arena then go to the gym . . . . Eat, sleep, basketball. Whatever free time I had was spoken for. I'd either be at a Team Meeting or with my family. Some might argue that it wasn't much of a life but it was mine and I enjoyed it. Now that my family and basketball have been suddenly extracted from the equation I don't really know what to do with myself.

When in Rome, right?

Everyone I'm surrounded by these days seems to be really into the trial so that's mainly what I've been doing to fill the hours. For the last couple of days my legal has been preparing me to take the stand. Typically, we work in two hour spurts. The first hour or so we go over direct examination. Mrs. Taurasi walks me through the types of questions she's going to ask me when I'm on the witness stand. She never asks me the questions verbatim because she doesn't want my responses to seem too rehearsed. When we reach a natural stopping point we take a break. After the break Mr. Taurasi comes at me as if he were R.F. Sanchez. He treats me as though I'm a hostile witness. All through the process my legal team is giving me pieces of advice:

*Now Sanchez will try to ask you the same question twice, but in different words, so make sure you're consistent in the responses.*

*You don't have to fill the moments of silence during questioning. That's their job.*

*Sit up straight. Look at the lawyer.*

*Take your time but not too much time. Keep your hands away from your mouth.*

*If it's a 'yes' or 'no' question then just answer 'yes' or 'no'.*

*You don't need to volunteer information. It's their job to ask for it.*

*Don't nod or shake your head.*

*If you don't remember it's okay. Say you don't remember.*

*Is that an approximation? Then tell him it's an approximation.*

*'Never' is an absolute statement. Are you sure you want to use that word? Sanchez might try to bait you into losing your temper. Do not take the bait. When you hear me say 'tell the jury.' I want you to look at the jury.*

*You don't have to guess.*

*There's an opportunity to establish eye contact with a juror.*

*When you're on the stand you're going to have to speak clearly.*

*When Sanchez' interrupts with an objection stop speaking immediately and don't say a word until the coast is cleared by either Judge Kosteniuk or me.*

*Don't look to anyone for help answering a question. Just tell the truth.*

\*

Arief is one of the last people I'd expected to come to see me. As he pulls up to the driveway a few news reporters ask him questions about the trial. Arief tells them "no comment" either not knowing or not minding that "no comment" is a comment in and of itself. I always had a feeling Arief liked me. Though he seems cold and calculated on the surface I knew that part of his personality was *only* the surface. The rare outburst he displayed on the bus ride home strengthened my resolve. He was greatly disappointed in the team and specifically me and where there is great love there is great disappointment.

He acknowledges the police officer's presence with a nod. The police officer quickly rifles through the grocery bag Arief is carrying then lets him pass. I open the door before Arief has a chance to knock. "No means no" He jests entering the Taurasi's private residence.

"And maybe doesn't mean yes." I counter.

Arief looks around and says, "Nice digs." The dog seems a bit star struck as she bounces around and sniffs at my teammate's feet. She's clumsy . . . in a cute way.

"So this (the dog) is head of security, around here." I tell Arief. "Come on in here." I introduce him to Mr. Taurasi and Mrs. Taurasi. They usher us into the kitchen. The dog follows the crowd. I didn't know Arief could cook. Then again I don't know anything about Arief other than he has nerves of steel and the guts of a burglar. Not to mention Arief has his shooting stroke down to a science. As a point guard it's such a relief to know that, when I break my defender down and get into the paint, there's a guy like Arief waiting behind the three point line. If Arief's his man decides to help guard me . . . booyah. Arief catches the pass, gets his feet under him, with even the slightest daylight, you might as well start heading the other way down court because the man is money.

I digress.

"The press on this are out of their minds." Arief points out. "How can you stand that? Did you guys ever consider asking the judge for a gag order?"

I can feel Mrs. Taurasi looking at me. She doesn't have to say a word. "Well, we're really not supposed to be talking about the case."

"Oh, I'm sorry" Arief says. "I know the rules. I'm just not used to . . ." I tell him it's okay and even okay-er that he took time out his busy schedule to come down and see me under these conditions.

Prior to Arief's arrival I had a talk with my legal team about bringing in character witness to testify on my behalf. The Forces of Reaction via the head of the team's legal affairs gave us a list of potential candidates. The list contained just about every active player, trainer, and coach. The team's dancers and mascot were even on the list. I thought Mrs. Taurasi would jump at the opportunity to parade these people in. Boy was I wrong. It was decided that we wouldn't bring a single one of them in to testify on my behalf. As it was explained to me character witness testimony would actually hurt my case more than it would help my case. The eventuality of cross-examination is the rub. Allow me to explain to you now and so that I may better understand it myself. Keep in mind this is a hypothetical situation.

Let's say Arief came in and testified that "Cal is a good man." Let's say he even offered testimony such as "At one of our games I forgot my shoes and Cal, being the same size as me, let me use his shoes." The jury wouldn't think much of these two statements because, at best, the former is generalized and the latter is anecdotal.

After that Sanchez would counterattack. He would be allowed to poke holes in Arief's credibility during cross-examination. "Did you know the shoes Caleb let you borrowed that day were reported stolen from an orphanage?"

Now, it would against the rules for a juror to judge me using the negative information Sanchez brought out during cross-examination. He would only be allowed to impeach Arief's credibility but you have to understand the psychology of a juror. What the juror would take with him/or her is not that 'Kingmaker' lent shoes to his teammate in need: rather that the guy accused of rape also stole some poor orphan's shoes. You see jurors tend to remember the negative. It's not necessarily because they're looking for a reason to hang me. It's just the way people process information. We tend to remember the negative over the positive; especially, when the negative is concrete, and detailed, and emotional.

Arief prepares for us gourmet macaroni and cheese: not knowing I hate cheese. He asks if I've been following their games. He tells me the players all miss me. He tells me that, since being subpoenaed, Bo has been like a new man. "It's weird. It's like he gave up on trying to push us around. No one wants to talk about it in fear that they'll jinx it."

As far as basketball is concerned the team has been making up for my absence via committee. Arief, for example, has been putting in more minutes than he'd like to. I'll remind you that Arief is the oldest player on the team. I understand that Coach has been playing with the idea of bringing a point guard in on a temporary contract. The idea hasn't manifested itself as yet. Arief then encourages me to participate in a big Charity Basketball Event that's coming up. I pull a 'Sojey' by making a noncommittal response. "Well, the guys miss you on the court and if you choose to play in the Charity Event there's going to be a spot waiting for you. Just give me a call and I'll make it happen."

Legally, I'm still allowed to play. I can't imagine playing with half the evidence of my case lurking around like some dark cloud. One thing that Arief and I have in common is that we're fairly private people. If there's a back or a side door to the arena I'll take it and Arief will be right behind me. If a sports person walks by, without recognizing me, it doesn't bother me at all. I thrive on flying below the radar. I'm pretty sure Arief could relate to that. He understands when I tell him "The last thing I need in my life is negative attention from non-sports people."

Mr. Taurasi puts on some music: George Bizet's *Carmen*. All the Taurasi's listen to is Classical music and it's beginning to grow on me. Though I have to admit that it's refreshing for the radio to go on and it play something other than *The Nutcracker*. In the last few days I must've heard it three times. It is winter. I find *Carmen* to be an interesting choice of background music. *Carmen* is an opera about a love triangle; involving, a soldier, a bullfighter, and a beautiful-young gypsy. Out of an act of jealousy the soldier strangles the gypsy to death.

Now, that's the shortest version of that story.

I probably shouldn't read too much into Mr. Taurasi's choice of night music. Anyway, he asks us if we would like something to drink. "No, thank you." Arief immediately responds for the both of us. Mr. Taurasi takes out two glasses. He then pours bourbon for himself and his wife.

Arief asks me if I remember the conversation we had on the bus. I tell him I do then ask him what that was all about. Seems like a harmless enough question. "My brother was in the gulag." He says. By the looks on the Taurasi's faces this is information we already have. Suddenly, I'm reminded that the head of the team's legal affairs gave us investigative reports on all the people on the list they provided. The Forces of Reaction have their own investigators. The team is a fraternity and before you are allowed into the fraternity you have to meet certain criteria. They keep track of all your little secrets. I imagine different teams having different standards of conduct. Things that would raise a red flag for my team are gambling and drug abuse. Arief's brother being in the gulag, however interesting it is as dinner conversation, isn't something that would get him released from the team. "They say my brother beat up his wife."

I'm sure I can read about this in one of our files but I'd rather hear it from Arief. "But he didn't beat up his wife." I state.

"My brother races bikes" he begins. "He has a few bikes. After races he and his friends like to have their fun. One morning, after a night of celebrating, his wife starts smashing beer cans in the driveway. My brother pleads with her 'What's wrong with you? What about our friends and neighbors? Do you want our daughter is seeing this?' You see my brother and his wife had been married for 16 years. They had been dating years before their marriage. She never had a problem with his celebrating before. Sometimes she would even accompany him. Then, my brother tells me, something changed. His wife changed. There she was pouring beer on one of the motorcycles. Can you imagine that?"

"I can," Mr. Taurasi chimes in. "You know my daddy had a saying . . ." "Let the man talk," Mrs. Taurasi orders. "I'm sorry. Please continue."

"Would you believe that it was my brother's wife who into the house and called the police? Then she went back to the refrigerator but the only beer that was left were in glass bottles. My brother tried to take the bottles away bring his wife back into the house. His wife resisted. The police arrived and took my brother into custody. His wife told the police that my brother was threatening her. She even told the police that my brother wouldn't let her leave the house."

"Let me ask you this," Mr. Taurasi asks. "Do you hate your brother's wife?"

"As long as it doesn't leave this house?" Arief pauses. "His wife is dead to me." "'Yes' then." Mr. Taurasi laughs.

"How is it that I never heard this before?" I ask. Arief nods and responds, "Gag order."

Arief's a smart guy but, at this stage of the trial, a gag order would be like bolting the stable doors after the horses have ran out.

Honestly, I used to the think Arief was creepy and a little pathetic. Some of the others would pressure him to be more social. In fact, we made Arief the focus of the one Team Meetings he attended. The team went to the mall. The first thing we did was have a few guys—Arief included—retire the mismatched clothes they loved so much. It wouldn't hurt for the Forces of Reaction to test their players for colorblindness every now and then.

So we went into men's clothing stores and we had the shy players order banana milkshakes. You see, it was part of their training. The point of it was to get them to loosen up and be accustomed to coping with disappointment. The dating game is tough and the response we men get is almost always "No." Some ladies could be completely dispassionate about loss.

They almost force you to accept what has happened and to move on. It's the sort of thing that can either build a man up or wear him out. Aware of the eventuality of the outright rejection the shy players would face we armed him with a mantra. Whenever they were faced with disappointment they were to tell themselves: *She and I are just going to be friends.*

The exercise got mixed results. I was impressed that they were able to do it with straight faces. "Hello, I would like to order a large banana milkshake." One of the ladies couldn't reply because she was laughing so hard. Another lady gave Arief directions to the food court. As an ad lib he even asked one of them if they had banana smoothies. These were the same ladies who were selling them clothes. I thought the least they could do was indulge us.

Banana milkshakes were only the beginning of our assault on shyness. Next we had the shy players smile and say "Hey" to as many ladies they could. If a lady responded we gave the shy player the follow up line "Do you like boats?" Scores were actually kept.

Saying "Hey" was 1 point.

Asking "Do you like boats" was 2 points.

Conservative body contact was 3 points.

Asking for a phone number was 5 points.

At first the shy players were a bit coy. You'd think we'd asked them to walk the plank. They would mumble or stare down at their feet. By the end of the day they had enough courage to approach *groups* of ladies. Can you imagine Arief (a 6", 5' 200 lbs. Indonesian guy) asking you if you like boats? To his credit, Arief turned on the charm and approached more than just a few ladies. After 10:00pm, though, his mother showed up and dragged him home.

After having dinner with Arief I believe that I'm the one who might be missing the point. There's a crowbar separation between the loner-by-preference and the *enforced* loner. There are two cavemen. One of them is something of a hermit. He sits by himself and thinks of one only thing: Why do the babies, in our tribe, keep dying? The second caveman doesn't bother himself with such thoughts. You see, the second caveman just keeps trying to make a baby. My question is: Which one of these cavemen is right? I think Arief simply *prefers* the living room over the ballroom. After spending some time with him I've come to the conclusion that he isn't just less sociable; he also engages the world in a different way. He's a cerebral guy who values ideas more than the nuances of social interaction. The sense that I get is that he's not a hermit he's just got a low need for affiliation.

And, ladies, he's still single.

# CHAPTER FIFTEEN

Surely there will be people who are going to think my outburst in court was staged. They'll say we did it to make it appear as though I was defending Sojey when, of course, I was. Mrs. Taurasi always gives me the heads up on what's going to happen in court that day but she couldn't possibly know her cross-examination of the traitor Lucas Ayers would go to the extent it did. Our plan was always to expose him as "the other man" and thereby shift blame from me to him. At the same time Sojey was to not share in that blame. I know this created a huge problem for my legal team but Sojey is still the mother of my children. She may be a horrible wife I still believe she's a good mother. What father wouldn't want to believe that? I have to believe that, don't I?

This morning Mrs. Taurasi reminded me to sit up straight and this time *not* show emotion. I'll be taking the stand today and she wants me to be at my best. "It's going to seem like everything is against you but—when we're in the courtroom—and I need you to keep your head up, remain calm, and pay attention." She then specifically, asked me to pause before answering Sanchez's questions. This is to give Mrs. Taurasi time to object if she sees fit. There are a few extra news trucks in front of the courthouse. When we get inside the public gallery is all filled up. Mrs. Taurasi tells me that the people in the gallery actually won their seat through some kind of lottery. I'm called as a witness on my own behalf. I should be scared but I'm not. The way I see it-it would be a shame if I went to jail for life without ever getting a chance to tell my side of the story. If I've learned anything from this ordeal it's that there's no stronger statement than one made under oath.

The bailiff duly swears me in and I state as follows:

BY THE COURT:

> Q Please state your name for the record?
>
> A My name is Caleb Escueta.
>
> Q And would you now please tell us how old you are?
>
> A Sure. I'm twenty-six years old, your Honor.

DIRECT EXAMINATION BY MRS. TAURASI:

> Q While you were in county jail did you speak with a man named Dexter Valez?
>
> A Yes, I admit I did.
>
> Q According to his testimony you confessed to sexually assaulting your wife. Was that a true and accurate statement?
>
> A No it was not. I said no such thing. to him or to anyone.
>
> Q While you in county jail did you speak with Dexter Valez about your case?
>
> A Valez approached me. He told me he read a newspaper article about an investigation. He said I was the basketball player who was under investigation.
>
> Q And, now, please tell the court how replied.

A I didn't reply to that. I never said a word about it to him or anyone else in M-Dorm. I never said a word about my case.

Q At that time, you didn't at least try to deny the allegation?

A No I didn't.

Q Why not?

A Prior to surrendering myself you advised me not to speak with anyone about my case. I took that advice very seriously. As much as I wanted to set the record straight I never said a word about it. Even to deny it would be to talk about it.

Q Thank you. Now, the complainant in this case Sojey Escueta is your wife. Is that correct?

A Yes it is.

Q Do you remember the day of December Twelfth?

A Yes I do.

Q Did you sexually assault her?

A No I most certainly did not.

Q But you did enter the kid's room with the *intention* of having sex with your wife?

A Yes. I admit I did.

Q Did you have sex with your wife on the day of December Twelfth?

A Yes but, like I've always said, it was consensual.

Q Mr. Escueta have you ever taken and illegal drugs?

A Drugs? No. Never. No.

MRS. TAURASI:

Please the court, we'll direct your attention to Defense Exhibit Golf. These are Mr. Escueta's toxicology reports going back as far as two years. These tests were administered by team doctors. As you can see they've all come back negative of any illicit narcotics.

Q Were you drinking alcohol on December Twelfth?

A No. I rarely drink and, when I do, it's on a special occasion.

Q How often is that?

A Maybe once or twice a year; certainly, not on December Twelfth.

Q Was your wife asleep when you entered the kid's room?

A I thought so.

Q Yes or no.

A If I had to choose I would say 'yes'.

Q Was she awake when you had sex with her.

A Yes. Absolutely. Yes she was awake. When I told her the kids were asleep she turned and looked right at me.

Q She turned towards you?

A Yes. She was on her side when I walked in.

Q Was she on her side when you had sex with her?

A No. She was on her back.

Q Did *she* roll over from her side to her back or did you roll her over?

A It was sort of both of us.

Q Would you please clarify that for the court.

A I got in bed with her, and under the covers, and I started to . . . you know . . . kiss her and touch her.

Q Did she kiss you back?

A Yes she certainly did. She was awake and she kissed me back.

Q Did your wife touch you back; that is in a sensual way?

A Yes she certainly did.

Q How can you be so sure she touched in that way.

A Because she helped me . . . penetrate.

Q She helped put your penis in her vagina?

MR. SANCHEZ:

Objected to as leading.

THE COURT:

> Overruled. I'll allow it but I don't think we should proceed very far in that direction, Mrs. Taurasi.

MRS. TAURASI:

> I understand, your Honor. I don't intend to, either.
>
> (Question repeated by stenographer.)
>
> A Yes. She usually did.
>
> Q 'Usually' you say?
>
> A Well, a majority of the time she does because sometimes it doesn't happen right away.
>
> Q You mean sometimes you're not able to penetrate right away?
>
> A That's right. So she has to . . . you know . . . help.
>
> Q Is that what happened on December Twelfth?
>
> A It is. That's exactly what happened. She put it in.
>
> Q Did she at any point communicate to you that she didn't want this to happen?
>
> A No. She certainly did not. If she did I would have stopped. In fact, there were times in the past, when she was finished, she asked me to finish and I would.
>
> Q To clarify, in the past, and at her request, you would stop right in the middle of sex?

A Well, I would hurry up and finish.

Q Did she make such a request on December Twelfth?

A Absolutely not. If she did then I would.

Q If she told you to stop you would do your best to stop.

A That's correct.

Q Did she—physically—try to stop you.

A No, she did not. If she did I would have stopped.

Q Do you remember what she was wearing that day of December Twelfth?

A Yes. She was wearing that brown t-shirt that says 'Will Work for Chocolate', panties, black spandex shorts, and a pair of white socks. She usually wore socks to bed.

MRS. TAURASI:

Your Honor I'd like to admit these items as Defense Exhibit Foxtrot. May I approach the witness?

THE COURT:

Yes you may.

MRS. TAURASI:

Q Mr. Escueta, are these the clothes you just mentioned?

A Yes, they are.

Q Are they torn?

A No, they aren't.

Q Are they stretched?

A No they're not.

Q Are they stained?

A Not at all.

Q Do they appear to be mangled in any way?

A No, they're not because I didn't 'mangle' them during our act of consensual sex.

Q Prior to having intercourse did you play any music for your wife?

A No. I admit I didn't.

Q Did you light a candle or hand her a rose or anything to that affect?

A No. I admit I didn't. In retrospect, maybe I should have.

Q Did you ask her if she wanted to have sex?

A I didn't but that wouldn't be the norm, anyway. You see, we don't talk about it before or after. It just sort of happens.

Q According to your wife this was *not* the norm. Did she talk to you about it afterwards?

A No, she didn't.

Q Prior to law enforcement arriving at your house your wife never accused you of raping her?

A No, she didn't. I found out when through the detectives. I had to learn about it through them.

Q Did she ever communicate discomfort or her being scared before, during, or after the event?

A Not to me. If that were the case I wish she had told me.

Q What would you have done if she had told you?

A I'd do something to keep her from feeling that way. I would have somehow accommodated her. I loved my wife.

Q You say 'loved'? Is that intentionally past tense?

A Yes, that's past tense.

Q So, you don't love her anymore?

A Not after what I've heard, here. This isn't the woman I married. I can't imagine a person who would cheat on her husband while she was pregnant with his child and accuse him of rape and tell her family our friends that I raped her. I would never marry such a woman if I had the knowledge that she capable of such a thing.

Q I can imagine, Mr. Escueta. The person you marry is seldom the person you divorce. So, you never suspected . . . .

A We were in a dark place in our relationship but I was still attracted to her. Yes, I was attracted to my wife and I wanted to be intimate with my wife. I don't think that's in itself is anything to be ashamed of. On December 12th I still loved my wife.

Q But not anymore?

A But not anymore. Sojey's repulsive to me. I can't even think of her, in that way, anymore. I don't know how it happens. I mean you have sex with me you tell me you love me then you have sex with him and tell him you love him? That's insane. You're the mother of my children. I mean, at least, show a little class. If you don't love me, fine. Tell me that. Leave me. Don't keep the whole thing going the way you did. Did you think you could have it both ways: a biological father who loves your children more than life itself and this back-door idiot? You can't have it both ways. Well, apparently, you can. I guess, if you have your way, you will.

MR. SANCHEZ:

I object to that, if your Honor pleases.

THE COURT:

Sustained. Please instruct your client to refrain from addressing the plaintiff.

MRS, TAURASI:

My apologies you Honor. It won't happen again.

Q Thank you for sharing, Mr. Escueta, I appreciate how difficult it all must be. Now, after you had consensual sex with your wife what happened?

A We laid there for a while, like we usually do, then I left.

Q You didn't say anything? You didn't tell her you loved her?

A No. I admit I didn't but that wouldn't be the norm. Perhaps it should have been the norm.

Q Did she say anything to you?

A No, she didn't.

Q Did she try to leave the room?

A No. We just laid there for a while.

Q About how long did the two of you lay there?

A It was a while, maybe, twenty minutes. Keep in mind I was still in love with her at the time.

Q And after that time what happened next?

A I left the room. I went outside to work out.

Q Where did you go exercise?

A I have the equipment set up just outside the bedroom window so I could watch the kids.

Q What type of exercises did you do?

MR. SANCHEZ:

Objection. That's immaterial.

THE COURT:

Sustained. You don't have to answer that. It should've never been asked.

MRS. TAURASI:

Your Honor, we sat and listened to the prosecution ask the complainant . . . . I withdraw the question.

Q Mr. Escueta, you heard your wife's testimony. What did your wife do in the time between the alleged incident and the time she went to work?

A She stayed in bed. Like she said she works grave shift so it's important for her to get her sleep.

Q Yet you woke her up to be intimate with her?

A With our conflicting schedules it's difficult to get any quality time together.

Q Where do you work?

A I'm a professional basketball player.

Q Were you working on December 12th?

A No. It was *supposed* to be a day of rest.

Q Going back to those missing ten hours. Do you recall your wife doing anything else?

A She made some phone calls, got something to eat, showered, got dressed, and went to work? It was nothing out of the ordinary.

Q And you know she did all this, how?

A I can also see into the kid's room from where I work out. Just out of habit I check in.

Q Does the window in the kid's room have blinds?

A Yes they do.

Q Do those blinds work?

A Yes. She could've shut them if she wanted to. In fact she probably should have so she could get some sleep.

Q Mr. Escueta, did you work on December 13th?

A Yes, we had an early game.

Q Who is the 'we' in question.

A Oh, my team and I.

Q When was the first time you heard that your wife was accusing her of rape?

A Like I said, it was when the detectives came to the house.

Q And when was that?

A The next day, December 13th.

Q What happened then?

A The detectives questioned me. Then they asked me to go downtown for further questions. They gave me a penile exam. I've been meaning to ask, is that a legitimate test, judge?

(No response.)

Not important.

Q Mr. Escueta, what did you tell the detectives?

A I told them that the intercourse was consensual; that I did not, never have, or never would, rape my wife or any woman for that matter. It's not me. I'm not that guy. I did not rape her.

THE COURT:

Well, I will tell the jury to disregard all this. It is immaterial.

MRS. TAURASI:

I want to get it in that . . .

THE COURT:

But you've got it into evidence already; that your client made no admission of guilt; that he always protested his innocence. If there was any claim that he made an admission of guilt this would be material but such is not the case. Now let us proceed with the understanding that the defendant vigorously protested his then and does so now. Let that be understood and conceded.

THE WITNESS:

With respect, your Honor, you allowed Dexter Valez to sit in this very chair and testify that I made an admission of guilt to him. I think that it is within my right to say that I made no such admission and that I did *not* rape my wife.

THE COURT:

Strike the witness' last statement from the record.

MRS. TAURASI:

Thank you, Mr. Escueta. No further questions. Stay there Mr. Sanchez has some questions for you, now.

CROSS-EXAMINATION BY MR. SANCHEZ:

Q Mr. Escueta, when was the first time you heard that your wife was having the alleged affair?

A It was during this trial. My attorney informed me that it was more than a mere possibility; that there was overwhelming evidence of infidelity on her part.

Q The court is to believe that you didn't know the woman you were living with had this alleged double life?

A The court ought to believe it because it's the truth. I didn't know about the affair until we investigated it for purposes of this trial.

THE COURT:

Now, counselor, how is *this* material?

MR. SANCHEZ:

If your Honor pleases, it speaks to the defendant's state of mind on the day in question. I ask for a little levity.

THE COURT:

Of course, the jury understand that they must pass on the credibility of the witnesses, and the court has only to rule on the questions of the law as they arise, and I say only what I deem it necessary to say, in view of the cross-examination of counsel for the defendant. It is not intended to limit his right, or prejudice the defendant in any way, but to keep the real issue before you. The real issue here is whether he did or did not assault his wife in the way she claims, and he says that he did not, and that he is innocent. Now, is that clear, Mr. Sanchez?

MR. SANCHEZ:

Yes sir; that's perfectly clear.

THE COURT:

Okay, then, I'll allow this for now.

MR. SANCHEZ:

Q Now, you've heard all the testimony. Your wife didn't go to great lengths to hide the sexual relationship she had with Lucas Kyle Ayers. People in her own family and your own friends saw the two of them together. Is it your testimony today that not one of them bothered to mention it to you?

A I can see how that might be difficult for you to believe.

Q Well, that's as spot on as that suit and tie combination, Mr. Escueta. It *is* difficult to believe.

MRS. TAURASI:

Move to strike that out.

THE COURT:

Strike out that last statement.

MR. SANCHEZ:

I was merely offering your client a compliment.

Q How often did you see the people I previously mentioned?

A Almost daily but you'd have to understand the culture.

Q Please explain it to the court 'the culture'.

A Well, we don't exactly act as a single coherent entity. I don't want to say too much but there are things that go unsaid. I suppose they had their reasons for not telling me that my wife might be having an affair. After all, nobody wants to be the bearer of that type of message. Look, infidelity has probably around since the beginning of man. I'd venture to guess that many of the people in this courtroom have been touched by infidelity in some way. Did I know about my wife's affair on the day in question? No I did not. Does it upset me, now? Yes it most certainly does.

Q Very well. Mr. Escueta, is it possible that the intercourse you had with your wife on December 12$^{th}$ began as consensual but then changed?

A 'Changed'? No, that's not what happened.

Q Is it your testimony, here today, that such a situation is impossible?

(No response.)

Q Yes or no, Mr. Escueta. Is it possible?

A Yes, I suppose it is possible and—for the record—so is time travel.

Q Do you believe a partner has the right to say 'no' at any point of intercourse?

A Of course.

MR. SANCHEZ:

(To Mrs. Taurasi.)

Don't do that again.

MRS. TAURASI:

Do what? Are you inferring that I acted inappropriately?

MR. SANCHEZ:

You were signaling to your client.

MRS. TAURASI:

When the witness began to answer I leaned in to catch his response—nothing more.

MR. SANCHEZ:

There was apparent signaling to the witness.

MRS. TAURASI:

I wasn't trying to convey any impression to my client and I resent the implication. I think these little tricks as we go along ought to be stopped. We all know why it's done. It's for the benefit of the jury but it isn't fair to my client. If this is going to go on I'll be on my feet for the rest of this trial.

THE COURT:

> That won't be necessary and certainly not without the court's permission.

MRS. TAURASI:

> I am going to be on my feet every time opposing counsel makes an insulting remark of that kind. I ask the court's protection from such insults.

THE COURT:

> I haven't noticed you signaling to her client. If I did I'd say something. At the same time I don't think you ought to be so sensitive. Now, let's move on, shall we.

MR. SANCHEZ:

> Q Mr. Escueta, is it possible your wife told you to stop but you just didn't hear her?

> A When you phrase the question like that it's impossible to say no.

> (Question repeated by stenographer.)

> A In that small context; that is given the limits of your question . . .

MRS. TAURASI:

> I object to the form of the question. Your Honor, the prosecution is crossing the line.

THE COURT:

> I'll be the judge of that, Mrs. Taurasi. I say the court will wait for an answer.

MRS. TAURASI:

> Exception.

THE COURT:

> Exception noted. Thank you. Please take your seat.

MR. SANCHEZ:

> Q Mr. Escueta, just one more question and a simple yes or no will suffice. Is it possible your wife told you to stop but you just didn't hear her?

> A Yes.

MR. SANCHEZ:

> No further questions.

RE-DIRECT EXAMINATION BY MRS. TAURASI:

> Q Mr. Escueta, is it possible your wife told you to *continue* but you didn't hear her?

> A Yes.

> No further questions.

*H. Valencia*

THE COURT:

The witness may step down.

MRS. TAURASI:

Your Honor, I renew my motion, may it please your Honor, made at the close of the people's case. Further upon the ground that there is no evidence, on the part of the prosecution, that shows that a rape had occurred.

# CHAPTER SIXTEEN

I've come to accept that the law doesn't operate in a vacuum. I'm being brought to trial not only before Judge Kosteniuk and her jury but also before the court of public opinion. Through radio, television, newspaper, and tabloid the public have gavel-to-gavel access to the trial. Every one of those people, if they so choose, gets to cast a vote on the legal and moral aspects of the case. I trust my legal team but I have a feeling this case may very well be won or lost on the courthouse steps.

Up until this point Judge Kosteniuk has started court precisely at 9:00am. You could measure coral by it. This morning, she's late. We're bringing a few witnesses in who weren't on our original list. Among the people on the new list is the traitor Lucas Kyle Ayers. We'll be recalling him as a hostile witness. I'll admit he's not my favorite person, right now. In fact I'm willing to sign an affidavit to that effect; that is, I'm willing to declare under the penalty of perjury that I don't like him.

Now, I may have told my legal team that Sojey is off limits. Lucas Ayers, on the other hand, can kiss my ass. I have little doubt that Assistant District Attorney Sanchez is in chambers, right now, trying to keep my witness' from testifying. After about an hour, Mrs. Taurasi tells me that Judge Kosteniuk granted a continuance. Sanchez has got two days to stop this train from running him over.

"Mind if I run something by you, real quick?" I ask my lawyer. "Is it about this case?"

"It is but it isn't." I jest. "It's a grey area thing . . . not unlike this case." She doesn't respond. Before all this started I would've assumed her lack of response to be a sign of consent. Nowadays, I prefer consent be written down, and signed under oath, before a notary public, or someone authorized to take oaths.

"Shoot." Mrs. Taurasi says.

"Let's say Sojey is lying. I know you want to stop me right there but you'll need to save your lawyering for until you hear the whole thing. If Sojey's lying then she doesn't love me. If Sojey doesn't love me then the collapse of this marriage isn't really much of a loss. If I haven't *lost* much then the *hurt* shouldn't be much. My question to you is: why do I feel like a have a huge hole inside?"

Mrs. Taurasi asks if we can have lunch before she answers. I grant counsel a continuance. "You were in chambers, huh. Tell me. What was Judge Kosteniuk wearing under the robe? You can tell me. Was she in her pajamas? Jeans and a t-shirt?"

After a couple of sandwiches, my lawyer is ready to respond to my initial question. "I follow your logic. It follows. By any rational calculus you feeling a huge hole in your chest is illogical. You're absolutely right. No rationally-calculating person, weighing the costs and benefits of being with a woman who would do such a horrible thing, would feel such angst."

I put my hand on my chest. "This is you making me feel better?"

"You're not a calculator, Mr. Escueta." She points out. "This woman has been a significant part of your life for over 5 years. You had 2 beautiful children by this woman. To the best of your ability you loved the woman you *thought* your wife was. I've seen some things in my life and one thing you can bank on is that, more often than not, love is going to trump logic."

I think about that for exactly two days.

*

Trial continued . . .

The first witness is Father Duncan. He's the priest who's been sitting behind Sojey during the entire trial. Mr. Taurasi, as it turns out, is a very good investigator. He's excellent with computers and, over the years, has accumulated favors from people in law enforcement. Contrary to popular belief, it's not easy to find dirt on a priest. In fact, the jury would probably frown on my legal team attacking him on the stand. After Father Duncan is duly sworn in Mrs. Taurasi prepares to walk a very fine line.

DIRECT EXAMINATION BY MRS. TAURASI:

Q What's your definition of an atheist?

A In layman's terms, an atheist is an individual who—not unlike your client—has no fear of god and no absolute moral code.

Q Yes or no, Father: Are atheists capable of morality?

A Yes.

Q So, a man cannot be accused of immorality simply because he rejects formal religion. Is that correct, yes or no?

A Yes.

Q In fact, some of the greatest leaders in history did *not* accept formal or even informal religion. Is *that* also correct, yes or no?

MR. SANCHEZ:

Objection. This is immaterial.

THE COURT:

Sustained. Strike that last question from the record.

MRS. TAURASI:

Q Father can we equate morality and religion?

A Yes, we most certainly can.

Q 'Most certainly'?

A Some of the greatest moral teachers in history were religious.

Q Indeed, and some greatest moral *sinners* in history were not only religious but also *sinned* in the name of their religion.

MR. SANCHEZ:

If your Honor pleases, I object to this as irrelevant and argumentative.

THE COURT:

Sustained. There's no need for that, Mrs. Taurasi.

MRS. TAURASI:

Q The complainant testified that she often confided in you. Was that a true and accurate statement?

A Yes, it is. I heard her confession, regularly.

Q In those confessions did she ever tell you she was having an affair with Lucas Ayers?

A At this time I'd like to take the Fifth.

Q You are an ordained priest. Is that correct?

A Yes, I am.

Q And only an ordained priest can absolve sins. Is that also correct?

A Yes, that's correct.

Q Speaking in the hypothetical, if I confessed to you that I was having an affair. As an ordained confessor it'd be in your authority to absolve me. Is that correct?

A Yes, I would be within my authority but it's not that simple.

Q I see. You'd also have the authority to advise me to admit this infidelity, to my husband, for the purposes of reconciliation. Isn't that right?

A Granted every situation is different, I'll stipulate.

Q So, if Mrs. Escueta *did* confess her affair then you either didn't give her that advice or she ignored it?

MR. SANCHEZ:

Objection.

MRS. TAURASI:

Withdrawn.

Q You'd also have the authority to advise me to stop committing adultery, wouldn't you, Father?

A Yes, I would.

Q Lucas Kyle Ayers also testified that he often confided in you. Was that a true and accurate statement?

A Yes, it is.

Q In any of those confessions did he ever tell you he was having an affair with the Sojey Escueta?

A I'm taking the Fifth.

Q Speaking in the hypothetical, if I confessed to you that I was having an affair with a married man. As an ordained confessor it'd be in your authority to absolve me. Is that correct?

A Yes, again, it would be.

Q You'd also have the authority to advise me come clean about the whole thing, to get it all out in the open and end the secrecy. Isn't that correct?

A Again, I'll stipulate.

Q You'd also have the authority to advise me to stop committing adultery, wouldn't you, Father?

A Yes, I would.

Q Did Mr. Ayers ever mention the name Soledad del Rio?

A I'm taking the Fifth.

Q Did Mr. Ayers ever mention the name 'Jimmy'?

A I'm taking the Fifth.

Q Hypothetically, if Lucas Ayers confessed to you that he assaulted Soledad del Rio, you could absolve him. Isn't that correct?

(All whisper.)

A Yes, but you see . . .

Q Hypothetically, if Lucas Ayers confessed to you that he assaulted Soledad's boyfriend Jimmy, you could absolve him for that as well. Yes or no, isn't that correct?

(All mummer.)

(Gavel raps.)

A Yes.

Q Now, tell the court, as an ordained confessor what obligation are you under in regards to reporting crimes to law enforcement?

A According to canon law, the sacramental seal is inviolable; therefore it is absolutely forbidden for a confessor to betray in any way a penitent in words or in any manner and for *any* reason.

Q And if you felt so compelled to report the crime, anyway, what would be the consequence of such a violation?

A If an ordained confessor were to break confidentiality it would lead to his automatic excommunication.

Q Let's circle back to the hypothetical confession. Lucas Ayers just told you that he beat up Soledad del Rio. Who knows if he's done it before? Who knows if he'll do it again? Wouldn't you be in a position to advise him to surrender himself to the proper authorities?

A I suppose.

Q You 'suppose'? Wouldn't you be in a position to ($1^{st}$) get the victim out of harm's way and ($2^{nd}$) have *her* report the crime to the proper authorities? A Yes.

Q Wouldn't you be in a position to get either the victim's or the assailant's permission to notify the proper authorities yourself?

A Anything is possible.

Q Well it's too bad we'll never know if you were in that position, Father.

MR. SANCHEZ:

Object. Move to strike out the Monday morning quarterbacking. Your Honor, this is all conjecture.

THE COURT:

I'll strike Mrs. Taurasi's last statement but the rest of it will remain in evidence.

MRS. TAURASI:

No further questions.

CROSS-EXAMINATION BY MR. SANCHEZ:

Q Father Duncan, you testified that an atheist has no fear of god and no absolute moral code. What is there then to prevent an atheist—like the defendant—from committing a crime like spousal rape?

A One way to look at it is that Caleb would adopt the set of ethics that is common to his society. If it's a culture of rape then, without an absolute moral code, Caleb would see nothing wrong about committing spousal rape.

Q But we don't live in such a culture, Father. Quite the contrary.

A That's correct. So it doesn't serve Caleb's best interests to commit spousal rape because it wouldn't take long before he was penalized, by society, for the crime. But ethics are ever-changing. In one century it's not a crime to rape your wife; meanwhile, in the next century the same act is a felony. So if we were to ask Caleb, if spousal rape were right or wrong, he could only tell us his opinion based on the current trend.

Q Let me see if I'm understanding this correctly, Father. Without a set of moral laws from an absolute god by which right and wrong are judged the defendant would simply do whatever works best for him in the society he is in?

A Yes. To Caleb morality would be a standard of convenience—not absolutes. Another way to look at it is Caleb does only what was right in his *own* eyes.

H. Valencia

Q That sounds awfully self-centered?

MRS. TAURASI:

Objection. Your Honor this entire line of questioning bares no weight on the case; furthermore, it prejudicial against my client.

MR. SANCHEZ:

You Honor, the issue here is the basis of the defendant's moral beliefs and how those beliefs affected his behavior on December 12$^{th}$.

THE COURT:

Objection overruled. I want the jury to hear this.

MRS. TAURASI:

Exception.

MR. SANCHEZ:

Q Please continue, Father Duncan.

A Belief systems are important and absolutes are necessary. If morals are relative, then behavior will also be relative. As an atheist Caleb cannot claim any moral absolutes, whatsoever.

No further questions.

RE-DIRECT EXAMINATION BY MRS. TAURASI:

Q I'll ask the witness to confine his responses to either yes or no.

THE COURT:

Very well.

MRS. TAURASI:

A Since you brought it up Father Duncan, is my client capable of governing his own moral behavior and getting along in society?

A Yes.

Q And to your knowledge he's done so his entire life. Isn't that correct?

A Yes.

A Regardless of his belief system, is my client subject to the same laws of our land as you and I?

A Yes.

Q You see this is where I'm confused. I hope you can help clarify this for me. Is it your testimony here, in a court of law, that belief in god is an absolute requirement for ethical behavior?

A Not absolutely, what I . . .

Q Yes or no, please, Father? Does a person have to believe in your god in order to be ethical?

A No.

Q So Caleb Escueta is perfectly capable of making ethical decisions; in fact, he *has* been for his entire life. Isn't that correct, Father?

A Yes.

Q And, finally, is Caleb Escueta *also* capable of developing his own moral standards and codes?

A Yes.

MRS. TAURASI:

Well, I have no further questions.

THE COURT:

The witness may step down. Mrs. Taurasi are you prepared to bring in your next witness?

MRS. TAURASI:

Yes, your Honor. The Defense calls Soledad del Rio as a witness.

[Soledad del Rio is duly sworn.]

DIRECT EXAMINATION BY MRS. TAURASI:

Q Soledad, did you have a sexual relationship with Lucas Kyle Ayers?

A Yes. I did, for a while.

Q How long did your relationship with Mr. Ayers last?

A We had a sexual relationship, on and off, for about three years.

Q Were you aware that, at the time, Mr. Ayers was also having a sexual relationship with the plaintiff?

A Yes, I was aware, but it didn't bother me. Lucas and I weren't serious. It was an open relationship.

Q Please explain to the court what an open relationship is.

A There were no strings attached. No commitments to speak of. He and could see whoever we wanted to.

Q During your open relationship with Mr. Ayers were you seeing anyone else?

A I was seeing someone else but like I said Lucas and I weren't serious. He was seeing someone else, too.

Q Thank you, Soledad, for the record what is his name of this *other* person you were seeing?

A His name's James Splitter but he prefers to be called 'Jimmy'. He's my boyfriend.

Q To your knowledge was Mr. Ayers aware you were with Jimmy?

A No. He didn't know about Jimmy, at first. He didn't know until recently.

Q And what was Mr. Ayers' reaction to hearing the news?

A Lucas flew off the handle; like I told you before.

Q Can you please tell it to the court, now?

MR. SANCHEZ:

Objection.

THE COURT:

    Is there a reason to you objection, Mr. Sanchez?

    (No response.)

    The witness can answer.

THE WITNESS:

    A Lucas grabbed me and threatened me.

MRS. TAURASI:

    Q And what were the exact words Mr. Ayers used to threaten you?

MR. SANCHEZ:

    Objection your Honor. This is hearsay.

THE COURT:

    No. That's quite a proper question. Objection overruled. I want to hear this.

THE WITNESS:

    A Lucas said [redacted].

    (Public gallery whispers.)

    (Gavel bangs.)

    Q Did anyone else hear Mr. Ayers say that?

A Oh yes, Jimmy was there. Lucas tried to go after Jimmy, too, but Jimmy kicked his ass ha-ha-ha.

MRS. TAURASI:

Thank you, Ms. del Rio. No further questions.

THE COURT:

Does the prosecution wish to cross-examine this witness?

MR. SANCHEZ:

The prosecution has no questions, your Honor.

THE COURT:

You can step down, Ms. del Rio, but please stay in the vicinity of the court, as you might be called again. Mrs. Taurasi I assumed you're prepared to bring in your next witness?

MRS. TAURASI:

The Defense calls Jimmy . . . I'm sorry . . . James Splitter.

[James Splitter is duly sworn.]

DIRECT EXAMINATION BY MRS. TAURASI:

Q Good morning, Jimmy. Can I call you Jimmy?

A Yes ma'am. Please do.

Q Did you have a sexual relationship with Soledad del Rio?

A Absolutely. She's my girlfriend. We are still having a sexual relationship to this day. In fact, only last night . . . .

(Inaudible.)

(Public gallery laughs.)

THE COURT:

I'll not tolerate that, Mr. Splitter.

THE WITNESS:

I'm sorry, you Honor. You see, I've never testified in court before. When I get nervous I make jokes. It's a stress reaction so you don't have to put me in jail.

(Pubic gallery laughs.)

THE COURT:

Officers of the court, would you please clear the public gallery. I'd like to keep this trial open, and fair, and seen as such; having said that, the public will only be removed from the court for this witness' testimony.

[After the gallery is emptied.]

MRS. TAURASI:

Q Jimmy, were you aware that Soledad was also having a sexual relationship with Lucas Ayers?

A I most certainly was not. I found out the hard way. Lucas showed up ready to throw hands.

Q Did Lucas say anything to Soledad?

A He threatened her. He said [redacted]. Then he came after me.

Q What happened when 'he came after you'?

A Well, I kicked his ass. It was self-defense, though. I want both of those facts to get on the record, too.

Q I'm sure the record shall so reflect. Jimmy, did the police get involved? A No, they didn't. There were no cops.

Q You say it was self-defense, Jimmy. If Mr. Ayers made those threats then why didn't you report it to the police?

A Because I just kicked the guys' ass. Suffice it to say, you don't call the cops on a guy whose ass you just kicked.

MRS. TAURASI:

Fair enough, Jimmy. I have no further questions.

THE COURT:

Mr. Sanchez, do you wish to cross-examine this witness?

MR. SANCHEZ:

I have no questions.

THE COURT:

You may step down but don't leave the court precinct. Bailiff, please let those people back in.

[Gallery is seated and quiet.]

Mrs. Taurasi, moving right along. Your next witness, please.

MRS. TAURASI:

The Defense recalls Lucas Ayers.

[Lucas Kyle Ayers is duly sworn.]

DIRECT EXAMINATION BY MRS. TAURASI:

Q Did you have a sexual relationship with Soledad del Rio?

A Yes I did.

Q Was it true love?

MR. SANCHEZ:

I object, if your Honor pleases.

MRS. TAURASI:

Your Honor, Ms. del Rio testified to their relationship being 'open'. The Defense would like to know how this witness classified their relationship.

THE COURT:

Q Mr. Ayers did you consider the relationship open—to use the jargon?

A Yes, your Honor. I did.

MRS. TAURASI:

Q So, it was an open relationship yet you were you upset—very upset—when you learned Soledad was seeing Jimmy?

A I guess so.

MR. SANCHEZ:

Objection. Leading.

THE COURT:

The witness already answered, Mr. Prosecutor.

MRS. TAURASI:

Q When you found out did you go over to Soledad's house?

MR. SANCHEZ:

Objection. Counsel is leading the witness.

MRS. TAURASI:

This is a hostile witness, your Honor, though I'm more than happy to rephrase the question.

THE COURT:

Very well. MRS.

TAURASI:

Q Mr. Ayers, what did you do when you found out Soledad was seeing Jimmy.

A I drove over to her place.

Q Soledad testified that you threatened her. Is that true?

A No it isn't.

Q She and Jimmy both testified that you threatened her with the words [redacted]. Is that true?

A I most certainly did not. They're lying.

Q So they're *both* lying; yet, it's the same lie?

(No response.)

So now's your chance, Lucas. Why don't you let the truth come out? Why don't you tell the court what happened?

THE COURT:

You're aware that you don't have to answer that.

THE WITNESS:

A I went over there and told Soledad our relationship was off. Then me and Jimmy got into it. It wasn't like he said. I never threatened anyone.

Q Jimmy testified that he 'kicked your ass in self-defense'. Was that a true and accurate statement?

MR. SANCHEZ:

Objection. That is irrelevant and immaterial.

THE COURT:

I tend to agree, counselor.

MRS. TAURASI:

Q Soledad also testified that Jimmy 'kicked your ass '. Was that a true and accurate statement?

MR. SANCHEZ:

If your Honor pleases, I object to that on the ground that it is incompetent, immaterial, and irrelevant; that even if such were the case, which is not true, but if such were the case it would have no material on the case at bar.

THE COURT:

Mrs. Taurasi, I'm finding this line of questioning to be immaterial. Do you have any other questions for this witness?

MRS. TAURASI:

Yes. I do, you honor.

Q You, previously, testified to having a sexual relationship with Mrs. Escueta. Were you aware; that is, did you know Mrs. Escueta was still having a sexual relationship with her husband?

A I knew. I know that your client raped Sojey, too.

(Public gallery gasps.)

THE COURT:

The witness' last statement will be stricken from the record.

MRS. TAURASI:

Q You testified that when you found out Soledad was seeing Jimmy you drove right over to her house, broke off the relationship, and got into a fist fight. And, like you said, that was an 'open' relationship. You also testified that Mrs. Escueta is your 'true love'. Knowing that Sojey was still sleeping with Caleb upset you, didn't it?

THE WITNESS:

Do I have to answer that, Judge?

THE COURT:

Yes, you do.

THE WITNESS:

A Of course it upset me. Cal didn't really care about her.

MRS. TAURASI:

Q Did you let complainant know how much it upset you?

A I guess.

Q Yes or no?

A Yes.

Q So it, in turn, upset her?

MR. SANCHEZ:

> Objection. Calls for speculation.

THE COURT:

> I agree. Objection sustained.

MRS. TAURASI:

> Q Let's say—for the purposes of this discussion—that I'm unfaithful in my marriage. The man I'm having an affair with tells me that if I sleep with my husband again I'll [redacted]. Is it *reasonable* to say that—in this perceived desperate situation—I would lie to protect myself?
>
> A No.
>
> Q 'No', it's not reasonable?

MR. SANCHEZ:

> Objection. Asked and answered.

MRS. TAURASI:

> Withdrawn. Mr. Ayers, is everything you've testified to in this trial truthful?
>
> A Yes it is.
>
> Q Every single word? A Yes, all of it.
>
> Q Equally truthful?
>
> A Let's not be absurd. Yes, equally truthful.

Q I have one final question. Did you confide any of this—your complex relationships with Soledad, Sojey, Jimmy, and Caleb—to Father Duncan?

A I'm going to plead the Fifth on that one, counselor.

MRS. TAURASI:

I'm done with this witness.

CROSS-EXAMINATION BY MR. SANCHEZ:

Q Mr. Ayers, did you ever threaten Sojey Escueta?

A No I did not.

MR. SANCHEZ:

That is all.

THE COURT:

The witness is excused.

MRS. TAURASI:

That's our case your Honor. The Defense rests.

# CHAPTER SEVENTEEN

So, I'm in Mrs. Taurasi's office. I'm looking for the last name of Geoffrey the polygraph examiner. His name is on the tip of my tongue and it's bothering me. Green. His name is Geoffrey Green. Underneath the Geoffrey Green document I find a stack of hate mail. I rifle through the letters. I don't mind saying that I've never seen so many, presumably, intelligent people be so over the top. It's all due to the vigilante atmosphere that this case has created. One of the letters is addressed to Coach.

> *What if your wife was next? Some things are more important that winning basketball games. Trade the rapist. You'll be a better coach for it.*

It would appear my legal team's media responses have fell on deaf ears. All I'm thinking at this point is: *Thanks people. Thanks for not waiting for the actual verdict or, at least, for reason to assist your emotions.* Another letter is written to Mrs. Taurasi from . . . apparently . . . no one.

> *Taurasi,*
>
> *I do not know you, but I am learning more about you. I understand you are a distinguished defense lawyer, but your effort to demonize a victim of rape is grotesque. It's a travesty that a pagan like your client can afford top legal representation, but since*

> *you had a choice, as to whether or not you would represent him, I fault you.*
>
> *In choosing to represent a known atheist and an alleged rapist you attach the entire religious community to your action. You have a right as a private citizen to express your point of view—that is a right which we all possess. But to use the court of law and your public position as an agent of the court to advocate for an alleged rapist is a flagrant abuse of that right. My tax dollars help to support the legal system, not to promote your own personal agenda.*
>
> *Shame on you as you proceed to mount a passionate defense for such an ungodly human being.*
>
> *Shame on you.*

I don't want to read anymore hate mail. It's unconstructive. You know, now that I think about it, maybe presuming *guilt* ought to be a crime. Don't I sound like George Orwell? I can't entirely fault these people for their presumptions. We're all entitled to our own opinions. For instance, I think those people are cowards for writing those letters. Yet, how many times have we seen a defense lawyer go on television and swear up-and-down that his client was innocent? It's almost cliché. What's Mrs. Taurasi supposed to say, "You don't understand; this time my client really *is* innocent"?

\*

Trial continued . . .

Once upon a time I was an important man; however, the longer the trial goes the less my legal team needs me. After giving testimony—which the Taurasi's advised against from the very beginning—there really isn't anything else I can contribute to the case. All the pertinent information has already been added to the sum of knowledge. All I can do now is let it run its course.

After, Mrs. Taurasi briefed me about the morning's events I took the time to tell her that—no matter what the outcome—I really feel she did me justice. From what I witnessed she controlled the tempo and *forced* Sanchez to prove his case. Every time Sanchez tried to prove his case Mrs. Taurasi was all over him.

This morning, she tried to explain something to me and I'm still trying to wrap my head around it. If I understand her correctly—and I'd like to think that I do—Judge Kosteniuk has the authority to overturn the jury's verdict.

Let me explain.

Let's say that by some act of mass insanity this jury finds me guilty. If the judge feels that there isn't enough evidence to support such a verdict she can simply ignore it and give me the big not guilty. Just wait because it gets even better. If this jury were to find me not guilty Judge Kosteniuk would *not* have the authority to overturn that verdict. Actually, it's not that difficult to understand. Why my lawyer decided to explain this to me, now, I *don't* know.

THE COURT:

Let's get right to it then. Mrs. Taurasi, your closing argument.

MRS. TAURASI:

Thank you, your Honor. Ladies and gentlemen of the jury, I'll try to be brief.

My learned friend began his case with a promise. He promised that there would be nothing he claimed that he wouldn't prove. Let's take a moment to see if he kept that promise. First he had the complainant come up here and claim she was raped by her husband. Then, when I asked her if she was raped she testified that she couldn't remember whether or not she consented. She couldn't prove a thing: 0 for 1.

Next the prosecution brought in a jailhouse snitch who supposedly heard my client confessing to the crime. You all saw what happened when I asked him if he was lying. That's 0 for 2 as far as the prosecution's promises are concerned. Then, because my client has no criminal history of violence they dragged his teammate in here to say he's a violent man by profession. When I asked him about Caleb Escueta's conduct on the basketball court he testified that Cal made him a better player. Now, that's the ultimate compliment you can give not just a basketball teammate but a coworker, a spouse, a friend, even an enemy. My client made him a better player and my client will be the first to tell you that he doesn't even like Reginald Bo. Imagine what Caleb Escueta can do for someone he *does* like?

Then who'd the prosecution bring in? They brought in the couple's therapist. All she did was offer testimony that the Escueta's were going through a tough patch in their marriage. Well, that was conceded from the outset. Why else would they have gone to couple's therapy—to brag? So, I asked this witness whether or not Caleb Escueta was capable of the crime he is being accused of. The prosecution's own witness testified that he was not.

I'm starting to see a pattern here, are you? You see, lawyers shouldn't be making promises they don't intend to keep. It's a large part of what gives us such a bad name.

At long last my learned friend brought in the doctor. The only physical evidence the doctor could offer was a ruptured hymen. First, the complainant was sleeping with more than one person around the time of the alleged incident so there's no telling who or what could've caused the injury. Second, a ruptured hymen can be a result of consensual sex.

To believe the prosecution's version of December 12th you'd have to suspend all reason and logic and accept the *least* likely explanation of the evidence. Some of you may or not be asking yourself why this young woman make an unfounded rape accusation. How could she? She's so beautiful. Well, this is *not* a beauty contest. This is a court of law and you can't just play the victim. In a court of law you have to prove, beyond a reasonable doubt, that you've been the victim of a crime. The prosecution proved no such thing.

If you have any doubt in your mind that Caleb Escueta committed the crime then it's your civic duty to come back not guilty. This is a classic case of 'he said, she said'. This time 'she' doesn't remember; while 'he' has been trying to tell you the truth from the very beginning.

I've been a lawyer for a very long time; longer than some of you have been alive. I've dealt with many of these cases and I can tell that every unfounded allegation of rape increases the plight of those who are genuine survivors of this brutal crime. The unfounded allegation against my client is an insult to actual rape survivors. As a juror you've been placed in a unique situation because, you see, you can do something about it. You have the power to send a message. By acquitting Caleb Escueta you'll saying 'It is *not* okay to falsely accuse a man of rape.' By acquitting Caleb Escueta you'll be saying 'I'm *not* going to let this injustice happen.'

THE COURT:

Mr. Sanchez, your closing argument.

MR. SANCHEZ:

Thank you, again, your Honor. Members of the jury, it says something about the sophistication of our democracy that this should ever reach the courts. Instead of the customary heated debate between the prosecution and the Defense going head-to-head in passionate argument we have spent this trial in absolute agreement with one another. Now why is that? Is it because the defendant has no other choice? He finds himself up against a mountain of evidence which he simply cannot contest; and not just technical forensic evidence but public witness evidence pertaining to the most important elements in any rape case: motive, intent, and medical evidence.

So let us remind ourselves of the facts that we all agree upon. On the morning of the December 12th the defendant put his two children to sleep—fact. He then entered a room in which his wife was sleeping—fact. He had one thing one his mind. He woke her up, undressed her, and raped her—again—all uncontested facts.

So what does he come up with? His wife wanted it. That was his defense. No evidence, no arguments, no witnesses, no proof. Just the crazy notion that this beautiful young woman, who told her therapist she was no longer sexually attracted to him, somehow wanted to have sex with him on that day. Oh, and that she and one, Lucas Kyle Ayers, conspired to accuse him of rape to get him out of their lives.

No, the whole Lucas Ayers sideshow was about something else entirely. It's a desperate attempt by the defendant's legal team to blame an apparently immoral individual of concocting a conspiracy. Don't be fooled. The defendant's first line of defense was "I didn't do it." His second line of defense was "I *did* do it but it was consensual."

Members of the jury, let's be clear about one thing: this was not a conspiracy. The Lucas Ayers sideshow was just another smoke screen to distract you from the obvious conclusion; namely, that the defendant is guilty. Caleb Escueta is guilty as all the evidence shows.

It's the state's burden to prove beyond reasonable doubt that the defendant committed rape on the day in question. You need not draw inferences. Here we have the victim. Let us not forget that we have a direct eye witness to the crime. When you consider the overwhelming evidence we submit that you can only draw one conclusion and that is that the defendant is guilty as charged. I now ask you to do the responsible thing, as privileged citizens of this society, and return a guilty verdict.

In the broader sense, spousal rape is a persistent and devastating problem. I would even go as far to say that the heinous nature of this crime should make it a hate crime. Husbands raping their wives aren't just the problems of women. Letting spousal rape go unpunished is a crisis of how I define myself as a man. When I am in a relationship of control over my spouse; go into a room where she is sleeping, strip off her clothes, and rape her, I cannot be free. I cannot be free to enjoy life, I can't be free to be who I am, or to enjoy the sunshine, I can't enjoy anything, because I am in a relationship of control. Only when the truth is known and justice is served can I become liberated.

Finally, we have the victim Sojey Escueta. You heard it in her own words 'All I could do was wait for it to end. Ever since then my body doesn't feel like my own.' What I'm asking you to do now is bring this criminal to justice and help this victim begin the long process of recovery.

# CHAPTER EIGHTEEN

With closing arguments behind us Judge Kosteniuk addresses the jury. "Ladies and gentlemen I'd like to thank you for the attentiveness you've displayed throughout this trial. Now, you've just heard a case that is as complex as it is emotive. Indeed, spousal rape is among the most serious of charges that are tried in our criminal courts. You've heard all the relevant testimony and I've read and interpreted the law to you as it applies in this case. It's now your civic duty to sit down and try to separate the facts from the emotions. A woman claims she' was been raped by her husband. If there's a reasonable doubt in your minds as to the guilt of the accused then you must come back not guilty. However, if there is no reasonable doubt, then you must, in good conscience, find the accused guilty."

The jury members are required to follow the judge's instructions in reaching their verdict. With local news reporters in attendance Judge Kosteniuk called on the six men and six women to use their common sense and logic. She specifically instructed them to make their decision based on the facts of the case and not appeals, made by either counsel, to sentiment or emotion. The judge seemed adamant about that particular point. The reading of instructions continued for about an hour. The judge ended by saying, "Such a decision can never and must never be arrived at in haste but reflected upon long and hard." At long last, Judge Kosteniuk handed the case over to the jury. The twelve of them went into a special jury room to elect a foreperson who would to lead the deliberation.

So, court will not be called back into session until the jury reaches their decision. This gives me the opportunity to exercise the "Love the Game Clause" in my contract. This morning's Charity Basketball Classic is open to all players throughout the league. It's an excellent opportunity for the fans to see players, who are ordinarily teammates, square off against one another. This year The Charity Basketball Classic is a league-sanctioned event so, technically, The Forces of Reaction can't object to player participation. Ultimately, this game is for the fans. It's our way to back to the communities that support us throughout the season. It's also a way for us to help raise money for a good cause.

During warm-ups I look into the stands. I see fans wearing shirts and jerseys of their favorite players and teams. I can't help but wonder how these fans are going to react to my surprise return. I'm excited to see the 5000 or so people who came out to watch us do what we do. Some of these are fans I've played in front of since I turned professional two seasons ago.

I remember the last game I played in this arena. How can I forget? It was the game that resulted in the players-fans altercation and, ultimately, my suspension. I always hated having to leave it like that way.

To make matters even more awkward an officer of the court is on standby; should the jury come back with the verdict I'll have to leave. If the jury finds me guilty my basketball career is, basically, over. So, for me, the Charity Basketball Classic *is* my last game. Of course, I want to win this one. I think every player hopes to win their last game.

We didn't hold a practice for this game but we did have a little shoot-around. We walked through the one or two set plays we'll be running. I asked the players on my team if I could play a ton of minutes in this game. I knew it was an odd request but the guys seemed to understand. In fact, they said I could play the entire game if I wanted to. I don't even know if I could do that. I've been sitting around the house urinating in my dog's bed and reading my annotated version of *The Constitution*. I guess we'll have to see how that all affects my performance.

THE FIRST QUARTER:

The referee throws the ball goes up and Bo tips it towards me. Our strategy, if you want to call it that, is simple. We want to get Arief the ball: early-and-often. The idea is to get him going offensively. Generally, when outside shooters are in a good rhythm the defense has to honor it. They can't stand around the middle of the floor. They have to spread out. In the long run this creates opportunities for offensive players to attack the middle. Arief comes off a screen and we score on our opening possession—so far so good.

The opposing team comes down court and it's time for us to play a little defense. They dump the ball into their big man and I come over to double team him. They swing the ball over to the opposite side of the floor (where my guy has been left unguarded). Our defensive rotation is late and we give up an open jump-shot. The battle lines have been clearly drawn. It's going to be our motion-type offense versus their inside-out offense.

On our *next* possession we run the same play we ran on our *previous* possession. This time the defense makes an adjustment. The ball finds its way back into my hands. An offensive team is given 24 seconds to shoot the ball. If they don't get a shot of within that time they lose that possession. I look at the shot clock and it's winding down. 5, 4, 3 . . . not every player can create their own shot (ordinarily it requires a team effort). Even less players can create their own shot so late in the possession. This is a play Coach likes to call, "What the hell was that?" I take two or three hard dribbles, to the left, and pull up for a jump-shot. My attempt falls short and hits the front of the trim. A few of the fans seem unusually pleased that I missed.

A few plays later I find myself, once again, double teaming the opposition's big man. I pop the ball loose and we come up with the turnover. The crowd begins to boo our/my effort. We score in transition and the crowd is obviously against us/me. The player I'm guarding (my best—est friend and Javaman) brings the ball up court. I imagine Javaman is being driven by conflicting imperatives. I gamble for a steal and it pays off. We force another turnover. As I dribble down the open floor the crowd boos in disapproval. I lay the ball into the basket and it feels just like I've never been away. When the public address announcer calls my name I hear a distant bleat of "rapist" from a fan.

\*

Javaman looks like a bouncer but he's really a big-old teddy bear. It's funny how it works out that way. I never met a single player who didn't like and respect Javaman and I'll tell you why. The first time I played against him was at a scrimmage. I drove the ball to the basket and Javaman blocked my shot. There was also a lot of body contact I didn't appreciate. In my mind it was a cheap shot. If you know anything about me then you know I was obliged to get him back. Later on in that scrimmage I got my chance. I saw Javaman about a step or two from the basket which was exactly where I wanted him to be. I came down the lane and elevated. When I jumped up for my shot I sort of extended my right leg. I gave Javaman a little nudged that sent him backwards. I thought, for sure, he and I were going to have an altercation.

To my surprise the only thing Javaman said was, "*That* was a tough shot." The very next defensive play I got caught on a switch. Javaman posted me up, backed me down, went into his drop step move, and scored. While we were trotting back to the other side of the court he smiled at me and said, "I think when you kicked me it woke me up." I couldn't believe my ears. I remember thinking *did this guy just insult me in Islam?*

300

If this incident happened with anyone else it would've escalated into a huge Alpha-idiot pissing contest. The scrimmage would've been over and that would just be the beginning of a bitter rivalry. Javaman doesn't operate like that. It's just not who he is. He's a true professional. He never talks trash and he seldom ever does anything to validate an opponent's aggression. In two years I've never seen Javaman lose his composure on the basketball court.

\*

Every time I touch the basketball a small but loud portion of the crowd chants "no means no." These upstanding citizens seem unhinged by the prospect of me being acquitted of the crime of which I'm accused.

I just keep playing. What else could I do but keep going? We run another screen for Arief and he hits another open jump-shot. The opposing team calls a timeout and the tension, in the arena, is palatable. I've played in hostile environments before but never anything quite like this. It's all so personal.

This is supposed to be a charity game but some of the fans are treating it as though it were a political demonstration. In the huddle my teammates offer me their words of support. "Just go into next play mode." One says. "Don't listen to those idiots." And. "Use it." And. "It says more about their mothers than you ha-ha-ha."

I imagine there are a few fans that support me; although, I don't suppose they are the types to scream obscenities. I think people ought to, though. I don't mean people should act obnoxiously. I mean people ought to be comfortable enough to disagree. Given the circumstances that might sound self-serving but, as a principal, I believe that what's right is right. Let's set my case aside, for a moment, and speak in more general terms.

Let's imagine there is an organized group of people protesting in the streets. For the purposes of this discussion let's say that they are arguing that the Earth is flat. Now, I don't think the correct response would be to deny that group of people the right express themselves. I think the correct response is for sensible people to respond with a *stronger* argument.

People have every right to claim "the Earth is flat" but (if we learned anything from my trial it's that) claiming something doesn't make it true. It doesn't matter how *many* people say "the Earth is flat" and it doesn't matter how *loudly* they say it. It just ain't true.

Whether you be a minority of hundreds, or a minority of one, the truth is the truth. Nothing else matters.

I digress.

Back at the Charity Basketball Game action is set to continue. The opposing team prepares to inbound the ball. One of the things you look for in team is the play they run *after* a timeout. Ideally, a good team should come out of that huddle and get a decent shot. After *this* timeout our opponents don't get a good shot: they get a great shot. They make two or three crisp passes and our defense gives up an easy lay-up. The crowd cheers in almost sarcastic manner.

This is my first time playing on the same team as a few of these guys. We're have to try to keep everything as simple as possible. We rely, primarily on two set plays (1) *Shooting Guard Take* for Arief and (2) *Shuffle Rub Center* for Bo. There are players who whine that their team(s) "don't really have a system." I couldn't disagree more. It's true that there are teams that don't run set plays. There are teams that play as though it were every man for himself (a sort of "me first" attitude). Even the worse teams in the world have a system. If you're on a team that consistently dribbles down court, ignore one another, and takes poor shots then—guess what—*that's* your team's system. It may not be an effective system but it's a system nonetheless.

By the end of the quarter the score is close. My team has a slight lead of 18 to 14. I grab the stat sheet and take a quick peak at the numbers. The only statistic that really stands out is our precise shooting. As a team we shot 81% making 9 out of 10 shots. If I made my pull-up jump—shot we'd be 10 for 10. We are but perfectionists in an imperfect game.

Also of note, the player I'm guarding (Javaman) scored a total of 9 points; that's the highest scoring total of a single player from either team. There are a few valid explanations for my best-est friend's efficient scoring. (1) His offense was exceptionally good. (2) My defense was exceptionally poor. Then there's a third preferred option. (3) My defense was good but his offense was better.

Also of note: I threw ball away three times. Three turnovers is a high number for a single quarter of play. It wasn't my fault; though, my imaginary friend kept calling for the ball.

THE SECOND QUARTER:

We open the next quarter with another steal. I managed to poke the ball loose and Arief hustles the other way and scores an easy lay-up. The crowd is booing again; though, this time the booing seems stronger.

On the next possession the opposing team runs a play for Javaman. I chase him through three screens. It's like hitting three brick walls. Then Javaman hits a jump-shot right in my face. It's a bit embarrassing, for me, and the crowd seems to enjoy it. I'm smiling because Sojey's grandmother hits harder these guys.

The next time the opposing team gets the ball they all clear-out for Javaman. He's feeling it and he wants to take me one-on-one. As you know my legs are fresh from sitting around the on house arrest. Maybe that has something to do with me beating Javaman to the spot he wanted to get to. I stand in his path and he knocks me down. The referee blows her whistle and calls Javaman for an offensive foul. We'll be getting the ball back. A little kid runs onto the court and wipes up the spot on the floor I just landed on. The buzzer sounds announcing a substitution of players. As all this is happening I hear a chorus of "no means no."

The hecklers want me off the court but it doesn't work that way. My team isn't going to take me off the court just because a couple of hecklers want me off the court. So long as I'm being productive I'm not going anywhere. The hecklers must be forgetting what drives athletes. Athletes use whatever they can to motivate themselves. So, the more the hecklers taunt me the harder I intend to play.

Our opponents are digging a little hole for themselves. At halftime the score is 34 to 26.

We're ahead by 8 points and we shot 73% in the quarter.

THE THIRD QUARTER:

We open the 3$^{rd}$ quarter like we opened the 1$^{st}$ and 2$^{nd}$ quarters. We run Arief off of a screen and I pass him the ball. The defense—having seen this play several times—double-teams

Arief. Arief, anticipating this adjustment, finds the open man. The result is another easy basket.

Javaman receives a pass and makes a three-pointer. To make matters worse he made the shot in my face, again. The crowd roars in appreciation and I'm beginning to sense a theme. Most players would want to come back at Javaman and score; therein, making it some sort of a duel. It's not who I am. I'm not going to go on a personal vendetta (scoring-wise) just because the player I'm guarding wants to embarrass me. I'm going to come back at my opponent with my entire team. It's basic arithmetic: five beats one. Not to mention, at this point in the game, we're winning. It would be foolish to stop doing what we've been doing up to this point.

My *team* comes back the other way. We proceed to run that same play for Arief. I pass him the ball and they double-team him, again. You'd think you were watching a video and this were a replay but you'd be wrong. Arief finds the open man. The opposing team—not wanting to give up another easy basket from this play— fouls the open man. It's a hard foul but my teammate takes it in stride. Our precise ball movement has managed to silence this hostile crowd but I have a strong feeling that the sobering silence is only temporary.

The buzzer sounds ending the quarter. A group of female dancers run on the court and perform their choreography. The music serves to drown out the chants of "no means no". The game has to be stopped because someone in the crowd actually has a rape-whistle (so much for the presumption of innocence). For those of you who have never attended a rape prevention seminar a rape-whistle sounds just like any other whistle. In fact, play can't be resumed because the rape-whistle might be confused with the referees' whistles. After about 20 minutes the rape whistling ends.

We've played 3 quarters of basketball. My best-est friend Javaman leads all players with 22 points. My teammates don't look worried. They're of the opinion that Javaman's high-scoring is taking the rest of his team out of the offense. They've been doing a lot of standing around and watching.

I think my teammates are just trying to play the situation down. It's embarrassing. During the season, I'm the starting point guard. Javaman is the back-up point guard. He shouldn't be out-playing me. Anyway, I just hope *The Law Office of Gisele Taurasi* have better defense than I did in those first three quarters.

## THE FOURTH QUARTER:

We're going into the final quarter ahead 51 to 44. Up to this point we've been doing an excellent job of moving the basketball. In the back of my mind this is the last quarter of my life. I talked with my teammates about this earlier. No matter what the score was I wanted to look to be more assertive on the offensive end. I want break my opponent down and take the ball to the basket.

In addition, we're going to run more pick-and-rolls. The pick-and-roll is an offensive play in which a player sets a pick for a teammate handling the ball and then slips behind the defender rolls to accept a pass. This simple play has become my bread and butter. Though I've been playing the entire game there hasn't been a single play called for me. That's about to change.

This may just be a glorified pick-up game but we're all highly competitive people. Both teams want to win this game. Most of my life has been dedicated to the sport of basketball. One of the things I've learned is that you do *not* motivate players with speeches. It's a myth. It's a myth that you can teach competitiveness. Players either have it or they don't.

We come out for the 4th quarter and set up a high pick-and-roll. We read and execute the play to perfection. Two basic passes and we get the result he had intended. A few possessions later we run pick-and-roll again. This time I take the ball hard to the hole, score, and get fouled.

This is my first time going to the free throw line, today. This is, also, the first time the crowd is going to get a really good look at the guy they've been reading about in the newspapers. The chant of "no means no" is at its loudest. My free throw goes into the basket and I get a feeling of satisfaction. The hecklers wanted nothing more than to see me miss. The best way to get even people like that is to succeed and move on.

The opposing team calls a timeout. Our players are giving one another high-fives. When the crowd is against your team, or a member of it, you have to pull together. You have to stick up for one another in those situations. Bo was right when he testified that basketball is a fraternity. We meant it when we told Arief that we're a family.

There's just over two minutes left to play. Our offense has been running as efficient as Swiss time. The result is that we're ahead by 12 points. It's unlikely that we're going to relinquish this lead. We don't intend to simply self-destruct. It's time to slow the game down and play for time. We work the 24 second shot clock down to about 10 seconds. Bo comes over and he and I run pick-and-roll. This time the defense tries to blitz me. This means that both Bo and my defender rush at me. I take a few extra dribbles to create space and an angle to Bo. He and I have done this a million times before. They leave the big man wide open: bounce pass, catch conversion, easy basket.

Later, the opposition goes into full-court pressure. Javaman wants to guard me for the entire 94 feet of the court. The idea is to get me to rush or make some type of mistake. Good luck with that. I don't think that's going to get the result they want but you never know. We don't rush our offense. Once again, we run the 24 second shot clock down to about 10 seconds. Bo comes over and we run another pick-and-roll. I dribble to an open spot and take a jump-shot. Javaman jumps up gets a piece of my shot. The blocked shot falls short and I hear "air ball" from the hecklers. I'm not too worried because we're up by 12 and there's only a little over a minute left to play. There's no real pressure for us to score, anymore.

Though it's all but impossible for the opposing team to catch up to us they stick with their full court pressure. We have time for one last pick-and-roll. This might be the last play of my life. I'm thinking *don't mess this up*. We run the play to perfection and Bo is, again, the beneficiary. He *emphatically* slams the basketball and the hecklers boo. The louder the hecklers boo the more satisfied I feel.

H. Valencia

I'm guessing Javaman ran out of energy because he has only scored 2 points in this final quarter. It's not how you come in: it's how you go out. The final buzzer sounds and the only statistic that matter, now, is the final score and that score is definitive. We win by 14 points.

After the game we shake hands with the opposing team. For obvious reasons I've got extra security. I get off the court as soon as possible. Only later do I learn that I've been selected to be the Player of the Game. Javaman was the frontrunner but, technically, the honor can only be given to a player from the *winning* team. I was probably lucky enough to be selected because I played every minute of the game and had 12 assists to show for it.

I enjoy just being one of the guys in the locker room. I let it all sink in. All day, in the back of my mind, I've been thinking *last time for this* and *last time for that*. The best part of a game, for me, is sitting in the locker room after you've won on the opponent's floor. This is as about as high as it can get.

*

After getting the opportunity change back into my street clothes I find myself cornered by a local newspaper reporter. I remember his newspaper being balanced, sincere, and brutally downbeat in their assessment of the case. The reporter says, "Congratulations Caleb. Was it difficult to focus on the game with the jury currently deliberating your guilt or innocence?"

I tell him, "I want to thank the people who came out and supported this event. I understand we were able to raise nearly twice as much as was projected for this good cause. I'm grateful to be named Player of the Game and am happy with our performance. I know I couldn't do it without my teammates, though. We played like a well-oiled machine. The guys knew how much I wanted to play well today with all that's been going on off the court. With respect to your question—I realize you're just doing your job—since the matter is now the subject of a legal proceeding, my lawyer has advised me to make no public comment about it. I'm sure you understand."

\*

Trial continued . . .

THE COURT:

Ladies and gentlemen of the jury, have you reached a verdict?

JURY FOREMAN:

Yes we have, your Honor.

THE COURT:

Foreman, may I have the verdict slip please?

[After examining the document.]

Would the jury foreman please rise. Would the defendant please rise and face the jury. In the matter of the State versus Caleb Escueta, on the sole charge of spousal rape, is he guilty or not guilty?

JURY FOREMAN:

We the jury find the defendant, Caleb Escueta, guilty as charged.

(All chatter.)

In regards to sentencing; we recommend the maximum penalty.

MOIRA DEL ROSARIO:

Yes. Thank you. Thank god.

[Over half the public gallery stands up and walks out of the courtroom.]

THE COURT:

(Gavel bangs repeatedly.)

Court officers, please clear those people from the court precinct. Bailiff the courtroom is to remain closed for the duration of the proceeding. I'll have no one else going in or out. Foreman, please take your seat.

(After order is restored.)

I cannot hide my feeling that the verdict of the jury is perverse.

(Loud sigh.)

Before I rule, will the court clerk please poll the jury?

THE COURT CLERK:

Right away, your Honor.

[After polling the jury.]

9 jurors vote 'guilty'. 3 jurors vote 'not guilty'.

THE COURT:

9 to 3. Okay. Thank you. At this point I'm going to make the ruling. You must keep in mind that this ruling is in the interest of justice. I have decided to take the unusual step of *vacating* the jury verdict of guilty for the . . .

(Inaudible.)

SOJEY ESCUETA:

No. You can't do that, Judge. This isn't fair. The jury already found him guilty. This case has been decided. You can't change the verdict simply because you're the judge.

THE COURT:

I can and I did, Mrs. Escueta. Take your seat; furthermore, if you address the court in that manner again I'll have you held in contempt, so fast, your lawyer won't have time to leak it to the press. Now, sit down and be quiet.

(The plaintiff sits down.)

Now, Mr. Prosecutor, I strongly suggest you get control of your client.

MR. SANCHEZ:

(Stammering.)

Yes-yes, your Honor.

THE COURT:

> As a matter of law I find no evidence proving beyond a reasonable doubt that, on the 12th of December, Caleb Escueta raped his wife Sojey Escueta. Of course, I'll have a complete text of this ruling to be published in due course. Ladies and gentlemen of the jury, the court thanks you for your service. Mr. Prosecutor, I suspect you will in turn wish to file motions. I give you leave to file whatever you like. As for Mr. Escueta, you've been found not guilty of spousal rape. You are hereby discharged by the court. Court dismissed.

> (Gavel raps.)

*

Perhaps there will come a day when I can again hear the phone ring without feeling this sense of dread. Perhaps there will also come a day when the solutions to my problems will not require a defense attorney or a court stenographer. As for today, I feel vindicated. I got the outcome I wanted but this acquittal won't necessarily make my life, or even tomorrow, any easier.

About the same time I'm discharged Assistant District Attorney Sanchez is also makes his way outside the courtroom. He's accompanied by my wife and her entourage, as it were. I have little doubt that Sanchez is going to file motions in an attempt to overturn the judge's decision. I have no doubt that if the judge's verdict of not guilty sticks my wife is going to push for a civil trial.

Suddenly, I recall the words of Aristotle: A tragedy is an action which is serious, complete, and of a certain magnitude, in which a person of substance is reduced to ruin by a flaw in his/her character revealed under the tensions of the stage. When the trial began I, in my naivety, thought my day in court would magically resolve everything. I thought the trial would bring closure. I was going to set the record straight and things would go back to normal. At best this case has merely shifted the blame. In the beginning, people were pointing their fingers at me and now others are suspect, as well. After all is said and done, Judge Kosteniuk may have closed the case but she couldn't close life. As I take my first breaths as a new man a local news reporter sticks a microphone in my face and asks "Mr. Escueta, do you care to comment on the outcome?"

LOCAL NEWS REPORT:

Love him or hate him the Kingmaker is a free man. There has been a recent and shocking development in The Kingmaker Case. Judge Reena M. Kosteniuk has vacated the jury's guilty verdict convicting a Caleb Escueta (also known as Kingmaker) of sexual assault. Following the high-profile trial, court records show, jurors found the basketball star guilty and they recommended the maximum penalty of a 10 year prison term. Then, Judge Kosteniuk took the *unusual* step of vacating the verdict and found Escueta not guilty. She stated her decision was "in the interest of justice".

The judge ordered Caleb Escueta to be immediately released from house arrest. The ruling is welcome news for the Kingmaker's legal team but the case is not officially over. Judge Kosteniuk gave Assistant District Attorney R. F. Sanchez 60 days to decide whether he wants to retry the case. Sanchez said he didn't know when he would decide but said it would not take 60 days. Judge Kosteniuk also gave Sanchez 21 days to file any objections to her ruling. In a 22 page ruling that accompanied the order she stated "The evidence of guilt was weak and the defendant had a plausible claim of innocence." She ended the document by stating, "What was displayed in my courtroom does a great disservice to all the actual survivors of this brutal crime."

Story adjourned . . .